She War

Joanna Dodd is fascinated by toxic friendship and family groups and the long shadows cast by old secrets. She lives in London and enjoys acting in plays, running very slowly, and spending time with her (lovely and not at all toxic) family and friends.

Also by Joanna Dodd

The Summer Dare
She Wants You Gone

SHE
WANTS
YOU
GONE

JOANNA DODD

hera

First published in the United Kingdom in 2025 by

Hera Books, an imprint of
Canelo Digital Publishing Limited,
20 Vauxhall Bridge Road,
London SW1V 2SA
United Kingdom

A Penguin Random House Company

The authorised representative in the EEA is Dorling Kindersley Verlag
GmbH. Arnulfstr. 124, 80636 Munich, Germany

A CIP catalogue record for this book is available from the British Library.

Print ISBN 978 1 80436 845 9
Ebook ISBN 978 1 80436 844 2

Printed and bound in Great Britain by Clays Ltd, Elcograf S.p.A.

Look for more great books at
www.herabooks.com
www.dk.com

For my first reader

Prologue

It takes seconds to die. A quick death. That's supposed to be a good thing, isn't it? It's what we all want — for ourselves, for our loved ones. But it's the speed that's the horrifying thing to me. Your life can change in less time than it takes to boil a kettle for a mug of tea. Someone else's life can end in that same time. Think about how short a second is. Now think about how long it is. Because that is the worst part of all. Seconds still give you time to make a difference.

I think about the seconds while she was dying. The seconds in which I could have done something to stop it, if only I'd grasped what was happening. Most days — every day — I try to work it out by counting in my head. I try to decide when it was too late.

One, two, three, four, five. I can hear her the whole time. *Six, seven, eight.* It's not like I'm far away, after all; I'm right there. *Nine, ten, eleven, twelve.* If I'd been far away, what happened would have been a tragedy, but it wouldn't have been my fault. *Thirteen, fourteen, fifteen, sixteen.* I'm not looking at her yet, but I know she's still alive at this point, because she's making a noise. I can hear her above the other small everyday sounds. *Seventeen, eighteen, nineteen, twenty.* It's gone quiet by this point. It probably isn't too late, though. Not yet. *Twenty-one, twenty-two, twenty-three.*

This is when I look. When I take in for the first time what's happened and try to make it make sense.

But even then, I use up more precious seconds. And when the image of her lying there comes back, as it does every time I close my eyes, because it is branded on my eyelids, I wonder: how long did I stare at her? How many more seconds did I waste standing there, trying to make the picture mean something else, before I rushed forward to help her? And how many seconds did I spend trying to find my phone to call the ambulance? Fumbling to dial the numbers. How many seconds before the call connected? The seconds while they explained how to carry out CPR. Seconds she didn't have.

Always, I'm counting. Counting is all that stands between me and the terror and the guilt. Counting is all I have left now.

Chapter One

Suffolk Life Blog

Today on the blog we're catching up with new Suffolk resident and baking wizard Beth Montgomery, who runs the Instagram account @BethLoves2Bake.

Welcome to Suffolk, Beth! We've been checking out your bakes online and it's making us feel hungry just looking at them. Could you tell us a bit about how you started inventing your own recipes?

I guess it's a classic example of something good coming from something bad, because I started doing it during the pandemic. Baking's always been my safe place during tough times in my life, so when lockdown began, I spent hours in the kitchen. I was working for a food magazine at the time, testing out recipes, but after a while I decided to try creating some of my own. And then I got obsessed with making them as good as possible. Friends started asking me to share the recipes, so I posted some pictures of what I was making on Instagram, and it just kind of grew from there. I keep it really simple – a series of before, during and after shots, and a link to the recipe on my website, but people seem to enjoy it.

They certainly do! Your account has nearly three thousand followers already. What do you think appeals to people most about your recipes?

3

I think they like the fact that I go for really classic recipes – the fluffiest scones you've ever tasted, or the gooiest chocolate cake. Quite a bit of baking has got a bit zany recently and my recipes are the total opposite of that. Not that there's anything wrong with zany if that's your thing of course, but sometimes instead of making a cherry, peanut butter, unicorn dust brownie, people just want a brownie – the perfect brownie – and my recipes help you to make that.

We hear it's been a big year for you in other ways too. Is it right that you got married a few months ago?

Yes, to the most fabulous guy. He's called Noah and I actually met him through my Instagram account. Noah's a photographer and he replied to one of my posts with some suggestions about how to take better photos of my bakes. To start with, I was a bit annoyed. I mean who was this guy I'd never even met who was telling me what to do with my pictures? So I sent him some fairly grumpy replies, but he took it well. It turned out he lived just up the road from me, so we ended up going for a coffee together and he was sweet and funny. And totally hot. When I looked back on the meeting later that evening, I realised I had to see him again, and luckily it turned out he felt the same way.

And you're a stepmum too, to thirteen-year-old Dolly. How's that going?

It's going great. Dolly and I are still getting to know each other, of course, and that takes time. I definitely don't want to fill her mum's place, but I do want to be there for her. I think a lot of step-parents probably understand how that feels. But there's a chance to do things differently too when you're a step-parent.

It can be a different kind of relationship. It's brilliant just hanging out together, like when Dolly helps me set up the shots for my Insta, or we go shopping together.

And you're all making a big move to a new home, right here in the lovely county of Suffolk. What prompted that?

It feels like the right time to start a new life together in a brand new place. The three of us, and our dog Bluebell, are all off to live in a tiny village in the middle of the Suffolk countryside. It's where Noah grew up, actually. His old childhood home. It's going to be very different from the life we've been living in London, but I'm looking forward to having the headspace to focus on being creative and work on some new recipes. One day I'd love to be able to write a recipe book, and I think this move could really help with that. For now, I'm planning to start my own baking business so people can commission me to make the bakes I post online.

How exciting! So can we expect Noah and Dolly to inspire some new recipes?

Well, Noah loves all things chocolate, so I think you can assume that there's going to be a big focus on chocolate from now on. I'm working on perfecting a triple chocolate cookie recipe right now that I know Noah's going to go crazy for. And Dolly's a big fan of my breakfast pancakes – she's always trying to persuade me to cook up a batch for her.

Is blending a family a bit like blending the ingredients in a cake?

I suppose in some ways it is! You've got a whole lot of different components to consider, and it's about finding the best way to meld them together and make them even more special. That's exactly what we'll be doing when we move to our new home.

Chapter Two

Beth

'Some of it isn't even true.'

'Come on, Beth, you're not telling me that Suffolk Life would make stuff up?'

Noah, tanned, golden-haired and indubitably hot – some of the blog *was* true – twists round to face me from where he's sitting in the passenger seat. His brown eyes framed by the dark rims of his glasses are laughing at me.

'It's making me cringe.'

'It's going to make you the owner of a successful new baking business.'

'Yes, okay, okay. I get it,' I say, putting my foot down and pulling out to overtake a Yaris moving at a glacial pace. We're in what I still think of as Noah's BMW, even though he keeps insisting it's *our* BMW. This joint ownership thing is still a novelty. It's even more of a novelty for me to be driving a car that actually accelerates. 'Why did they have to make me so gushing and wholesome though? I'm sure I didn't sound like that on the phone.'

'I'm guessing that's what they think baking fans want.' There's a pause, while I pull back into the inside lane. I can feel Noah's eyes still on me. 'You are excited about the move though?' he asks, a trace of anxiety in his voice now.

'You know I am. I can't wait to get out of London. It feels like time, for all kinds of reasons.'

'Some of which you definitely can't tell Suffolk Life.'

'Well, no. I don't think being mugged at the end of my street would tick the gushing and wholesome box.'

'Is it still keeping you awake?'

Now there's no mistaking the anxiety in Noah's voice. I know he feels terrible that he wasn't there to help me when I stumbled home that night a few months ago.

'Not really. I think about it sometimes, of course I do. I know they were just kids, but it was still scary. But that wasn't the main reason I want to get out – that was just the prompt. You do know that don't you?' I'm determined to make him understand. 'The bit in the blog about the move and a new start, that's all true. I just didn't realise they were going to include so much of the personal stuff, that's all. When I spoke to the lady, I thought she was going to focus mainly on the baking. But it's fine. Honestly. I'm being a diva. I can't believe there even is an interview with me.'

Noah studies me in silence for a few moments.

'There's a lot going on for you, you're definitely allowed to be a bit of a diva.' His tone lighter, he adds: 'I'm just worried you might start having palpitations being so far outside Zone 3.'

I've lived in London all my adult life and it's true that there have been various points over the past couple of weeks when I've felt genuine panic at the thought of leaving sweaty Streatham, with its chicken shops and five-pound flat whites, for the delights of the Suffolk countryside. But mainly I know this is the right move for me – for us – so I try to match the lightness of Noah's tone as I reply.

'I'm too busy looking at all the green stuff out there.' I gesture out of the car window. 'What's it called again? And those big black-and-white things eating it – what are they? Pigs?'

'I can tell you've been listening to *The Archers*.'

'You're the only *Archers* fan in this car.'

I glance in the rear-view mirror. The car is piled high with luggage, even though the removal van took most of the stuff down to the new house last weekend. In the middle of all the boxes and big blue IKEA bags are Dolly and Bluebell. Bluebell is my – our – Staffordshire Bull Terrier: clumsy, white with brindle ears and smelly. Dolly is Noah's daughter, and not so easily summed up. She's currently listening to something on her phone, probably K-pop, which everyone at her school seems to be obsessed with at the moment. She's the same build as her dad, tall and slender, but her colouring is different. Where his skin is golden, hers is very pale, almost translucent, and her long, thick hair, today worn in a French plait, is white-gold. She's like a beautiful ghost, albeit one wearing Urban Outfitters joggers, a cropped pink T-shirt and expertly applied eyeliner. I raise my voice slightly.

'We know his shameful secret, don't we, Dolly?'

Her eyes meet mine in the mirror. Startling, deep blue eyes. Then she turns her head slowly and looks out of the window.

Noah twists round even further in his seat and says: 'Everything all right in the back?'

Dolly removes her earbuds.

'What's that?'

'Beth was talking to you.'

'Oh sorry, I didn't hear.'

Our eyes meet in the mirror again.

One of the least true things in the blog is the bit about Dolly. Things are emphatically not going great. I'm not even sure it's true to say Dolly and I are getting to know each other. One of the first rules of being a stepmum to a teenage daughter: don't push it. There's a whole article about this on My Blended Family, the website I've taken to doomscrolling in the small hours of the morning when I can't sleep. It's called 'Moving through the gears'. Apparently, you have to allow your stepchild to choose their own gear, and move at the same pace as them. I'm starting to suspect that Dolly's preferred gear would be reverse.

'What did you ask me, Beth?' Her voice polite, like I'm a family friend she met a few hours previously. She's nearly always polite in front of Noah.

'It doesn't matter,' I say cheerfully. I'm determined that Dolly and I are going to get on, today of all days. This is the start of our new life together and I don't want to begin it with a silly row. 'Just a stupid joke about *The Archers*.'

She shrugs and replaces her earbuds. Noah raises an eyebrow at me and I smile back, reassuring him that everything is fine. He's so desperate for us to get on. And I want us to get on too. I'm pathetically eager for Dolly to like me – as though I'm the thirteen-year-old in this relationship. Mainly, I want Dolly to like me because I love Noah, and he and Dolly come as a package and I'm determined to make this work. But I have to confess that there's also a small part of me that wants her to like me because I'm usually good at making friends. Everyone has their talents, and if you pressed me on mine, I'd probably say baking and friendship. Obviously this is different, though. I'm not making friends with Dolly exactly, but neither am I trying to be her mum. It's complicated. Way more complicated than I'd expected.

The road has narrowed to a single carriageway at this point, and we're stuck behind a horsebox, crawling past vast fields and the odd village, most of them boasting a pub and occasionally a village shop. The heat is beating down outside – according to the dashboard it's thirty-one degrees – and Noah asks whether he should crank up the air con. His voice is low, but the response from the back is instant:

'No way, Dad, it's freezing in here already.'

She heard that okay, says a petty voice in my head before I can stop it.

Blending a family is nothing like blending a cake. When it became obvious that Noah and I were serious, several of my friends pointed out the irony that I of all people, who'd made up my mind about not wanting children, had ended up in a relationship with a man who already had one. I'd defended myself indignantly. There were all kinds of reasons why I'd decided I didn't want children of my own, but it wasn't because I didn't like them. As I follow Noah's directions to pull off the A12, I replay one of those early conversations in my head.

'It's not like she's a baby or a small child.'

Barely suppressed glee came from the rest of the group, nearly all of whom were parents themselves.

'Oh, that would be so much easier!'

My best friend Sasha, mother to a fourteen-year-old daughter and an eleven-year-old son, was so excited she spilt half of her Negroni as she rushed to add her helpful contribution.

'Teenage girls are monsters.'

'Well Dolly isn't – she's lovely.'

'You've met her once. You wait.'

Actually, even our first meeting had been disconcerting. Noah had taken us both out to lunch at Pizza Express in Clapham Junction. Something low key, on neutral territory, so we could get to know each other. Dolly had indeed been lovely, very chatty, answering all my questions about school and what she liked doing and even asking questions of her own about baking and my Instagram account. Right up until the point when Noah had gone to the toilets. And then she'd just sat in silence. I tried to keep the conversation going, asking her about her favourite subject at school, but it was like she hadn't heard me, and I worried that repeating the question might make the whole thing feel even more awkward, so I rambled on for a bit about how I'd loved chemistry and then we sat in silence for what felt like for ever, but was probably only a few minutes. She literally didn't say a word the whole time, just played with the crust of her pizza. Once Noah came back she snapped into life again.

At the time, I decided she was probably way more shy than she'd initially seemed, but over the past few months, I've come to recognise it as a familiar tactic. Only a couple of days ago, we met some of Noah's old art college friends in a pub garden in Kennington. Dolly was there too and on her best behaviour. When I went to the bar, one of the women came with me to help carry the drinks and made a point of telling me how sweet she thought Dolly was. She wasn't there for the bit later when Dolly and I walked to the tube station and I tried to ask her about her dad's college mates, and she simply gave a small shrug and turned her face away to look at something suddenly fascinating on the other side of the road. When Noah caught us up a few minutes later, she told him what a great afternoon it had been and how much she'd loved meeting everyone.

It's one of the reasons why this is such a good move for us. We need a fresh start, in a new place. Now we've left the A12, there are fewer and fewer houses and the lanes we're travelling down are getting narrower. They're like tunnels with the trees overhanging them and dappled light. Eventually, we see a sign on the right: *Fortune's Yard, 2 miles*. Our future home. Beneath it is a smaller sign: *No Through Road*. I indicate.

'Almost there,' Noah says.

I feel a rush of excitement that I'm finally here. On the brink of my new grown-up life in the country, with my new husband and my stepdaughter. Slowly, I pull out to overtake a woman riding a gorgeous chestnut horse. You don't get that in Streatham. She looks about my age and gives a cheerful wave of thanks. Maybe I'll even learn to ride. As I pull away, I glance in the rear-view mirror for another look at the horse. Dolly is looking right back at me. And in her deep blue eyes there is something cold and hard, and way beyond her years.

Chapter Three

Extract from Explore Suffolk website

Fortune's Yard is a hidden treasure of the Suffolk countryside. Barely warranting the description of a hamlet, it's a tiny, picture-perfect collection of three houses and a pub, arranged around a millpond, buried deep in the country lanes, three miles from the coastal village of Orford. Fortune's Yard is a place to take a deep breath, throw off your everyday cares, and enjoy the serenity of the beautiful countryside surroundings that seem like they belong to another century.

A settlement on this spot was recorded in the Domesday Book, although little of the older village remains and most of the current buildings date from the early 1800s. If you're approaching Fortune's Yard along the lane (cars not recommended), the first dwelling you'll encounter is the old watermill. Built of sand-coloured stone, and today an attractive family home, it stands opposite the millpond, with its resident pair of swans. Immediately past the old watermill, you'll reach a crossroads. Here, you can turn right, down a wide sand track that becomes a footpath, to pass the beautiful red-brick farmhouse, which still has some of its original outbuildings. If you're lucky, the owners might have put out eggs for sale from their collection of rare-breed hens.

Retrace your steps and this time head in the opposite direction at the crossroads, and you'll come across the final home that makes up this miniature community: what used to be a workman's dwelling and is now everyone's idea of a perfect country cottage, complete with requisite roses around the door. Beyond the cottage is a small country pub. The Fortune's Arms is the only remaining part of the older village that originally stood on this site, but having served as a haven for walkers for centuries, it sadly closed its doors in 2022 and is now looking for a new owner.

As well as the charms of the place itself, there is much to enjoy in the area surrounding it. The community is bordered on three sides by Fortune's Woods, which are criss-crossed by a warren of foot-paths and home to a host of wildlife. On the other side there is marshland. As you stand beside the millpond and look around you, there are no other buildings in sight, and on a quiet day, you might start to feel there are no other buildings in the world. Fortune's Yard is a true haven from reality and a place where you can let your imagination run wild.

Chapter Four

Beth

'What do you think?'

Noah is already out of the car. I haven't even turned the engine off yet.

'Give me two seconds.'

One of the things that drew me to Noah from the first time I met him – apart from the aforementioned hotness – is his positivity. For a man of nearly forty, he's refreshingly free from mid-life weary cynicism and keen to seek out new experiences. He wants to share the things that are special to him. Fortune's Yard is one of those things. It's where his parents still lived until a few months ago. It was his family home, and now it's going to be ours. And mainly, I think as I take a deep breath and turn off the ignition, that is a brilliant thing, and if it's also a little bit terrifying, that's totally understandable.

I unbuckle my seatbelt and get out, my legs cramped after three hours of driving. Dolly and Bluebell clamber out of the back, the latter belting over to a patch of interesting grass on the other side of the lane and Dolly following and calling her name. Noah, who's gazing lovingly at the converted watermill built from warm amber stone, reaches out and puts an arm around my waist. I'm all clammy and crumpled, despite the air con, but I lean into him and look around me. I know what I'm meant to say and I say it.

'It's perfect.'

And it is perfect. Like something from that romcom with Cameron Diaz where she swaps her busy life in the uncaring city for Kate Winslet's cottage deep in the English countryside. *The Holiday*. Except this is for keeps.

'Really? We're doing the right thing?'

'Of course we are. It's so…' I search for the right word. 'Still.'

'Still?'

'Peaceful.'

I've been here before, of course. I'm not so mad that I'd move somewhere without at least visiting it. But only once. That was a few months ago, when Noah and I came down to look at the house just after his parents had moved out. It was evening and we seemed like the only souls on earth. At that point, it had all felt like a huge and slightly unreal adventure. We'd explored the half-emptied house, going from room to room, and then we'd driven back to Aldeburgh, where we were staying, and talked through the decision to move here, permanently. Noah twists round from looking at our new home, aptly named the Old Watermill. I follow his gaze. Behind us, Dolly is facing the other direction, surveying the millpond that stands on the opposite side of the lane. Bluebell is near her, still furiously sniffing at the grass and wagging her tail.

'Come over here a minute, Dolly,' Noah calls to her and she obediently wanders over to stand beside us. He reaches out his other arm, so that he's hugging us both to him – a tight family unit.

'I love this place,' says Dolly. She sounds relaxed, happy even. Right from the start, she's been positive about the idea of the move. I thought she'd hate the idea of leaving London, with all its distractions, but I'm probably just projecting my own worries about leaving the city onto her. It's not like she spends her evenings exploring the capital's cultural life. She's thirteen. She spends most of her evenings on her phone, something Sasha tells me is pretty much standard.

Of course, Dolly knows Fortune's Yard already – her grandparents used to live here. She and Noah came down last weekend, with the big removal van, while I was away in Brighton for Sasha's fortieth, and ever since then, she's been talking about how she can't wait to come back. I feel a surge of hope, despite that weird moment in the car. Perhaps a fresh start really is all we need.

'It's like a million times better than Streatham,' Dolly says.

Noah laughs.

'I'm glad you approve.'

'Did you see the swans?' she asks.

'Wait till Bluebell notices them,' I say, 'They're going to blow her mind.'

'We'll have to point out the *No Bathing* sign to Blue-bell,' Noah says, pointing to a notice by the millpond. 'You know how she likes a dip!' Dolly and I both laugh at the same time. A phenomenon sufficiently rare for me to notice it and one that seems like a good omen. Noah beams back at us, also delighted by our joint reaction.

'Good morning all!'

The voice that greets us is unashamedly posh and confident. We all swing round, the family group more ragged now. Standing in front of us, wearing gardening gloves and holding a pair of vicious-looking shears, is a small woman with wavy cropped hair and big burgundy-rimmed glasses. I'd put her in her mid-fifties.

'Noah, how are you? You're looking well and very tanned. And Dolly, how are you, sweetheart? Good to see you again.'

'Hi Aunty Meg,' Dolly says, easily, as though she's known this woman all her life – and maybe, it suddenly occurs to me, she has.

Meg smiles at me with what seems like genuine warmth, but there's something about her expression that's making me ever so slightly uneasy, as though she's assessing me to decide whether I'll pass some kind of test. Her eyes behind the Gloria Steinem spectacles are sharp with intelligence.

'Aren't you going to introduce us Noah?' she demands.

'Of course, I'm so sorry.' Noah is standing at my elbow, and places a hand on my arm. 'Meg this is my wife, Beth. Beth, meet Meg. Meg and Stuart live just round the corner in the old farmhouse. See, just over there.' He gestures to a red-brick Victorian building emerging from the trees. I can't help noticing that it is, as Noah says, just over there. I don't remember the houses being so close together last time we came down. 'They've lived here almost as long as my parents.'

'Coming up for forty-one years in November.' I mentally readjust Meg's age – she must be at least in her early sixties. 'We brought up all our kids here.'

'And now those kids have kids of their own,' Noah says.

'It's terrifying,' Meg says. 'Beth I won't hug you because I don't want to impale you with these shears – you caught me mid-way through cutting back one of our hedges, I saw you from up my stepladder – but I want you to know you're very welcome. Oh, and I almost forgot to

19

say, Stuart and I have left you a little surprise in the back garden. A sort of housewarming present. I hope you like it.'

'That's really nice of you. You didn't need to.'

'Well, we're so pleased to have you all. It can get pretty lonely here in the evenings, once the walkers have left, so we're a tight-knit bunch. Anyway, I should let you get on. I only popped over to invite you round for drinks this evening. Nothing fancy, you understand. Just a chance for us to say a proper welcome and for you to meet your other neighbours.'

'That's very kind of you, Meg,' Noah says.

'Seven o'clock suit you?'

I don't think Noah and I even knew the names of the people we lived next door to in Streatham, and here we are on night one in Fortune's Yard having drinks with the neighbours.

'Seven sounds perfect,' I say. 'Thank you.'

It's the second time I've used that word since I arrived. And really everything should be perfect. But for some reason I'm beginning to feel uneasy. The stillness has started to feel slightly oppressive. In an effort to shake the unsettling feeling off, once Meg has said her goodbyes, I say brightly, 'Why don't we go and have a look at Meg's housewarming present before we unpack the car?'

'Good idea. Are you coming Dolly?' Noah asks.

'I already know what it is. Aunty Meg showed me last weekend. Please can I go and see my room?'

While Noah is looking for the house keys to give to Dolly, I make my way down the gravel path to the left of the Old Watermill, which I remember from last time leads to the back garden: a quarter of an acre of well-tended lawn and flowerbeds, backed by woodland. With the exception of a concreted yard about half a metre wide and three metres long at the back of my old ground-floor flat in Clapham, and the square of fake grass at our rented house in Streatham, it's the only garden I've ever had. London doesn't really lend itself to gardens. I suppose Noah and I are going to have to learn how to look after this one; we can't rely on the after-effects of his parents' loving attention to keep it in order for much longer. I'm looking for a plant of some kind on the half-moon shaped stone terrace immediately at the back of the house, but there's nothing other than the impeccably maintained garden furniture. Maybe Meg and Stuart planted their gift somewhere?

I look around me. That's when I notice. There are three people at the bottom of the garden, down by the woods. They're not moving. In fact, they look like they're watching something. The heat shimmers around them and the sun is in my eyes making it difficult to see them properly, but I think they're facing this way. Are they watching me? Surely there's not a footpath through the garden – Noah would have mentioned that, wouldn't he? I suppose they could have found their way in by mistake, but why are they just standing there, staring?

I call out an uncertain 'Hi,' and take a couple of steps in their direction, but they neither move nor respond, and heart thudding, I stop again, wary. There's a malevolence to the stillness of their gaze – to their silence. Despite the warmth of the day, I feel a chill inch down my spine. There's something really not right about these people. About this place.

Just as I'm thinking this, Bluebell shoots around the corner of the house and bounds off across the lawn, making straight for the little group. It's not a conscious decision, but when they still don't move, I start to follow her and this time I don't stop. As I make my way over the grass towards them, I realise what I'm seeing.

The tallest of the figures is dressed in a navy-blue sweatshirt and slacks and has his arm around one of the two female figures. A pair of glasses have been safety-pinned to his sackcloth face. The middle figure has string hair, and is wearing a flowery long-sleeved dress and a scarf that makes me stop dead in my tracks. There's a big grin drawn on her face. The smaller female figure has plaits and is dressed in leggings and a pale pink shirt. There's even a sackcloth dog on a baler twine lead.

'They're scarecrow versions of us,' Noah says from behind me.

'They're really creepy,' I say, finding my voice.

'It's a kind of tradition.' He sounds a bit hurt. 'Apparently my parents made a scarecrow family for Meg and Stuart when they first moved to Fortune's Yard. There's an old photo somewhere. Meg was telling me about it last weekend. I had no idea she and Stuart were going to go to all this trouble though.'

'I sort of wish they'd stuck to a bottle of wine.'

'I suppose they are a bit unnerving. We'll have to leave them up for a while, or they'll be offended, but don't worry, I'll think of something. We can put them in the shed maybe.'

'It's not a big deal,' I say. 'Sorry. It's just not what I was expecting, that's all.'

My eyes are drawn back to the scarecrow version of me. Bluebell is busy sniffing round her scarecrow counterpart and I call her over. When she ignores me – a common occurrence when she's found something interesting – I snap at her, and she comes at once, tail between her legs.

Noah is watching me, his steady brown eyes, so calm and different from Dolly's startling blue ones, full of concern.

'What's wrong Beth?'

'That scarf. The one on my scarecrow.'

'What about it?'

'It's really like the one I was wearing that day, that's all.'

'What day?'

'The day of the mugging.'

Chapter Five

Beth

'Are you two ever coming inside?'

Dolly's tone as she shouts down to us from an upstairs window is exasperated but not unfriendly. Despite most of my mind being preoccupied with the scarf, I note the 'you two'. It's a phrase I don't think I've heard her use before, and it gives me another little surge of excitement. It suggests that she sees Noah and me as a couple, which we are of course, but I've never been sure that's how Dolly thinks of it, even after our marriage. There's a photo of the three of us standing on the steps of Lambeth Town Hall just after the marriage ceremony. Dolly is looking very young in bunches and a pink sundress and beaming for the camera as if she's delighted about the whole thing, but once the pictures had been taken, the smile had vanished as quickly as the photographer, who was running late for another wedding.

'On our way!' Noah says, and takes my hand, leading me back across the grass. Bluebell trots happily in front of us. I do my best to put the unsettling housewarming present, the scarf, and the wider feeling that there's something not quite right about Fortune's Yard firmly behind me. It helps that there's an instant distraction in the form of the Old Watermill itself. Apart from the kitchen, I don't remember much about the interior of the house. I didn't even take photos when Noah and I came before, so all I've got to go on is my memory – and strangely, I can remember the hotel we stayed in in Aldeburgh much more clearly than my future home. It's like my brain refused to take it in properly last time.

We go around to the front door and the first thing that hits me as we step inside is just how much room there is. There's a proper hallway – not a tiny pocket of space rammed full of shoes, bags, umbrellas and other crap, like in our rented house in Streatham. It has a tiled black-and-white floor and a wide staircase, with pistachio carpet and elegant mahogany banisters. There's a welcome coolness to the interior after the heat of the garden. It smells faintly, and not unpleasantly, of furniture polish. Even inside, you can hear the rush of water from the stream that still goes past the building – a reminder of the days when it was a working watermill, although the wheel itself has long since ceased to turn. I try to fix it all in my mind: the big moment when we start our new lives.

'Shall we do a tour?' Noah says, making me jump, and I remember that although this is a big moment for him too, it's not quite the same. In a sense, this is already his home, and now he wants to show it off to me. 'We can unload the car later.'

'Of course,' I say, at the same time as Dolly hurtles down the stairs in a tangle of teenage limbs and says excitedly:

'Come and see the kitchen first, Beth! You're going to love it.'

It's sweet of her and I don't want to spoil the moment by telling her I already saw it on my previous visit, even if a small part of me suspects that the display of enthusiasm is largely for Noah's benefit. She opens the door to the left of the hallway. The kitchen is vast. The entire downstairs of our Streatham terrace would probably fit in its footprint. Noah told me his parents had it refitted a couple of years ago. The floor is made up of terracotta flagstones, picking out the colours in the exposed stone wall that runs down one side of the room. The cabinets are handmade and painted a warm cream. The overall design is probably a bit more rustic than I'd have chosen, but it's stunning. A huge stone sink sits under windows that look out onto a view so perfect that it's hard to believe it's real: the mill-pond shimmering in the bright afternoon sunshine and the swans gliding across the water side by side. Removal boxes are piled up against the far wall and I'm itching to start unpacking so that I can bake something, but I know Noah will want to tour me round the rest of the house first.

'I can't get my head around the fact that I'm actually going to be cooking in here,' I say, as I follow them back out into the hallway, Dolly bouncing ahead, almost unrecognisable from the child who sat in the back of the car with her earbuds in, glaring at me from hostile blue eyes.

Apart from the kitchen, my favourite room downstairs is the library. It really is a library, with actual bookshelves and everything. I feel a bit like I'm going to be living in a game of Cluedo. I'm not sure I'll ever get used to having all these rooms. It's not just my London life. Even growing up I lived in a small 1930s semi, and my main memory is of me and my parents all living on top of each other, overhearing each other's conversations and tripping over each other's things. It felt like a place where it was impossible to have secrets. Which is ironic, of course, in the light of what I discovered about them later.

The library has a large leather sofa and glass doors leading straight out to the garden. It's full of light and I know that this is where Noah and I are going to end up relaxing. There's also something Noah and Dolly call 'the posh sitting room' at the front of the house, on the opposite side of the hallway to the kitchen. It features some garish floral wallpaper and a swirly patterned carpet that makes my head ache. It feels more stuffy and old-fashioned than the rest of the house and now that I have the luxury of a choice of living spaces, I definitely prefer the library at the back.

Trailing in Dolly's wake, we head upstairs where she informs me that she has already chosen the bedroom at the back, which used to be her dad's when he was a kid. There are five bedrooms in total and I feel a sudden panic about what we're going to do with them all.

'Have lots of people up to stay,' Noah says cheerfully when I voice what I'm thinking. And of course that's exactly what we should do, although it suddenly seems impossible to imagine any of our London friends in this place. London itself – with its relentless noise, its grime and its life – already seems like a distant memory, and I feel separated from it by far more than the three hours we've spent in the car. But this is better, I tell myself. This is clearly better. Who wouldn't want space? And quiet? And although Fortune's Yard itself makes me feel a little claustrophobic, the house doesn't. At least the downstairs didn't. Upstairs, I notice, the ceilings are lower so although it's still quite roomy, it's also a little oppressive, like the house is slowly pressing down on us. And somehow the very expanse of it is increasing my anxiety. Is it possible to feel smothered by too much space?

While Dolly plans out where she's going to put everything in her new room, Noah takes me back along the landing to his parents' old bedroom at the front of the house. He seems to take it for granted that this should be our room and I suppose it does make sense: it's clearly the main bedroom and it even has its own en suite. And at least I won't have to look out on the scarecrows. But I also feel slightly uncomfortable about simply adopting all his parents' old choices, as if we have no agency of our own. As we stand in the doorway, there's a sudden machine-gun burst of barks. Bluebell, who we've all forgotten, has clearly spotted something exciting outside.

'I'll go!' shouts Dolly from her room. We hear her thunder down the stairs, but the barking continues.

'I'd better go and find out what's going on.' Noah gives me a quick kiss. 'You finish exploring up here.'

But when he leaves me, I don't move. It's all so over-whelming. I feel like I'm on the brink of something huge, and before I step forward and embrace it, I need to be sure I'm ready for it. In my throat, I can feel a small lump of doubt threatening to expand and choke me. Yes, we needed a change, but isn't this too much of a change? And why can't I rid myself of the nagging feeling that there's something wrong here – that the whole village is hiding something? The barking has stopped and all I can hear now is the soft sound of water rushing past the building and beneath it the numbing hum of silence, stretching ahead for hours, days, months.

I look around Noah's parents' bedroom, trying to focus on what's immediately in front of me. I take in the brass bed frame, the uneven ceiling that slopes down to the old windows with their Cath Kidston wild poppy curtains, the warm buttermilk paint on the walls and the faint marks where pictures that hung for decades have been taken down. It's a really nice room. I'm not sure I like Noah's parents' taste in curtains – way too flowery – but I approve of the general colour scheme, which makes me feel like I'm bathed in warmth. I take a deep breath. Maybe this is going to be okay.

I whisper the words out loud to myself, like an affirmation: 'I can do this.'

I feel a bony hand on my shoulder; I cry out and whip round.

Chapter Six

Beth

'Welcome to Fortune's Yard!'

It's later the same day and we're at Meg and Stuart's. Meg holds the front door open wide and this time she does hug me. A powerful hug for a small and apparently slight woman. It's hard to hug her back as I'm carrying a box of raspberry macarons that I just made, but I do my best and actually, although I still can't entirely shake my earlier feeling that Meg is assessing me for some sort of unknown test, and I seriously dislike her taste in housewarming presents, there's something about her enthusiasm that is instantly welcoming. I already feel like I've known her for ever, even though I met her for the first time this afternoon. Dolly allows herself to be hugged too; she even shows signs of enjoying it.

'I made you this,' she says shyly, and hands Meg a homemade card. I look over her shoulder. The front is filled with a picture of the millpond, complete with two large swans, presided over by a sun with a big smile on its face – reminding me unsettlingly of the smile on my scarecrow – and inside the message reads: *I'm really looking forward to living here – thank you for making me welcome. Dolly xx*

'Sweetheart, that's so kind of you,' Meg says. 'I'll treasure it.'

It's a thoughtful gesture and I feel a rush of pride in Dolly. She'd nearly given me a heart attack earlier when she'd crept up on me in the bedroom, and I still feel mortified at the thought that she might have heard me whispering to myself. She'd apologised straight away – she hadn't meant to frighten me, she said, she just wanted to let me know that her dad had started unloading the car. She thought I'd heard her coming up the stairs, and it's strange that I didn't, although I suppose I'd been in a world of my own. It had taken several minutes for my heartrate to return to normal and, as I went down to help Noah, I made a mental note that in a house as big as the Old Watermill, you don't necessarily hear people coming.

Meg makes room for the card on the Lancashire dresser, which is covered with post, old copies of *Country Life* magazine and bits of fruit. When she turns around, I can feel her inspecting me again.

'Beth, you look lovely,' she says. 'Where did you get that – what do you call it? My daughters would tell me off for forgetting. Playsuit?'

'Oh, thank you,' I say, relief coursing through me. I'm wearing a bright red jumpsuit that I always worry is slightly too tight on me, but it was the only vaguely smart thing I could find when I started unpacking my clothes and I want the neighbours to think I've made a bit of an effort. 'I actually got it off Vinted, but I think it's from Reiss originally.'

'What fun! I read an article about Vinted in the *Telegraph Magazine* and I keep meaning to try it. Look, you've baked for us too, how marvellous! Whenever did you find the time?'

'Oh, they don't take long and I thought I'd try out the new kitchen.'

The line in the blog about baking being my safe place is one of the things that made me want to die of embarrassment when I first read it, but, although it's not exactly how I put it on the phone, it's a pretty good summary of how I feel.

Once I'd helped Noah unload the car, I needed to do something to shift the feeling of uneasiness that had crept over me since our arrival and that had not been improved by the discovery of the three creepy scarecrows at the bottom of our garden and Dolly appearing out of nowhere behind me in the bedroom. Baking was the obvious choice and macarons are one of my favourite things to make. Just whisking the egg whites has an instantly soothing effect. It's no wonder I was feeling a bit on edge; however much I've been looking forward to the move, there's no getting away from the fact that it's a massive change. By the time the tiny pale pink domes were cooling on Noah's parents' state-of-the-art marble work surface, I was already feeling better.

'Your kitchen is beautiful. Not like mine – total chaos I'm afraid.' Meg looks around her cheerfully. I follow her gaze. I'm always interested in other people's kitchens and I used to get kitchen envy when I saw how much space and storage some people had. Now I have more space than I know what to do with, but it's probably going to be hard to shake the habit. Meg's kitchen is the sort of size I could once only have dreamt of, with very high ceilings, but the windows are also set high up making it rather gloomy. It's not just the Lancashire dresser; there is clutter on every work surface. Mugs, plates and packets of food jostle for room with dog leads, sunglasses and insect repellent.

'Now, tell me, did you love the scarecrows?'

'They must have taken you ages,' I say, making my voice as warm as I can. I'm never going to love, or even like, the scarecrows, but I'm feeling much better about them now. There are loads of silver scarfs like that. I happened to be wearing mine the day a group of kids stole my bag, and for me, it would be for ever associated with that moment. Meg putting a similar scarf on the scarecrow was just a stupid coincidence, and coming on top of the stress of moving no wonder it panicked me. 'Thank you.'

'We had a lot of fun doing it. Did Noah tell you that his parents did something similar for Stuart and me when we first moved here? We treasured them for years, until they finally succumbed to the weather.'

Noah and I exchange glances. So much for putting them in the shed after a few weeks.

'Aunty Meg, is Laura here?' Dolly says eagerly, as soon as there's a pause in the conversation.

'Not at the moment, sweetheart, but she'll be back tomorrow and I'm sure she'll be thrilled to see you again.'

Dolly's face falls.

'Laura is our youngest,' Meg explains to me. 'Dolly went for a walk with her last weekend.'

I feel a slight puzzlement about ages. Is Laura Dolly's age? When Meg talked about her children before, I'd assumed they were all adults. Didn't she say something about them leaving home? But Dolly certainly seems keen to see Laura, so maybe I misunderstood. It would be nice for her to have a friend living in Fortune's Yard. As if reading my mind, Meg adds, 'You'll meet her before long, Beth, and I think you two will really get on. She's about your age.'

33

I mentally put Laura back in the adult category. She's clearly just an adult whom Dolly has taken to. Whatever Laura is doing, she must be doing a good job of it and I make a mental note to ask for tips when I do meet her. I like the idea of someone my own age to hang out with, even if Laura isn't a permanent resident of Fortune's Yard.

'How's everything going with the baby?' Noah asks. 'I didn't get a chance to talk to her last weekend.'

Meg's face clouds over.

'It's exhausting in the early months,' Noah says sympathetically. 'You're so sleep-deprived you can barely function. I know exactly how Laura and— what's her husband's name again?'

'Ewan.' She hesitates, still looking troubled. 'But I'm afraid things aren't in a terribly good place right now.'

The door to the kitchen opens and a tall, balding man, in his late sixties comes in, accompanied by a very enthusiastic border collie, who weaves in and out of our legs. The kitchen suddenly feels much busier, despite its size.

'Ah, here's my errant husband,' Meg says. 'Beth, meet Stuart. And this is our dog, Drake. Just push him away Dolly if he's bothering you.'

'You're very welcome, Beth. Welcome one and all! The rest of us are in the other room. We were wondering where you'd got to.' Stuart beams at us.

'I was just explaining about Laura and Ewan.'

'Ah yes,' Stuart says, his voice suddenly far less jovial. 'No need to go into all of that now is there? We don't want to depress Noah and Beth on their first evening.'

'Noah was asking after them.'

'Well then,' Stuart says. And the tension in the room is suddenly almost tangible. Stuart and Meg are wordlessly communicating something. I catch Noah's eye. We've

34

only been here five minutes and we seem to have inadvert-
ently stumbled onto the awkward topic of conversation.
You can tell we're not used to neighbourly drinks.

'Laura and Ewan are spending some time apart,' Meg
says, putting us out of our misery. 'At least that's what
Laura says, but I actually think they've split up permanently.'

'Oh, I'm sorry,' Noah says. I wonder how well he
knows Laura and her husband. He's never mentioned her
to me that I remember.

'It's obviously a very difficult time for her. Stuart and I
are doing everything we can to help.'

'I'm sure it makes a big difference having the two of
you to support her.'

'That's what you do for your children, isn't it?' Meg
says. 'You're always there for them, no matter how old they
are.' Noah takes my hand and gives it a gentle squeeze. He
knows parents are a difficult topic for me.

'Is Laura staying up here?'

'Well she's back at work, so she's in London during the
week, but she's up here most weekends, and she's got some
leave coming up next week, thank goodness.'

'Laura's a lawyer,' Noah explains to me. 'One of those
big city firms.'

'This place has become a bit of a harbour in a storm for
her, I think,' Stuart says, but he still seems uncomfortable
and the next moment he changes the subject. 'Shall we
shut Drake out here, Meg? He nearly sent Ralph flying
just now.'

'Yes of course. Ralph seems a bit unsteady on his feet
tonight, doesn't he?'

'Anyone would be unsteady with this menace around,'
Stuart says, giving Drake an affectionate rub on the head.

The collie wags his tail enthusiastically. The tension has vanished almost as quickly as it arrived. 'Do we have any elderflower cordial, Meg? I thought I took it through earlier, but I can't find it on the tray and Ralph wants a glass.'

'It's by the breadbin, over there.'

'Ah yes.' Stuart retrieves a bottle from the sea of vaguely culinary detritus. 'Don't hog our guests of honour too long out here in the kitchen. Let them come through to the living room and I'll fetch them a drink.'

He disappears out of the door again.

'Stuart's right – I'm being very rude keeping you out here when there are people dying to meet you next door. Let's go through shall we and put them out of their misery.'

Meg and Noah leave the kitchen first – Noah asking Meg something alarming to do with septic tanks; not something that troubled us in Streatham – and I follow. Dolly is stroking a sad-eyed Drake, who's sitting in the middle of the kitchen floor, and telling him we'll be back soon. I glance back at her – she really is good with animals – and then follow Meg and Noah. The kitchen door clicks as Dolly closes it behind her. Noah and Meg disappear through a doorway on the left. I'm just about to plunge after them when I hear Dolly's voice, low behind me.

'You look really fat in that jumpsuit.'

Then she brushes past me into the living room.

Chapter Seven

School report for Dolly James
St Mark's Secondary School, Streatham
Summer Term 2024

We're so sorry Dolly is leaving us at the end of this term. She's been a tremendous asset to St Mark's since she joined us in Year Seven, and has grown from a rather shy and withdrawn eleven-year-old to a confident thirteen-year-old who demonstrates a positive attitude to all aspects of school life. This is all the more remarkable given the personal tragedy she has suffered.

Dolly is popular with staff and students alike. She's been an enthusiastic participant in our mentor scheme, taking two Year Seven pupils under her wing and helping them to settle into secondary school life. She also led an interesting assembly for Kindness Week, focusing on the difference even the smallest acts can make to someone's day.

Drama continues to be a particularly strong subject for Dolly and her performance in this summer's production of Alice in Wonderland demonstrated a real talent for inhabiting a part. Academically, Dolly has gone from strength to

*strength. She has a love of learning and, from what
I read of her subject reports below, I'm sure Dolly
will thrive at her new school. We wish her all the
best as she goes on to study for her GCSEs.*

Chapter Eight

Beth

I take a sip of the fruity Cabernet Sauvignon Stuart handed me a few minutes earlier when I stood frozen in the doorway, wondering if I'd somehow misheard Dolly, and try to focus on what he's telling me about the history of Fortune's Yard.

You look fab in that jumpsuit.

That would sound very similar wouldn't it? It's my own paranoia surely that heard fat. After all, Dolly's never said anything horrible to me before. During the two months we lived together in Streatham, she went out of her way to avoid my company and when she was forced to spend time with me, she alternated between extreme politeness when Noah or anyone else was present, and silent indifference when we were alone. For all kinds of reasons, not least that I'm standing in a room of people I barely know, I want to believe that I'm wrong about what I thought I heard. But somehow, the idea of Dolly telling me I look fab is even harder to believe. Stuart is asking me a question which I barely hear over my own thoughts.

'There's a local history society, if you're interested in that kind of thing, Beth?'

'Oh great. Yes.'

I'm not sure what kind of thing I'm expressing an interest in, but I don't want to be rude to Stuart by asking him to repeat himself.

'I have an extremely rare journal, written by one of the previous residents of this farmhouse. It's a kind of local history, going back several hundred years, and it's got a whole chapter about Hannah Fortune – she's the girl I was telling you about. It's quite hard to read the handwriting, but it's well worth the effort. I must show it to you some time.'

I take another mouthful of wine and force myself to concentrate.

'I'd like that, thanks.'

'Our kids used to love reading it when they were Dolly's age, especially all the gory details. It's good to know about the place where you live, don't you think? Of course, I'm a history teacher, so I'm biased.'

At the mention of Dolly, I glance round the room, to see where she is now. Like the kitchen, the living room is cluttered with seemingly random objects and is quite dark – not helped by the fact that the walls are papered in a rusty red print and, even though it's still light outside, the blinds have been pulled down, creating a Stygian feel that the glow of two faint table lamps can't quite extinguish. There's a lot of stained dark Victorian furniture and two big sofas, covered in gold brocade, arranged at right angles in a V-shape. One of them contains a thin, bird-like woman, and next to her, chatting away, is Dolly.

Following my gaze, Stuart says, 'I'm so sorry Beth, here I am boring on at you and what I should be doing is introducing you to Ralph and Evelyn. They live in Workshop Cottage, just the other side of the crossroads.' It really is just the other side of the crossroads. We saw it as we walked over, a tiny cottage built from the same sandstone as the Old Watermill. Stuart lowers his voice slightly. 'You and Noah are very honoured. Evelyn is a bit of invalid and she hardly ever leaves the house. She tires very easily, poor woman, and I'm afraid she's getting more and more confused. I know Ralph worries a lot about her. We weren't expecting her to be able to come tonight, but Ralph said she was determined to meet you all. Come with me and I'll introduce you.'

As soon as Dolly sees us making our way towards her, she springs up and heads over to the window where Noah and Meg are talking to a slightly stooped man with a full head of silver hair, who must be Ralph. Stuart introduces us and Evelyn pats the place next to her on the sofa. Her grey eyes are slightly cloudy. She has thin, stark-white hair pulled back into a bun and is wearing a jade cardigan with a beautiful silver brooch that shows an elaborately worked tree. She's clearly made an effort for her evening out, and suddenly I'm glad I did too, whatever Dolly thinks of my outfit.

I obediently sit. Stuart takes Evelyn's glass away to refill it. She instantly takes my free hand in hers, and squeezes it with a strong grip that belies the age-mottled skin. Her wedding ring, a plain gold band, is digging into my flesh, but I don't want to pull away.

'I've just been talking to Dolly. What a delightful child she is. You hear such terrible things about young people nowadays, especially in London, how they all carry knives and go shoplifting. It's a pleasure to meet one who has such good manners.'

'Oh, I'm glad you liked her,' I say, gently extracting my hand. Because what else can I say? Strangers nearly always do like Dolly. *I* like Dolly, I remind myself. I just wish she showed any indication of liking me.

'Your husband must be very proud of her.'

I think of the lovely card she made for Meg.

'We both are.'

Her cloudy eyes fixed on mine, she suddenly asks: 'Tell me, when are you going to start a family of your own?'

'I'm sorry?'

'I'm wondering when you are going to start a real family,' she says unmistakably, her voice thin but clear. Out of the corner of my eye, I see Dolly leaving the room and wonder if she's going to check on Drake.

'We're a real family already,' I say brightly.

'Make sure you don't leave it too late,' Evelyn continues as if I hadn't spoken. 'I had my two before I was thirty, but you young women nowadays seem to think you have all the time in the world and then before you know it you've missed your chance. I know you must think I'm an interfering old woman, but sometimes interfering old women really do know best.'

'Well,' I say, reminding myself that Evelyn is not only our new neighbour but a very old lady who rarely leaves the house and has done so tonight specifically to meet me and Noah, 'I suppose there are lots of reasons why people might not have children of their own.'

'I think one of the main problems is that people are too selfish nowadays.'

I search for some way of rescuing this conversation.

'Do your own children live locally?'

'Oh no. You see, Ralph and I aren't from this part of the world originally. We moved up here six years ago when Ralph retired. Our sons don't live near.' All of the animation leaves her voice and she says, almost to herself, 'We don't see them very often.'

'That's a shame,' I say, feeling sorry for her. 'You must miss them.'

'They have lives of their own now,' she says, the wistfulness still in her voice. 'And children of their own.'

I fear we're about to start again, so I'm relieved when she calls out to the old man who's walking towards us.

'Ralph, come and meet Bethany.'

'Beth,' I say standing up, and beaming at Ralph. At the very least, hopefully he'll lead to a change in conversation. Ralph doesn't beam back. In fact, I sense he's very much not a beamer. He has a pinched, sour face and hard grey eyes beneath his full head of silver hair, and my sympathy for Evelyn increases. He smells faintly of stale tobacco. Like his wife, he is smartly dressed, wearing a forest green tie and a matching V-neck sweater. I'm not sure whether it's my crimson jumpsuit or me generally that's making him wrinkle his face in disapproval.

'Pleased to meet you,' he says, looking anything but, and taking a seat on the edge of the other sofa. He's perched as though readying to spring up and leave at any moment, and I'm starting to know how he feels. When I sit down again, I shift position slightly so that I can see both him and Evelyn. My attention is drawn to a round side table, every inch of which is covered in old photographs. There are a lot of family shots, stretching back over decades. Variations of Meg and Stuart, their three children and a menagerie of dogs, captured in a succession of life events: children's parties, school photos, picnics on the beach, graduation shots. Pictures of babies and grandchildren. They look like a happy family, but I suppose that table is like the Instagram of yesteryear – it's only going to show me the golden moments.

Some of the photos feature other people too, and it takes me a while to spot that one of them is Noah. He looks so much younger; it must have been taken about twenty years ago. He's wearing black tie – not something I've ever seen him in in real life – and standing beside a pretty woman of about eighteen, who's in the other photos and must be one of Meg and Stuart's daughters. She's wearing a midnight blue ballgown and her fair hair is cut in a Twenties-style bob. Noah is clutching a bottle of champagne and both of them are laughing. It's weird seeing this younger Noah frozen in a moment of carefree joy from nearly two decades ago. I think I can even make out the millpond in the background, so the photo must have been taken here in Fortune's Yard.

'You're not overdoing it are you, Evelyn?' Ralph asks. 'I can take you home any time you'd like.' At least his concern for her seems genuine.

'Not at all. I've been having a lovely time talking to Bethany here, and before that to Dolly. Isn't she a sweet child?'

Ralph purses his lips, and I sense that, for once, Dolly hasn't necessarily made a hit. Mind you, having Ralph like you wouldn't be a badge of honour for anyone as far as I can see.

'Dolly was telling me all about the subjects that she's studying. She's taking music, Ralph. She listens to a lot of—' She breaks off. 'What was it she said? Some kind of foreign music she was telling me about. It sounded very interesting. I was saying she should ask you for advice.'

'Oh, are you a musician?' I say, pleased to have something to ask him about.

'Ralph sings in the church choir,' Evelyn says proudly.

'That must be fun.'

'It is a service I perform for God.'

That told me.

'Is there a church in Fortune's Yard?'

They both laugh, Evelyn a light tinkling and Ralph a noise like he has heard of laughing and is trying to imitate it.

'Dear me, no,' says Evelyn. 'We're a very small community here in Fortune's Yard. The nearest church is in Orford, but that's a fifteen-minute drive away.' She makes a fifteen-minute drive sound like an impossible feat. 'Are you a churchgoer, Bethany?'

'I'm afraid not.'

'You're not worried about evil?' Ralph asks, and it takes me a few seconds to process the question, which is asked in the same tone of voice he might use to inquire whether I'm worried about potholes. I almost wish Evelyn would start talking about families again. I'm finding our new neighbours pretty heavy going and, despite all my efforts to seem positive, I can feel the creeping sense that there's something wrong about this place starting to take over again.

'Um,' I say, when it's clear he actually does expect me to say something. 'I suppose I don't really think about it very much. I mean, obviously I know evil things happen sometimes.'

As I say the words, I realise that it's not even true. I think about evil more than most people, probably. Thanks to my parents, I have good reason to know that evil things do happen sometimes.

'People do evil things all the time,' Ralph says. I know it's ridiculous, but it's as though he has seen into my mind and is giving voice to my innermost fears. 'Even people who are close to us. There is evil here in Fortune's Yard.'

'Surely not,' I say, too quickly.

'Oh yes,' he says solemnly, and I can't help noticing he sounds very pleased about it. 'And you must be prepared for it when you encounter it.'

'I suppose when I encounter it,' I retort as brightly as I can, 'I'll just try to do the right thing.'

Ralph stares back at me, his grey eyes shining with dislike.

'"There is a way that appears to be right,"' he says, and something about his voice tells me it's a biblical quote, '"but in the end it leads to death."'

Chapter Nine

Beth

Usually I'm terrible at extracting myself from conversations, but the urgency of my desire to be away from Ralph and Evelyn lends fluency to my excuses. Once I'm free, I go over to join Noah and Meg, who are standing by the windows, discussing something in a low voice. I don't catch any of what they're saying, but I get the sense it's no longer the septic tank. When they see me coming, they draw apart and make room for me to join. After Ralph's unsettling diatribe on evil, I'm struck again by how hospitable and welcoming Meg is.

'So, who else are we expecting?'

'This is it,' Meg says.

'There are three houses, Beth,' Noah says, putting an arm around my waist. 'And we live in one of them.'

'Oh yes, I realise that, sorry,' I say, feeling like an idiot. I just don't think I realised what that would mean in practice. The entire population of Fortune's Yard, our new home, is currently in this living room. And it still feels on the cavernous side, which is partly, it has to be said, because the old farmhouse where Meg and Stuart live is built along generous, if somewhat gloomy, lines, but also because the entire population of Fortune's Yard is precisely seven people. And that includes the three of us.

'There used to be more people of course,' Meg says, 'when the pub was still open.'

'Yes, the poor old Fortune's Arms. When I was growing up,' Noah explains to me, 'it was owned by this lovely family called the Wrens and it was a proper old-fashioned pub.'

'The Wrens still own it,' Meg says. 'They retired two years ago, but they can't find any buyers. The whole place is starting to look a bit sad, I'm afraid. There was a bad leak inside just before Christmas last year. We think it had been going on for weeks, but we only found out when we saw mould on the outside wall. The Wrens had asked us all to keep an eye on the place, so we felt terrible. They even gave us keys. You'll have a set too somewhere I expect. Stuart and I pop in every so often to check everything's okay and I have to confess I sometimes sneak in there and use the space – I made your scarecrow figures there, Beth. It gets so chaotic here,' she adds, looking around her as if the mess is somehow nothing to do with her.

I'm very glad I never saw the scarecrow figures when they were in the abandoned pub – they were disturbing enough at the end of our lawn.

'What a shame it can't find new owners,' Noah says. 'I was picturing sitting in the pub garden with Beth and Dolly and some beers, though no beer for Dolly of course.'

'Do you think Dolly's all right?' Meg says. 'I hope she's not too bored, spending time with all us oldies.'

Dolly has come back and is sitting on an ottoman at the far end of the room, scrolling through her phone, her hair loose and hanging over her face.

'I'll go and check on her,' Noah says.

'Don't worry, I'll go,' I say.

After all, I'm the adult in this relationship and My Blended Family is big on keeping lines of communication open. I walk across the room towards her, shoulders back, trying to appear confident. Stomach ever-so-slightly held in. I sit down beside her. She gives no indication that she knows I'm there. The ottoman is uncomfortable, and somewhat dusty.

'Everything okay?' I ask.

For a moment, I think she's going to ignore me again, but then she lifts her head and smiles slowly.

'Yeah, it's good.'

She tucks a strand of white-gold hair behind her ear.

'Big change from Streatham, right?' I say, aiming for conspiratorial.

'I like it.'

'Did you often come up to visit your grandparents?'

'Sometimes we'd come up. They mostly came to London to see us though. But I love it up here.'

'That's great. It's nice that it already has happy memories for you.'

'And for my dad. He's got like a bond with this place.'

This is a good conversation for us. She's not usually nearly so forthcoming when it's just the two of us. Maybe I really did mishear her earlier.

'Yes, I bet. It's where he grew up. His childhood home. That's amazing.'

'I mean, he's got strong ties to the people here.'

'He must have known Meg and Stuart since he was a child, I guess.'

'That's not what I meant actually.' She looks directly at me, her eyes bright. 'Laura and my dad, they were a couple. She could have been my mum.'

Chapter Ten

Beth

I'm still taking in Dolly's announcement when the door-bell rings. Clearly there are more people in Fortune's Yard after all – even if only temporarily.

'Whoever can that be?' Meg says, shouting to be heard above a cacophony of barking from Drake, who's still shut in the kitchen.

'One way to find out,' Stuart says cheerfully. 'Back in a minute everyone.' He goes out, closing the living room door behind him. It's quite some time before he returns and when he does, he's accompanied by a slender, fragile-looking woman, with long fair hair in a middle parting. She's an older, more troubled version of the woman in the midnight blue ballgown in the photo with Noah. I'm sure it's all in my head, but she looks, to my newly opened eyes, a little like Dolly, who bounds towards her with the energy of a puppy whose owner has just returned home, her face lit up. It would be endearing if it wasn't so exactly the opposite of how she behaves towards me.

'Laura!' exclaims Meg. 'Darling, we weren't expecting you until tomorrow. Why didn't you tell us you were coming up this evening?'

Like the pull of some invisible magnet, we have all now gravitated towards Laura in the doorway. Even Evelyn has got up.

'I'm sorry, I didn't know you'd have guests.' Laura sounds a bit like she might cry. I'm guessing having a new baby, a job as a high-flying lawyer and an absent partner might be a bit much for anyone to take. 'I just really needed to get out of London and I managed to get away early from work so I thought I'd surprise you by coming up tonight instead.'

Laura is still in what I assume is her work outfit: a dark grey trouser suit that's beautifully tailored and probably expensive.

'You know you're always welcome,' Stuart says, putting an arm around her thin shoulders. 'Any time. And you've met everyone anyway, apart from Beth here.'

Laura turns her gaze in my direction. She doesn't look exactly pleased to see me. Her eyes as they meet mine are full of suspicion. *She could have been my mum.* Dolly's words are playing in my head, despite my best attempts to bury them.

'You're Noah's wife?' she asks, and the question comes out sharply.

'Lovely to meet you, Laura,' I say, trying to make up for her lack of obvious enthusiasm with bucketloads of my own. I don't know what Dolly wants me to read into her revelation that Noah and Laura used to be a couple, but whatever it is I'm determined not to take the bait. Laura's probably just tired from her journey up from London and countless sleepless nights. Plus, she wasn't expecting anyone to be here and now she has to be sociable when all she wants to do is fall into bed. I'm not going to take her lack of warmth personally.

'Good to meet you too.' Her tone is still not particularly friendly, but she doesn't sound like a woman who's holding a torch for Noah. At least I don't think she does. 'When did you move in?'

'We actually only got here today.'

'Mum was straight in with the drinks invitation then,' she says, and I think it's meant as a joke but it comes out slightly wrong – as if she's resentful of my presence. But perhaps it's just that jokes are an effort for her right now.

'She sure was. Our social life is going to improve dramatically at this rate,' Noah says, leaning forward to give her a peck on the cheek. An old friends type peck on the cheek. His hand lingers briefly on her upper arm. Laura greets Dolly with enthusiasm, and Ralph and Evelyn politely, inquiring after Evelyn's health.

'I'd love to see the baby, Laura,' Evelyn says. 'Is she asleep?'

'Yes,' Laura says abruptly, and I know at once that Evelyn inspecting her baby is the very last thing she wants. 'I've taken her straight upstairs. She fell asleep on the drive up.'

'We don't want to wake her, Evelyn,' Meg says, shepherding the older lady back towards the sofa. 'Or we'll none of us get any peace tonight. Stuart, can you get Evelyn another sherry.' Ralph hurries forward to take Evelyn's arm. 'And Laura darling, do you want a drink?'

'I'll have a glass of red.'

'Should she be drinking if she's breastfeeding?' Evelyn says to Meg in what she clearly thinks is a low voice. The rest of us pretend we haven't heard.

'Laura's stopped breastfeeding now.'

'That's very soon, isn't it?'

'Well she's back at work now, Evelyn.'

I catch Laura's eye. She looks exhausted, even a bit haunted, but she manages a wry smile, which I return.

It's a brief moment of connection, and it gives me hope that we might actually get on and tonight is just a bad time for her. She has big dark circles like bruises under her blue eyes, and she looks like she might fall over if you gave her a light tap on the arm, but despite this, there's something compelling about her; she's brought an energy to the room that was lacking before she arrived.

Stuart is explaining to Laura that I invent recipes.

'On Instagram,' I add, seeing Laura look confused. 'I'm about to launch my own baking business.'

'Oh, amazing.' She still sounds tired, but her voice is definitely a bit friendlier now. 'I'll look you up.'

'I didn't have you down as a baker, Laura,' Noah says. And instantly it's there again, that little niggle that Dolly's planted in my head. Noah knows Laura well enough to know what she likes and doesn't like – or thinks he does.

'God no, I'm not,' she says. 'But I like looking at the pictures and imagining eating the results.'

'Actually, Laura darling, you've arrived just in time to try Beth's macarons,' Meg says. 'I was saving them up as a treat. I'll go and fetch them.'

Dolly has been very quiet so far, but every time I've glanced in her direction, her eyes have been fixed on Laura.

'Laura, can we go on another walk tomorrow?' she asks, with a kind of fervour that makes her seem suddenly much younger than her thirteen years. I wonder whether this enthusiasm is all connected in her mind with the idea that Laura could have been her mum or whether there's something else about Laura that's captured her attention so absolutely.

'Dolly, Laura's just arrived and she's exhausted,' Noah says. 'Give her a chance to settle in before you bombard her with requests.'

'No, it's okay, Noah. I don't mind.' And she honestly doesn't sound like she minds. In fact, she sounds positively eager. The pair of them have matching faces, alight with something I don't understand – some kind of connection much more profound than the fleeting moment Laura and I shared earlier. 'We can go tomorrow afternoon, Dolly. There's something I want to show you anyway.'

'Are you sure darling?' Meg says. 'You don't want to get some rest?'

'Can we take the baby?' Dolly asks.

'See how you feel in the morning Laura,' Meg says. 'No need to decide now.'

Just as I'm wondering whether I can ask what it is that Laura wants to show Dolly, there's a cough from behind us.

'Evelyn and I must be going.'

I'd forgotten all about Ralph, who's gathered up Evelyn from the sofa.

'Oh, that's a shame. Aren't you going to stay for a macaron?' Meg asks. 'Beth made them specially.'

'I'm afraid Evelyn is quite worn out,' Ralph says, glaring at me and somehow making it sound like my fault. Evelyn, leaning on his arm, smiles faintly and regards us through her cloudy grey eyes. 'She can't be held up for macarons.'

'Of course not. Did you have coats, the pair of you? Let me come and find them for you.'

'We don't want to be any trouble.'

'No trouble Ralph. I need to come out anyway to fetch the macarons. Beth, if you come with me, we'll find a pretty plate to show them off.'

I follow Meg out to the kitchen, and Stuart, Noah and Dolly follow Laura over to the sofas. Evelyn walks slowly down the hallway, leaning on Ralph's arm and it takes Meg and me a while to reunite them with coats and see them out of the front door. It's almost dark now, but Ralph has brought a torch with them and at least they don't have far to go. They can literally see their cottage from here. They eventually depart with Ralph bestowing an almost cheery sounding 'God Bless' as they walk up the lane. Meg shuts the door behind them and leans on it, with an exaggerated show of relief.

'I'm afraid Ralph can be rather hard work, but he means well. He worries a lot about Evelyn. She really is almost totally housebound. Can you reach up into that cupboard just above the kettle and get me the big plate with the gold flowers on it?' Meg opens the box of macarons and her face falls. 'Oh, what a shame!'

'What's wrong?' Dolly says, appearing in the kitchen doorway.

'I think someone must have knocked the macarons off the worktop,' Meg says, passing me the box. 'I'm so sorry Beth. They're all broken.'

'Oh no, you spent ages making those,' Dolly says.

Her face looks as tragic as Meg's, but as I bend my head to inspect the mess of pink shards and blood-red raspberry jam, I think I catch an almost imperceptible smile playing across her lips.

Chapter Eleven

Beth

'Why didn't you tell me about you and Laura?'

'Me and Laura?' Noah echoes stupidly.

I'm lying in a tangle in his arms, on top of the duvet, the light from the moon coming in through the Velux window above us and making a rectangle on the king size bed. The sex was good and for a while it had driven all other thoughts out of my head, but now they're back. I promised myself I wasn't going to take Dolly's bait and ask about Laura, but now that I have Noah to myself, I'm unable to resist.

'You used to be a couple.'

He pulls himself up on one elbow and looks down at me, his face all shadows and angles. He looks naked without his glasses, which is a strange thing to think when he literally is naked.

'Who told you that?'

'It just came up at the drinks thing.'

I'm unwilling to say it was Dolly.

'I think couple is something of an exaggeration. As I remember, which I would have to say is not very well, we went out for about three and a half weeks when I was seventeen. Our entire relationship probably consisted of a couple of walks to Orford, a few mixtapes and some inexpert kissing. I think she dumped me for Andy Sullivan, who was captain of the rugby team.'

'There's a photo of you both together in Meg and Stuart's living room.'

'Is there?'

'An old photo. You've got champagne and she's wearing a posh dress.'

'Oh God, yeah, I think I remember that picture. I didn't know they still had it up. It was Laura's eighteenth. They had a huge party. Meg loved the photo because you can see a champagne cork flying in the air in the top corner – it's not because she still harbours hopes of me and Laura ending up together if that's what's worrying you. In fact, I'm surprised she even remembers anything about the two of us.'

It's interesting he assumes Meg told me, although I suppose someone must have told Dolly, and presumably it wasn't Noah.

'It doesn't really bother you, does it?'

'No, of course not.'

And in that moment I really don't think it does.

'Because I feel honour-bound to tell you that I also once kissed Lisa, Meg and Stuart's other daughter. I seem to remember she threw up afterwards, although in hindsight I think that had more to do with the litre bottle of cider we'd shared than my kissing. It certainly knocked my confidence at the time though. And my sister briefly dated both Meg and Stuart's son Jamie, and Adam Wren, the son of the people who used to run the Fortune's Arms.'

'At the same time?'

'I actually think it was, although you should check with her for the purposes of historical accuracy. It was all very incestuous. What can I say? We were six teenagers growing up in a very small hamlet.'

'We should probably be glad there's no one here for Dolly to kiss.'

'Very glad,' Noah says, lying back down again and cuddling up to me.

'Did the six of you all keep in touch – once you'd left home?'

'We did for a while. To start with, we'd come back anyway, for university holidays and so on. All our parents still lived here. So, we'd see each other then. But over the years the catch-ups dwindled to maybe an awkward drink at the Fortune's Arms on Christmas Eve. We all had our own lives to live and, moving away, it was like the spell of this place had been broken. My sister moved to the States, as you know.' Noah's sister Amy is one of the main reasons his parents have decided to move to San Francisco. 'And then Lisa, Meg and Stuart's oldest, moved out there too – I think she even found her job through Amy. Weirdly, they're probably the two closest. They live in different states, but I know they keep in touch. Jamie, who's Meg and Stuart's son, lives in Aberdeen I think, and works in oil. I know Adam was back here for a while with his family, he took over the day-to-day running of the pub. I saw him behind the bar a few times when we came down to visit my parents. But then his marriage broke up.'

'And Laura?' I say, even though it makes me sound paranoid. I wish I could simply draw a line under the whole thing, but I can't resist this chance to find out how well they know each other.

'Well, we both lived in London so I saw her more than the others. We'd go for the occasional coffee, but even that fell off over the years. She's very driven and her job is pretty intense so she was hardly ever about. Laura's always been a classic high achiever, even in primary school – top speller, fastest swimmer, star gymnast. You name it, she won it.'

'No wonder your relationship was doomed to failure,' I tease, relieved that I'm able to joke about this. Noah sounds so normal as he talks about her. I'm almost sure there's nothing to worry about.

'Anyway, by the time we were both living in London, Juliet and I had Dolly, so we had our hands full and we just kind of grew apart.' It's strange that I'm uneasy about Noah and Laura and not Noah and Juliet – the woman to whom he was married for ten years. I've never felt like the second Mrs de Winter. Maybe it would be different if Juliet was still alive, but I don't really understand how you can be jealous of a dead person. Laura, on the other hand, is still firmly in the realms of the living – although, from what Noah's telling me, it's been a long time since she's been part of his life. 'We'd still message each other occasionally. Before last weekend, the last time I saw her was probably when I came down to visit my mum and dad at Christmas. She was heavily pregnant at the time, determined to be the perfect parent and everything. She had this kind of ideal image of what motherhood would be like. No wonder she's finding the reality a bit challenging.'

'Did you ever meet her husband?'

'Ewan? Yes, once or twice. And that was plenty. He's a twat.'

'In what way?'

'He was always putting her down and making her question herself. I think he knew she was way more intelligent than him, and it frightened him. She's better off without him in my opinion.'

'It must be tough though. She's lucky to have such supportive parents.' Parents are a tricky subject for me, as Noah knows, and I don't want him to think I envy Laura hers, even though I do – in fact, particularly because I do. I long to have parents like Laura's, and Noah knows enough of my past to understand why, but although it was important to me that I felt able to tell him about it, I don't want him to feel sorry for me, or to think I'm fixated on what my parents did. I continue quickly, 'No wonder she likes coming down here.'

'Fortune's Yard has always been something of a haven.'

'Ha! That's what it says on that website.'

'The internet never lies, Beth.'

'It's what Stuart said, too. A harbour in a storm.'

'Stuart has always been one for a poetical image. You know he was my history teacher back when we were at secondary school?'

'No way! I bet he was a good teacher, actually.'

'He was brilliant, always weaving stories about the past.'

'What was it like?' I say. 'Growing up here?'

'Magical. It's a good place to be a kid – that's one of the reasons why I wanted to bring Dolly here. This place felt like another world, where we could do anything we wanted, believe anything we wanted, kind of cut off from reality.'

It's on the tip of my tongue to point out that they were almost literally cut off from reality.

'You weren't bored?' I ask cautiously.

'Maybe a bit as I got older. I craved the bright lights of Ipswich and Yates's Wine Lodge.'

'You crazy sophisticate,' I say kissing him gently on the lips.

We're silent for a few minutes and then he says, 'Are you sure you're okay with this Beth? I know it's a big thing I'm asking of you.'

'It's my thing, too. I wanted to do it. I needed the change.'

'And you like it here?'

My hesitation must last fractionally too long.

'Beth? Because it's not too late. We can tell my parents we've changed our minds. They'll understand.'

'No, I do. Of course I do. It's early days, that's all. We've just arrived, and it's a big move, like you say. It's just going to take a while until it feels like home.'

I struggle to find the words for what I want to say, which is essentially: *Don't you get the sense there's something not quite right here?* But I know he can't feel it. He's too caught up in his memories of what this place used to mean to him. And maybe I'm overthinking it. There's so much pressure to like this place – our brand new blended family home – that maybe my subconscious is rebelling and creating difficulties where there are none. I can feel myself succumbing to sleep, when suddenly another memory of the evening comes back to me.

'Noah?'

'Hmm?'

'What do you think happened to my macarons?' I say, Dolly's face and its strange little smile suddenly making me feel wide awake.

'I expect someone dropped them, and didn't like to say.'

But I know they didn't. They weren't just broken. They were smashed to smithereens.

Chapter Twelve

School report for Dolly James
St Mark's Secondary School, Streatham
Summer Term 2022

Dolly has made a good start at St Mark's, although it took her a while to settle in. It's not unusual for Year Sevens to find the move to secondary school a bit overwhelming, but, as we discussed earlier in the year, Dolly seemed quite withdrawn to start with, which caused us some concern. We're aware Dolly suffered a sudden bereavement in her penultimate year of primary school and wonder whether she may still be processing the trauma of what happened. She struggled to make friends initially, and, although that has now improved, we have observed that her friendships tend to be quite intense attachments. We've noticed that the lack of social contact during lockdown has understandably made socialising difficult for a number of our pupils, so Dolly is no different in this regard. In time, we're sure she will adjust and re-calibrate her approach to interacting with other children. We're not sure we've got to know the real Dolly yet, but she's finished the year in a much more confident place than she began it and her subject reports show real promise.

Chapter Thirteen

Beth

I wake early and abruptly. My eyes suddenly wide open, my heart racing. I can hear running water. Has a pipe broken? It's a while before my brain catches up with my senses. I'm in our new bedroom at the Old Watermill. Well at least that would explain the water.

Normally, I'm the kind of person who wakes up refreshed, with whatever has been troubling me the day before erased, temporarily at least. Noah teases me that I begin every day an optimist, however grouchy I was the night before. But today doesn't feel like that. I still have that ominous feeling that I failed to articulate to Noah last night. In an effort to shift it, I lie there for a few minutes trying to enjoy my surroundings. This is not like early mornings in Streatham. No sirens, no mopeds, no Co-op lorries doing a three-point turn outside my window, in fact no traffic at all. The sun is flooding in from the Velux window above our bed.

My phone, left on Noah's parents' bedside table, tells me it's six a.m. It also tells me I missed a call from my friend Sasha. Sasha is a literary agent and she's almost single-handedly persuaded me that my dream of publishing a baking book one day could actually come true. She's also my main source of social media advice and has helped me with my Instagram account right from the start. If I'd missed a call from any of my other friends, I'd assume some life-changing crisis was occurring – phone calls now only seem to signify bad news or someone trying to scam you. But it's not that odd for Sasha to call me, particularly at the moment when she's trying to help me build my followers. It is a bit strange that she called me at what my brain eventually processes was just before midnight though. Instantly my feeling of uneasiness returns.

I manage to inch out of bed without waking Noah, who looks shattered and is snoring gently with his mouth open. Once outside, I try Sasha's number, my toes sinking into the thick pile of the pale green carpet that runs throughout the house upstairs. It's early, but I'm worried now. There's no answer so I quickly tap out a WhatsApp.

> Hey – everything okay? Saw I missed a
> call from you last night xxx

I wait a few minutes, but the ticks remain stubbornly grey. She's probably asleep, like most of the rest of the world.

Definitely like Dolly. I walk past her room on the way to the bathroom. I don't want to wake Noah by using the en suite, so I head for the big bathroom at the rear of the house. I pause briefly outside Dolly's door, listening for signs of life and feeling vaguely guilty as I do, almost like I'm spying on her. Dolly is rarely up before nine unless it's a school day, feeding into all the teenager clichés – although Sasha says nine is early compared to her lot – and I can't hear any sounds of life this morning. I picture Dolly flinging open the door and finding me outside, and hurry on.

I calculate I've probably got a few hours to myself before the other two wake. I love this early part of the morning, before most people are stirring. Back in our house in Streatham, I'd got into the habit of sitting with a coffee, doodling and trying out recipe ideas. I'm tempted by this thought this morning, sensing the routine of it would be soothing, but I decide instead to try to get the kitchen straight, because I figure if I can feel at home there, that's going to help make me feel more at home in Fortune's Yard itself.

When I open the kitchen door, Bluebell is waiting right behind it and greets me with a display of tail wagging that wouldn't be out of place if I'd just returned from an expedition to the Arctic. I bend down to give her head a rub. It's hard to stay anxious when your face is being enthusiastically licked by a large Staffie, and I can feel my mood starting to improve. I let Bluebell out in the back garden and look around at what still needs doing. Noah did a lot of unpacking last weekend when I was away for Sasha's fortieth, and we worked our way through a few more boxes yesterday afternoon before we went to Meg and Stuart's, so we're off to a good start, but I'm keen to get rid of all the boxes as soon as possible and make the place feel like ours.

Perhaps because I've just been thinking about her, I can hear Sasha in my head reminding me about the importance of creating new content, so, as Bluebell gulps down her breakfast, I decide to take some 'Before' shots, complete with intriguing bits of kitchen and lots of removal boxes. First, I carefully arrange the boxes so that the labels saying 'Old Watermill, Fortune's Yard' are no longer visible. Privacy is important to me, because of my family history. My Instagram never includes photos of me. My hands might occasionally feature, but never my face. I'm the absolute spit of my mum when she was my age, something that gives me no pleasure, but which I can do little about. That's one of the reasons why I wasn't sure about doing the blog interview. But eventually Sasha persuaded me: she reassured me that I could ask them not to reveal whereabouts in Suffolk I was moving to – something that seems even more important here, in this tiny place – and I could pick the photo they used. In the end I sent them a picture with my head turned away from the camera, as I reach to get some flour down from the shelf. All you can see is my messy brown bob and the side of my face. Even if my parents did happen to see it, there's no way they would recognise me.

But Sasha says posting some personal stuff is a good way of building followers, so I'm doing my best and some kitchen pics without any identifying details can't do any harm. Snaps taken, I start work on unpacking. I feel another surge of excitement that this kitchen is actually ours, and a corresponding wave of gratitude to Noah's parents. We could never have afforded a place like this on the open market; the agreement is that we'll pay them back in stages.

I start pulling open drawers and working out where to put things. Through the window, I see Laura wheel a buggy past. Her head turns in my direction and I wave my hand in greeting, determined to be friendly. She hesitates and then waves back. She's dressed much more casually this morning, but still in neutral colours. Dark blue leggings, those cool New Balance trainers I keep meaning to try on and a long silver-grey shirt. Her fair hair is pulled back in a ponytail. She looks different in some other way too, something more profound than just a change of clothing. Her face is more relaxed than last night. Serene even. Maybe Noah's right and this place really is a haven. Or maybe she's just had a good night's sleep, with her parents to help out. There it is again: the parent thing. No use pretending – I envy Laura the kind of relationship she has with Meg and Stuart. *You're always there for them*, that's what Meg said in the kitchen last night. As I have done so many times over the years, I try to imagine what it would be like to have a mum and dad who felt like that. Noah has it too. Even though his parents are now living thousands of miles away, there's nothing they wouldn't do for him or his sister. I have no idea where my parents are living and I intend to keep it that way. I pull myself up. I don't want my brain to go there. Envying Laura isn't going to change anything and if anyone needs good parents right now it's her.

While I watch, Laura crosses the lane and pushes the buggy over to the millpond. The two swans are still asleep, their heads tucked under their wings, and I imagine her showing them to her baby. I can see her bending down to say something and pointing out across the water. Even at a distance, that compelling quality to Laura that struck me last night is still exercising its pull and it's hard to tear my eyes away. Perhaps that's the explanation for what makes Dolly so fascinated by her too. Laura is a strange combination of wired and exhausted, and even I find it hypnotic, so perhaps it's no wonder Dolly does too. I make myself go back to the unpacking and when I next look out of the window, Laura's gone.

Chapter Fourteen

Beth

'Hey, morning. I've made my secret pancake mix. The coconut ones you said you liked a while back. If you go and wake your dad, I'll start cooking them.'

Silence. I wonder if I've committed the fatal sin of trying too hard. My Blended Family has strong views about keeping it casual. But it also has strong views about insisting on basic politeness so I probably shouldn't let this one pass. Apparently, the trickiest point to build a relationship with your stepchildren is when they're in the twelve to fifteen age bracket. Younger and they're more open to accepting you into their lives; older and they already have their own. Some days I find it reassuring that this is meant to be difficult. That this is normal.

'Dolly?'

Her startling blue eyes flash in my direction.

'It's not that secret if the recipe's on your website.'

Which isn't exactly polite, but is at least a response. I try to keep my tone light.

'Ah, but this one's not on the website.'

'I'm not hungry.'

She's found the cupboard where I put the glasses and is getting herself some water from the tap. Her phone, never far from her reach, is on the worktop.

'No problem.' *Try to de-escalate any conflict. Remember you're the adult in the relationship.* 'Do you want to give your dad a shout anyway?'

As soon as the words leave my mouth I regret them, because I'm just giving her another chance to ignore me, and because that formulation always irritates me anyway – 'do you want to' normally means 'I want you to' – and now I'm using it on Dolly. But there's no need to worry, because a few moments later Noah pads into the room, in ancient slippers and a dressing grown, looking slightly ashamed and running his hands through his hair.

'I'm so sorry, I didn't mean to sleep that late. Wow, you've worked wonders in here Beth. Hasn't she Dolly?'

'It looks lovely,' Dolly says politely. Noah gives her a kiss on the top of her head.

'And what's this I see? Pancakes? You hungry?'

'Starving,' she says.

'I thought you said you weren't,' I say, before I can stop myself.

'Hmm?'

'You said you weren't hungry,' I say doggedly. 'Just now.'

'That was before I knew about the pancakes,' she says, not missing a beat. 'Are they the coconut ones? My favourites.'

'Just don't get too used to it,' Noah says. 'Beth isn't going to be able to make pancakes every morning. I'll fix us some coffee.'

I take the bowl of batter over to the high-spec Range-master that is going to make baking everything so much more precise than the ancient oven in Streatham. As I heat the pan, I replay the past few minutes in my head, trying to work out what I should have done differently. The pancake mix spreads over the surface of the pan, exactly the right thickness, bubbling slightly as it cooks. I scoop each one out onto a plate automatically, covering it with a tea towel to keep the pancakes warm. I'm dimly aware of Noah boiling the kettle and scooping coffee into the cafetière. Sometimes the way Dolly behaves when there are other people around is so different from the way she behaves to me when we're alone that I wonder if I'm imagining it. As we all take our seats at the kitchen table, I wonder whether it's possible to be gaslit by a thirteen-year-old.

'These look amazing Beth, thank you,' Dolly says, helping herself to two from the top of the pile.

'Oi, leave me some greedy guts,' Noah says. 'So, what are everyone's plans for today?'

'Laura and I are going for a walk,' Dolly says instantly, as if she's laying claim to her.

'Well remember Laura's down here for a break.'

'Don't worry, Dad. I know. I won't push it.'

'You should make a start on unpacking your boxes, too.'

'We're not going until this afternoon. I can unpack this morning.'

My mobile rings, making us all jump. I fumble for it in the pocket of my dressing gown.

'What happened to no phones at meal times?' Dolly asks. I dimly register this as a misstep on her part – she's hardly ever rude to me in front of Noah – at the same time as I feel a rush of relief: it's Sasha calling me back.

'Hey,' Noah says. 'If Beth needs to answer her phone it's because it's important.'

I take the mobile out into the hallway.

'Sasha? Is everything all right?'

Chapter Fifteen

Beth

'Yes, sorry, I didn't mean to panic you. I'd had a few drinks and I didn't realise it was so late. I just thought it might have upset you.'

'What might have?' I say, the relief ebbing away.

'You haven't been on Insta this morning?' Sasha asks.

My sense of foreboding increases. I meant to post the kitchen shots, but I haven't got round to it yet.

'Not since yesterday. Why?'

'Just some stupid troll. Someone who's clearly jealous of you. It's inevitable now that you're reaching a wider audience.'

My heart thumps. I've had my Instagram for more than three years, but aside from a couple of horrible messages at the beginning from someone calling themselves @Truth-Teller1001, I've been pretty lucky up until now. I know that social media can be vile, but in my experience, the trolls don't seem that interested in tips for the best way to get raspberry jam to set. Even Truth Teller 1001 got bored after the first few messages and left me alone.

'What have they said?'

'I can't remember exactly,' she says, and I can hear her deliberately keeping her voice light, 'but something along the lines of you're an evil bitch, your baking business is a giant scam and they're going to make sure everyone knows your secret.'

'Wow. Okay.'

'It's fairly standard kind of stuff. Just ignore it.'

The reference to a scam, coming just before the mention of a secret, is ringing warning bells in my head. Could this be someone who knows about my past? Sasha's voice interrupts my thoughts.

'Honestly, hun, it's not worth worrying about. Just block the account.' Her tone more upbeat, she says, 'We missed you last night.'

I attempt to push the troll to the back of my mind and focus on my friend. It's almost certainly just a random shot in the dark. Like Sasha said, it's pretty standard abuse, there are no specifics.

'Yeah? Where did you go?'

I wander down the hallway and into the library.

'That little place on the corner again.'

I picture the cafe-come-cocktail-bar on Streatham High Road, with its industrial light fittings, fifteen-pound Negronis and live-if-obscure music, and feel a wave of longing for my old life. It's so good to hear Sasha's voice, even though I last heard it only forty-eight hours ago.

'Who was playing?'

'That guy who looks like a second-rate Chris Martin and wrote that weird song about a red squirrel.' I even feel a flash of nostalgia for fake Chris Martin. 'How's day one in the country?'

'Good, I think.'

'You don't sound very sure.'

'It's a big move. It's going to take a while to adjust,' I say, conscious that I'm echoing what I said to Noah last night.

'So what's it actually like – the place I mean? Fortune's Yard.'

'The house is amazing, I'll send you some pictures. The place is…'

'What?'

'I mean it's perfect. It's at the end of this quiet country lane and there's a huge millpond that has actual swans on it, and there are just three houses and—'

'Wait, rewind. There are three houses in the whole place?'

'Yes,' I say, defensively.

'You didn't mention that before.'

'I guess I didn't really notice.'

'How could you not notice?'

'I just didn't really think about it. I mean there are other houses nearby, of course.' I'm not sure this is even true. Where is the nearest other house? I certainly haven't seen one, even from the upstairs windows, looking out across the woods and marshland. I decide not to mention the marshland to Sasha; it makes it sound like I'm living in *The Hound of the Baskervilles*.

'I've got this weird feeling about it though,' I say almost without thinking. 'About the place.'

'How do you mean?'

I hesitate.

'I can't really put my finger on it any more than that.'

'Maybe,' Sasha says, 'it's because something bad happened there in the past. Do you remember when I used to say that the area around Hyde Park had a bad vibe? Way back when we first knew each other and used to go to that pub just off Oxford Street. And then we found out that it used to be a place called Tyburn, where people were driven to be hanged. Maybe something similar is going on with Fortune's Yard – spiritual geography and all that kind of thing.'

So much for not making it sound like I'm living in a Sherlock Holmes story; Sasha now seems to be spinning a *Woman in Black* vibe.

'Almost certainly something bad happened here, it's an old village,' I say practically. 'But I think the feeling's connected to the here and now. Although Noah and Dolly both seem to love it, so maybe it's just me.'

'How is the wicked stepdaughter?'

'Don't call her that.'

'She's not there is she?'

'No, she's in the kitchen.'

'Which in your new house I'm guessing is several miles away.'

'Yes, it's so strange having space.'

'So how are things going?' says Sasha, who's nothing if not persistent.

I shut the library door, because even though it's a big house, I've already discovered it's the kind of place where people can suddenly appear behind you with no warning. In a two-bedroom terrace, you know where everyone is. Here, not so much.

'Okay, I guess. I'm trying my best to be understanding, but sometimes it's just really difficult.'

'Understanding of what exactly?'

I recount the pancake incident, and even as I describe it, I'm doubting my own memory. Sasha's response is instant though.

'Have you talked to Noah about this?'

'I mean it just happened.'

'But you are going to tell him, right?'

'I don't know, Sasha. It would feel like I was complaining about her behind her back.'

'You need to talk to him. She's messing with your mind, and you're letting her do it.'

Sasha's parenting advice tends to be a lot more robust than the sort My Blended Family dishes out. She's the only person I've really confided in about how Dolly behaves sometimes.

'I did challenge her about it.' She makes a noise I take to denote scepticism and I explain my attempt to pull Dolly up on what she said.

'Doesn't sound very challenging to me.'

'It's difficult. She's been through a lot. With her mum and everything.'

'I know Beth, but that doesn't give her the right to treat you however she chooses.'

'It's such a little thing. I don't want to come across as petty.'

'It's little, but it's strange. The whole being two different people act – I mean all kids do that to an extent, but she seems to be taking it to a whole new level. Dolly's power over you is because she knows you're not going to tell her dad. As soon as she knows you're going to call her out on that stuff, she'll stop doing it. The two of you need to present a united front.'

I think again about what I think I heard last night. *You look really fat in that jumpsuit.* I don't want to tell Sasha because it's just going to be even more grist to her mill, but why don't I want to tell Noah either? I wonder if on some level I'm worried that Noah is going to believe Dolly and not me. He's never given me any reason to think this, but I don't want to put him in a situation where he has to choose. If she simply denies it, which I'm pretty sure she will, he's going to have to come down on one side or the other. His daughter, or his wife? Not exactly a fun decision. But if Sasha's right, my reluctance to involve Noah is exactly what Dolly is counting on.

'Honestly, Beth, you should tackle it head on before it gets any worse. It's probably the source of your weird feeling, for a start.'

'No, it's not that. It's something else. It's not like I haven't lived with Dolly before. I mean I shared a house with her for two months before we moved down here.'

'But you're on her territory now, aren't you? She used to go down there to visit her grandparents, didn't she?'

'The odd visit over the years, yes, but I don't think that makes it her territory.'

'I'm just saying your instincts are telling you something is wrong and you should listen to that.' My instincts are definitely telling me something – I only wish I could work out what. We talk for a while longer, but as we're about to ring off, I revert to the question that's been preoccupying me since Sasha told me what the comment on my Instagram said.

'Sasha, you know the troll?'

'I knew you were going to worry about it.'

'You don't think it could be one of my parents' victims, do you?'

Chapter Sixteen

School report for Dolly James
Lord Lane Primary School, Battersea
20 December 2019

This has been a difficult term for Dolly. The very sad passing of her mother in October has understandably dominated. Dolly's grades have dipped, and she seems to have trouble concentrating in class, but this is all to be expected. We are trying to keep things as normal for her as possible. More concerningly, Dolly has become very withdrawn. We've all observed that at break she hardly ever plays with the other children. Instead, she usually chooses to remain in the classroom by herself, and in the circumstances, we've been reluctant to insist that she goes outside. It's clear she feels a large burden of guilt for what happened and grief counselling may help her work through this.

Chapter Seventeen

Beth

I've come outside for a break from all the unpacking. The three of us – a phrase I'm still not used to – made good progress this morning, and it really was the three of us, too. Sasha's right: Dolly is like two different people depending on whether I'm alone with her or not. She not only helped us to unpack, she even went into the garden to pick flowers for the vase Noah found at the bottom of one of the boxes. 'So it feels more like home.' They're pink dahlias and they look beautiful on the table in the kitchen. She's got an eye for things like that – her dad's a photographer and her mum was an artist so I suppose it's not that surprising. After lunch she headed off to meet Laura for their much-anticipated walk in the woods, taking Bluebell with her. It's hard to know which of the two of them was more excited: dog or child. And now Noah has driven into Ipswich to pick up various bits and pieces we seem to be missing. Although I continued to unpack for a while by myself, there seemed to be an inexhaustible supply of boxes – some of which probably contain the things that Noah has gone to buy afresh – and I felt like I needed some fresh air and sunshine, so I'm heading up the lane to inspect our local.

The Fortune's Arms is not at all what I was expecting. I know it's closed of course, but despite what Meg said, I think I was imagining somewhere that could easily open its doors again. This place looks almost derelict. The pub sign is just a metal pole, with a gaping hole where the actual sign should be. The building itself is clearly very old – much older even than the other buildings in Fortune's Yard – and looks like it's sinking in on itself, with a dip in the middle of the roof. The bottom windows have metal shutters over them, and the paint on the front door is blistering. Attached to the wall is an estate agent's sign saying *For Sale* and giving a phone number. Even the sign looks like it's been there a long time. There's a small car park in front of the pub, with grass growing up through the tarmac and old wooden picnic tables piled up haphazardly in one corner. It looks like the least inviting hostelry I've ever seen and I'm struggling to imagine it as a popular stop-off for walkers and sightseers, although to be fair, I'm probably not seeing it at its best. I take a photo and send it to Sasha.

> This is my local!

I get a shocked face and a laughing face emoji in return. Then:

> Don't post that on Insta – it's way too depressing.

> This is real country life!

Fake country life only please. There must
be something more picturesque.

Messaging Sasha reminds me I do actually need to post
something on Instagram. It's been two whole days, which
in social media land is an eternity. I checked my account
as soon as I came off the phone to her earlier. Sasha
had been unconvinced by my idea that the comment had
something to do with my parents. 'Way too vague,' she'd
said reassuringly.

All the same, my heart was thumping as I clicked
onto my account and scrolled down through the messages
under my most recent post. I found it about halfway
down: a snippet of nastiness among lots of posts wishing
me luck with the move. It was almost a relief to see the
name of the account: @TruthTeller1001. My old troll
from way back when I first started the account; not a
new enemy after all. I clicked through to the profile,
wondering if it would still be private like it was the first
time I looked, but to my surprise it wasn't. It didn't help
me much though. Truth Teller 1001 hasn't posted a single
photo or video. They aren't following anyone else either.
I try to remember if this was also the case last time I
checked. It's more than a little disturbing to think that
their sole purpose is trolling me, but hopefully they'll get
bored again soon and leave me alone.

I hadn't felt like posting anything after that, but now
I remind myself that I should be posting whether I feel
like it or not – that's the way I'll build my followers and
my new business. I need to take some 'After' pics of the
kitchen to go with the 'Before' shots I took this morning
and if I head back now, I can get the photos done before
Noah gets back from Ipswich.

On my walk to the Fortune's Arms, I'd scurried past Ralph and Evelyn's cottage, not ready to have another conversation with either of them, but on the way back, I linger a bit, needing an antidote to the abandoned pub. Sasha would love their house. A sandstone cottage with two tiny windows either side of a smartly painted green front door that has actual roses climbing round it. It's called Workshop Cottage, and I suppose once it might have been a workshop to go with Meg and Stuart's farmhouse, but it's way too pristine to be hosting any kind of workshop now.

I hear the voices before I see them. A man's voice. Staccato, loud. And a quieter, higher voice that's harder to make out. I try to work out where they're coming from. Once I pass the cottage, it becomes obvious. In the distance, where the garden of the cottage meets the line of the woods, and on what is presumably a footpath, I can see Dolly talking to someone, slightly hidden by the trees. They're about fifty metres away from where I'm standing in the lane. Dolly's white-gold hair, worn in a plait, is glowing like a beacon in the bright August sunshine and she's wearing her favourite neon pink sweater. As I watch, Dolly moves a few steps backwards and now I can see that the person she's talking to is Ralph. There's no sign of Laura, so either she's hidden by the trees or she's headed back to her parents' house already.

The two of them are clearly having some kind of disagreement. I can hear raised voices, but not what either of them is saying. A volley of barking, which must come from Bluebell, doesn't help. Ralph is pointing at Dolly now and she's backing away from him. My first thought is that I need to find out what's going on and get her out of there before it gets any more heated, but I'm briefly confused about how to reach them. I think I'd have to go up the drive to their cottage and into the garden, although there must be another way onto the footpath.

'Hey!' I shout. 'Everything okay up there?'

It so obviously isn't, but Bluebell is barking again and I'm not sure either of them has heard me. It surprises me how strongly I feel that I need to protect Dolly. As I head up the drive towards them, Dolly pivots and walks rapidly away, leaving Ralph staring after her. As she goes, she picks up her pace, practically running. I run too, my heart pounding, back down the drive and then along the lane, following her progress. I see her veer right and then she briefly disappears. I keep running and by the time she emerges through a thicket of trees about ten metres further down the lane, I'm already there waiting for her.

'Dolly? Are you okay? What was all that about?'

She thrusts Bluebell's lead at me and storms past, her face set, her expression hard to read. If I had to guess, I'd say she was frightened. As soon as she's handed over Bluebell, she starts to run again. I jog after her. Bluebell is looking confused, her tongue lolling out of her mouth, but, ever-willing, she trots along beside me. All kinds of thoughts are going through my head. I knew there was something wrong with this place. Was that feeling because of Ralph? What has he said to her? Or done to her? Surely it can't be anything sexual. He's an old man and she's a thirteen-year-old child. I don't want my mind to even go there.

When Dolly reaches the Old Watermill, she pushes at the front door, which doesn't open because I have the key. As I catch up with her, she's beating her hands against it in frustration.

'Dolly?'

83

'Let me in.'

'What happened?'

'Open the door.'

'Okay, give me a moment.'

She snatches the key from me, flings open the front door and rushes up the stairs. I hear the door to her room slam. I stand in the hallway, the bright August light flooding in from outside, Bluebell sitting panting at my feet. I wish Noah was here. I'm so out of my depth. But there's no way this can wait until he gets back. I turn and gently shut the front door, and then I take a couple of deep breaths, and follow impotently in Dolly's footsteps. As I walk down the landing, I think I can hear her crying, but when I get to her bedroom door it's all quiet again. I could, of course, open the door. I'm pretty sure there's no lock on it. But something warns me not to invade her space. I take a few moments to pick my words, and I hope I manage to sound considerably calmer than I feel as I speak to her through the door.

'Dolly, please tell me what happened. Are you okay?'

To my surprise, I get an answer straight away.

'I'm okay. He's just a stupid old man.'

'What did he say to you?'

'He said I'd go to hell,' she says, and this time I can hear an unmistakable sob in her voice.

In a sense it's a relief. And it fits too. From my brief encounter with Ralph yesterday, it seems so much more likely that he would choose to harangue Dolly with a religious diatribe than some of the other things I've had time to imagine and fear since I first saw them on the footpath. But it's also an utterly vile thing to say to a child. I'm suddenly furious on her behalf.

'That's totally unacceptable. Who does he think he is? I'll go and talk to him now.'

'No, don't do that!'

Her door opens, and she stands in front of me, her face tear-stained and her hair all messy and falling out of its French plait. I guess that she's been lying face down on her bed crying. She's wearing denim shorts with her neon sweatshirt and her legs seem impossibly thin and child-like. She looks younger than I've ever seen her and all at once I have an image of her as she must have been when she found out her mum had died.

'I won't if you don't want me to, of course I won't, but he's got no right to say such horrible things to you.'

'Promise you won't tell anyone what he said?'

'I promise, but Dolly, it's really not worth getting this upset about.'

'Maybe he's right and I will,' she says, sniffing.

'Of course he's not right.'

Almost every instinct is telling me to put an arm around her, but still I hold back. This is more vulnerable than she's ever let me see her before, and I desperately don't want to fuck this up. Her lip is trembling and her eyes are full of tears, threatening to spill over again.

'How do you know?'

'Well, for a start, I don't believe in hell.' She half turns away, and I know I've said the wrong thing. 'But even if I did,' I say quickly, 'I'm absolutely sure you wouldn't be going there. Hell, if it exists at all, is for people who've done truly terrible things.'

'You don't know me. You don't know what I've done.'

'Then tell me. I'm sure it can't be as bad as all that.'

She shakes her head. Her hand is still on the door handle, and she's twisting it backwards and forwards.

'I bet whatever it is I've done worse.'

She sniffs again, mild interest flickering across her face.

'Tell me the worst thing you've done,' she demands.

'I pretended I didn't have any parents.'

Dolly stares at me, astonishment briefly replacing all other emotions. I'm pretty surprised myself – I certainly didn't intend to tell her that.

'Why would you do that?'

'They did a very bad thing when I was not much older than you. And, to start with, it was easier to tell people I didn't have any parents than to tell them what they'd done.'

'What did they do?'

I'm already not sure I should have told her this much, but I can hardly stop now, or expect her to trust me if I'm not willing to trust her.

'My dad conned a lot of people out of a lot of money – their life savings in some cases – and my mum knew all about it. It was a big fraud case, a long time ago now. Roxeter Investments, that was my dad's company. It was all over the newspapers. My dad went to jail for a long time. One of his victims committed suicide.' It's difficult for me to say this, even now. For once, I have Dolly's total attention, though.

'What happened to all the money?'

'A lot of it was never recovered. Mostly my dad gambled with it, made risky investments with other people's money to try to make even more money. They had this entirely new life planned it turns out.' One that probably didn't involve me. 'But the whole thing collapsed before they got a chance to live it.'

'Where are they now? Your mum and dad?'

'I don't know. I haven't had anything to do with them for nearly twenty years, and I prefer it that way. They lied again and again – to me, and to everyone – and they destroyed a lot of people's lives, all out of greed. I decided a long time ago that I was better off without them.'

'Haven't they ever tried to find you?'

'My mum tried in the early days.'

'But you don't want to see her?'

I very much don't want to see her. It's the main reason I'm so paranoid about my photo being online. I don't want her to recognise it and somehow track me down.

'She doesn't want to see me because she cares about me,' I say, and I hate that my voice still sounds bitter after all this time. 'She wants to see me for what she can get out of me.' I did meet my mum once, two years after I'd left home, while my dad was still in jail. Six days after we met, I found she'd phoned my new employer and told them there was a family emergency and I needed an advance on my pay. I never answered her calls after that. I changed my number – I even changed my surname. 'They were only really interested in money.'

'Does my dad know?'

'Yes, I told him all about it. I'm much better at talking about it now.' This at least is true. Better, but still not good.

'He didn't tell me.'

'I suppose he thought it wasn't his story to tell. Now, will you tell me the thing that's worrying you?'

She twists the door handle again and looks away. I wonder if all of this has been for nothing.

'Dolly, you can trust me. Please tell me what you're frightened of.'

The tears spill down her cheeks. And then I do move forward, and put my hand on her shoulder. She looks straight at me and whispers:

'I killed my mum.'

Chapter Eighteen

Beth

It's not easy talking to your new husband about his first wife's death, but I know I have to do it, and quickly before I lose my nerve. Dolly's extraordinary revelation is still playing on a loop in my head. I think she regretted telling me as soon as the words left her mouth, because immediately afterwards she clammed up entirely. It was like she was so upset by her argument with Ralph that her need to confide in someone had overcome all her other instincts, but as soon as the confession was out, the shutters slammed right back down. I need to talk to Noah to understand why she feels so much guilt about what happened to her mum.

Noah told me about Juliet on our first proper date, which was in the fancy bar in the converted Battersea Power Station. We'd been for a couple of coffees before that, but mainly we'd talked about photography and other work stuff. I knew enough to know that he'd been married but his wife was no longer in the picture, and that he had a daughter who lived with him. I guess I assumed he was divorced. By our second martini, we were onto the usual first date subject of dating – the thing all single people have in common and so end up talking about. I think I brought it up and he asked jokingly how he was comparing, and I wanted to say that he was a zillion times better than my seven other first dates of recent times, but I didn't want to freak him out with my enthusiasm so instead I talked about how it was early days and I hadn't broken up with Pete that long ago and then we talked about the break-up ('we wanted different things,' the all-encompassing phrase) and finally, a bit tentatively I asked about his divorce. And then he went quiet and the laughter left his face, and I thought *shit*.

'I'm not actually divorced,' he said awkwardly.

Ah ha. I knew this was too good to be true. My face must have revealed what I was thinking because he said quickly, 'No, I don't mean that. My wife died four years ago.'

'Oh God, I'm so sorry.'

'Thank you. Sorry, bit of a mood dampener.'

'Don't be silly. What happened? That's if you're okay to talk about it?'

'I'm okay to talk about it, but we don't have to. It's quite heavy stuff for our first drink.'

His voice as he talked about Juliet was calm. It broke at times, but he managed to get it back under control. He described how she had gone to pick their daughter up from a friend's ninth birthday party down in Surrey. He'd been working on some wedding photos for a client on his computer and he lost track of time. He didn't even notice they weren't back when they should have been and the first he knew about it was when there was a ring at the door – I remember his voice shaking slightly as he said this – and he'd gone downstairs to find two yellow-jacketed police officers standing on his doorstep. Even then, he said, he hadn't thought that something bad had happened. He thought they were going house to house because there had been a break-in at the end of the road a few days earlier. When the police officers explained that there had been a road traffic accident and his wife and daughter had been involved, he stopped taking things in at all. In the police car on the way to the hospital, he kept asking how they were and they had to explain all over again that his wife wasn't expected to make it, but his daughter had only minor injuries and was being treated for shock.

When I heard this story, maybe what I should have done is made sympathetic noises and then run a mile. After all, I was a woman who'd just broken up with her boyfriend because he wanted to have children and she didn't, and I was about to get involved with a grief-stricken widower with a young child. But what I wanted to do was fold Noah in my arms and hold him tight, because I could see how devastated he was by what had happened, but also how hard he'd tried to deal with it all for his daughter's sake.

Thinking about this now, as I move around the unfamiliar kitchen, helping Noah to unload and pack away all the shopping he's bought in Ipswich, I want to hold him again, but I content myself with touching his back as he reaches up to put away a jar of peanut butter. His T-shirt feels soft to my touch, his back slightly damp and sweaty. He turns and smiles at me. When we've finished unpacking, I suggest we take the mugs of tea he's made us out into the garden.

Noah's parents have kindly left us their garden furniture, a big table and six chairs that must date back to the time when the whole family lived there. Bluebell is already stretched out on the crescent-shaped terrace, in a patch of sun. I lead us past the furniture and out onto the grass, feeling it soft and slightly scratchy beneath my bare feet. Noah puts his arm around my waist and we stand with our back to the house looking out at the woodland beyond, listening to the sound of running water. It really is a perfect view, a gentle slope of green leading away from the house, and only trees beyond. I even feel a strange affection for Meg's scarecrow family, regarding us steadily from the end of the garden. Someone – Noah, I presume – has taken the silver scarf off and got rid of it, which certainly helps. The water rushing past is the only thing in a hurry, everything else is the embodiment of peace. But the feeling of something wrong is still there, even though I can't put my finger on exactly what's causing it. Looking at the view reminds me of seeing Dolly and Ralph in the woods earlier – something tangible at least – and makes me realise I can't put this off any longer.

'Dolly and I had a bit of a chat when you were out.'

'That's good.' He pushes his glasses further up his nose. 'She seems happy down here doesn't she?'

'Overall, yes,' I say cautiously. His arm drops and he turns to face me.

'What is it? Did something happen?'

'She and Ralph had a bit of a run-in.'

'What kind of a run-in?'

'I'm not sure exactly. I saw them arguing about something, up on the footpath in the woods behind Ralph's cottage, but I couldn't catch what they were saying, and when I saw her afterwards she was really upset.'

'Did you ask her about it?'

'Yes, but I didn't really get to the bottom of it.'

'Poor kid. I wonder what Ralph's problem was. It's not like Dolly to fall out with anyone.'

'It *is* hard to warm to Ralph though.'

'You don't like him?'

'He's a bit self-righteous, don't you think?'

I move back to the terrace and settle on one of the chairs. It's hard and not particularly comfortable. Bluebell raises her head, gives her tail a brief wag and then flops back down again. Noah joins me, putting his mug on the table, which, now I look at it closely, could do with a good wash. Noah's meticulous parents moved out three months ago and the place has been empty since, so everything is a weird combination of pristine and neglected.

'Meg says he's a bit of a busybody but well meaning.'

'She said something similar to me. Had you met him before last night?'

'I've seen him to wave to a couple of times when I came up to visit my folks.' I try to imagine waving at Ralph; it seems unlikely he'd wave back. 'But he and Evelyn only moved up here about six years ago.' I notice that the passage of six years still makes you a newcomer in Fortune's Yard. 'All the time we were growing up it was a different couple who lived there – the Andersons – but they had to sell up when she went into a home, and I remember it was a big deal for my parents and Meg and Stuart, the whole "who would move in" thing. But then Ralph and Evelyn did and everything was fine again. My mum would occasionally mention something about Ralph, I think he helped her with some of her fundraising stuff, but they hardly saw Evelyn.'

'Ralph seems very religious. He even quoted the Bible at me.'

'Do you think that's what he was haranguing Dolly about? She's been a bit anti-God ever since Juliet's death.'

I wonder whether I should tell him about the going to hell comment. I promised Dolly I wouldn't tell anyone, but surely that doesn't include her dad who needs to know what's going on in her life so that he can look out for her. These are the kinds of things I can't decide and that I feel like I would know instinctively if I was an actual parent, rather than just trying to make it up as I go along. I compromise.

'Why don't you ask her about it? She might tell you more than she's willing to tell me.'

'That's nonsense Beth, she trusts you.'

'She did tell me a bit, but like I say, I didn't really get to the bottom of it.'

'Okay, I'll have a try. We can't leave it like that, anyway. This is such a small place. We can't start off on the wrong foot.'

He bends down to stroke Bluebell, his brown eyes troubled, but I know I can't leave it there.

'Noah?' He looks back at me. 'Do you think Dolly feels guilty about her mum's death?'

'What makes you say that?'

'Something she said when we were talking afterwards.'

'What did she say?'

This is obviously where I should tell him exactly what Dolly said, but somehow I can't bring myself to use her words.

'I can't remember exactly, but something that made me think she might feel somehow, I don't know, responsible.'

Noah looks stricken.

'How could she be responsible? She was just a child.'

'Of course. I just got the impression that that's how she feels.'

Noah glances upwards as if suddenly remembering that Dolly's bedroom is immediately above us, looking out onto the garden.

'It's all right. She's not up there.'

'Sudden grief, like the kind that Dolly's experienced, can take years to work through.'

The kind that you've experienced too, I think. I reach out across the table and lay my hand on his larger one, with its pale gold hairs and bitten down nails. Our fingers intertwine.

'It's even worse for Dolly,' Noah says, almost as if he can read my thoughts. 'She was there when it happened.'

His fingers tighten.

'I know. I can't imagine what she must have gone through.'

In that moment, I feel like I could forgive Dolly anything. She had a horrific experience at an incredibly young age. If anyone's allowed to be a bit messed up, she is.

'Does she ever talk to you at all about what happened?'

He shakes his head. 'She never talks about the accident. She never has. Perhaps it's a good sign that she opened up to you about how she's feeling, maybe it marks some kind of shift.'

I can tell that he's a bit hurt that she hasn't confided in him, but is also trying to find something positive to cling onto. He's a committed optimist, my husband.

'Well, she didn't say much.'

'It's a start though,' he says.

'I wonder if she's holding back from saying anything about it to you because she's worried about making you unhappy.'

'Maybe. I know she worries about me a lot. I do everything I can to try to let her know that it's good to talk about her mum. I talk about her myself – I remind Dolly of the things we did together and I encourage her to share her memories too, but it doesn't seem to make

95

any difference. She hardly ever mentions Juliet in front of me.'

'Was Dolly very close to her?' Noah pushes his glasses further up his nose and doesn't answer straight away. 'Sorry. Stupid question.'

'It's not a stupid question at all. Not everyone is close to their mum. Sorry, Beth,' he adds suddenly, realising what he's said.

'It's all right. Honestly. I guess my relationship with my parents is one of the things that makes me so curious about other people's.'

'The two of them were very close, but Dolly didn't always have an easy relationship with Juliet. It was difficult, at the beginning.' He hesitates. 'I don't think I've talked about this much before, but Juliet had a horrendous time giving birth and the first few months were a bit of a nightmare, if I'm honest. Juliet found it quite hard to bond with Dolly. But she eventually got some help from our GP and we got through it, and for a while it was all fine. But then as Dolly got a bit older they started arguing a lot. I think it's because they were both quite similar in some ways. They were both strong-willed, stubborn sometimes. It's one of the things I love.' I notice the present tense, but I don't mind that he talks about Juliet like this. It doesn't mean that he loves me any less, in the here and now. I'm more troubled by the contradiction in what he said and the fact that he seems utterly unaware of it: a few minutes ago, he told me confidently that it wasn't like Dolly to fall out with anyone and now he's telling me that she argued lots with her mum. 'They'd always make up though. Juliet used to read to her every night, kids' stories when she was little. She adored *Cops and Robbers*. And then other stuff as she got older. *The Lion, the Witch and the Wardrobe*,

Charlotte's Web. They'd sit there every night, Juliet doing all the voices and Dolly hanging on her every word.'

We're both silent for a few moments, imagining the scene he described, and then Noah says abruptly, 'Maybe moving down here has brought back some old memories for Dolly.'

'How do you mean?'

'Did I tell you that she came down to stay here immediately after it happened?'

He certainly didn't.

'After the accident?' I ask as I process this new piece of information.

'Yes, when she came out of hospital. Just for a few days. I thought it would be better for her to be out of London. Juliet's friends kept coming round, the house was full of people crying all the time, and everything was so chaotic. I figured it would be good for her to come down and stay with her grandparents. She always loved it down here.'

'But maybe moving down here has brought that time back?'

'I should have thought about all this before, but Dolly was so happy about the idea of moving down here, I never really questioned it.'

'I don't think that it's necessarily a bad thing that it brings back memories. It's just a lot for her to deal with. But it can't be good for her to keep those feelings buried, and if moving down here helps her to talk about it more, that could be a positive step, like you say.'

I'm trying to capture some of his optimism and I must succeed because his face visibly relaxes as I watch him.

'Thanks, Beth. You're the best.' He leans over and kisses me. 'I'll go up and have a chat to her now.'

'You can't. I said, she's not here.'

'Where is she?'

'She went over to see Laura.'

'Again?'

'I know. I did think about stopping her, but she seems fascinated by wherever they went on the walk this afternoon – something to do with some girl who used to live here hundreds of years ago – and apparently Laura has some book she's going to show her. Dolly was so upset earlier and I thought it would be a good distraction.'

Plus, I'm not actually sure I could have stopped her. My step-parental authority, if I have any at all, hangs by a thread at the best of times.

'It's fine I guess, if Laura doesn't mind. I'm just conscious she's got a lot to deal with right now, and she's come down here for a break.'

I try to gauge his tone. He sounds concerned about Laura, but in a friendly way, nothing more. I think back to Dolly's revelation and I realise it's not actually Noah's relationship with Laura that's making me feel uneasy right now, it's Dolly's. Dolly seems a bit obsessed with her, and I wonder whether I should mention this to her dad. But I've already worried him enough for one day.

Chapter Nineteen

Extract from Explore Suffolk website

For such a beautiful spot, Fortune's Yard does have a somewhat sinister history. Parish records make it clear that by the early seventeenth century there was a small but thriving community based here. The unusual name, Fortune's Yard, originates from this time and is believed to derive from the name of the family of farmers who owned most of the land. A Joshua Fortune is recorded as farming here in 1608.

At that time, Suffolk was in the grip of a peculiar kind of mania which took hold under the sinister eye of self-appointed witch-hunter Matthew Hopkins. Shortly after Hopkins's early death from tuberculosis ended his reign of terror in 1647, local legend has it that a member of the Fortune family accused her own daughter of witchcraft and was backed up by other villagers who insisted that the young girl was evil. Parish records show a Hannah Fortune sentenced to death for witchcraft in 1650, although there were repeated rumours that she survived, and that the powerful magic she once controlled can still be used by those who know the secret that unlocks it. What is certain is that Hannah Fortune is still a strong lure for visitors to Fortune's Yard, who are fascinated by her story and want to see the place where she lived and almost certainly died.

Please note, Fortune's Yard is at the end of a no through road. Parking is limited, and the hamlet is best approached on foot or bike. There is a beautiful five-mile walk from Orford (see the Suffolk Rambles website for a description of the route).

Chapter Twenty

Beth

'So, big change. How are you liking it so far?'

'It's great,' I say. 'So peaceful.'

Meg is striding out along the path. The dogs are running up ahead. It's Sunday morning, the start of our second full day in Fortune's Yard, and the sun is already blazing high in the sky. Thankfully it's a bit shady here in the woods and a faint breeze is making the leaves rustle overhead. Meg messaged me first thing and asked if I fancied taking the dogs for a walk. I haven't seen her since Friday night and I'm keen to be sociable – I'm missing Sasha and my other London friends even more than I thought – so I agreed at once.

'I thought I'd take you to Hannah's Grove. It's where Laura took Dolly yesterday.'

I remember the name from Dolly's account at dinner last night. The place had clearly made quite an impression on her, but given how upset she'd been after her encounter with Ralph, I was pleased that she was so easily absorbed in something else again, even if I was a bit worried by how literally she seemed to be taking the idea that it was a magical spot.

'Dolly certainly seems fascinated by it.'

'Laura was too when she was Dolly's age. She probably told her all the old stories.'

'So what *is* the story behind it?'

'Are you sure you're ready for it?'

Meg says this in the same brisk, confident voice that she says everything else, so it's hard to know how serious she is. I wouldn't have thought she was a woman for myths and legends – she seems far too practical and Noah told me she used to be a research chemist before she retired – although I suppose she did make us a life-size scarecrow family as a housewarming present, so clearly there's a strain of whimsy in her somewhere.

'Tell me all.'

'Well, Fortune's Yard is an ancient settlement. Most of the current buildings are early nineteenth century, but there was a village here before that – a bigger one. There was a farm here before our farmhouse was built and it was owned by the Fortune family for generations. The Fortunes had a daughter, Hannah, and people started noticing that Hannah seemed to have a powerful influence over life and death. She had an old nurse who was practically at death's door, some said she'd breathed her last, but Hannah went to visit her and the next day she was up on her feet again, as hale and hearty as ever. There was talk in the village that what happened wasn't natural. And if ever Hannah was annoyed with someone, bad things happened to them. It came to a head with a young boy who threw stones at Hannah's cat. The next day, he was paralysed on one side of his body. Three days later he was dead.'

There's something about Meg's no-nonsense delivery that's much more disturbing than any more elaborate attempt at creepiness. It's as though she's relating something that happened a few days ago.

'The rumours started to spread, but the Fortunes were quite a powerful family and no one wanted to make the accusation of witchcraft outright. They were frightened of what it would mean for their livelihoods and of what Hannah might do to them if she heard. Nearly everyone had noticed that every morning Hannah took a walk into the woods and it was said that when she came back her eyes glowed with a strange light. One day, a labourer on the Fortune farm decided to follow her. He said that she went to a clearing in the woods where there was a kind of altar made out of rocks. He saw Hannah summon the devil and he said that they conversed with one another in tongues. The devil called Hannah his handmaiden and said she must continue his work.'

'So he understood that bit,' I say, hoping to lighten the mood.

'What?'

We're walking through a patch of sun and Meg's burgundy-rimmed glasses glint as she turns towards me. Her face is totally serious and for a moment I wonder whether she actually believes this stuff.

'I meant if they were speaking in tongues.'

'In time,' she continues as if I hadn't interrupted, 'the Fortunes themselves came to hear the rumours about their daughter, and there was talk about what they should do. They thought about sending her away, but in the end, her parents told the villagers that if their daughter really was a witch, she should meet a witch's fate, so they took her to the grove and the villagers held their own trial and found her guilty. She was sentenced to be drowned.'

I'm really regretting asking about Hannah's Grove now. This definitely doesn't sound like a suitable story for Laura to be sharing with Dolly.

'So, they nailed her up in a coffin, weighed it down with stones, and placed the coffin in the water. Several weeks after that, Hannah's coffin washed up on the shore near Orford and some of the villagers went down there to see her body. And when they opened the coffin, do you know what they found?'

I shake my head.

'Nothing. She'd vanished. The only thing that was in there was the stones. Everyone thought the devil had worked his magic to save one of his own.'

'Is that what you think?'

Meg looks at me as though I've lost my mind.

'Certainly not,' she says briskly. 'I think her family saved her.'

'Right.' I'm rapidly trying to catch up. 'Yes, I suppose that makes sense. They spirited her away after all.'

'It's what you'd do, isn't it? For your own child?'

'Of course,' I say, still processing the story. 'Even if they were a witch,' I add lightly.

'Even then,' Meg says, and again her voice has a seriousness that is disconcerting. I like that Meg has assumed I will feel for Dolly what she feels for her children: it's the exact opposite of Evelyn with her 'real family' remark. At the same time, I'm thinking that I would do this for any child about to be drowned by a mob; they wouldn't have to be *my* child. Meg is still talking about the grove. 'Hannah's Grove has been a special place ever since. The kids used to love the stories when they were growing up. They became obsessed with the grove one summer and all they talked about for a whole month was summoning Hannah back from the dead.'

All my fears about growing up in the countryside confirmed, I ask, 'What's there now?'

'Nothing much. You'll be disappointed when we get there. The place has a very odd atmosphere, that's all.' That's more than enough for me. As far as I'm concerned, the atmosphere at Fortune's Yard is odd enough already. 'The rocks Hannah supposedly used to make her altar are long gone of course. There's just a clearing in the wood, and some old logs you can sit on and take a rest, and the tunnels.'

'Tunnels?'

'Oh, they're very small, just old rabbit warrens, but the children used to pretend they were where Hannah stored the ingredients for her spells.'

Chapter Twenty-One

Beth

Meg is right. Hannah's Grove is, after her stellar build-up, a bit of a disappointment: a circle of green space, perhaps fifteen feet in diameter, in a clearing in the woods. If it really has been here since the seventeenth century, there's something quite cool about that, but I don't get the sense that anything particularly terrible has happened here. In many ways, it has an air of genuine peace that for me is lacking in the hamlet itself, despite the adjective that I keep using to describe it when people ask me how things are going. It's somehow quieter than the woods that surround it; I can't hear any birds and even the rustling of leaves seems muted. Drake runs straight in and lifts his leg against one of the fallen tree trunks that Meg said we could use as a bench. We mutually decide not to sit on it.

Now that we're here, Meg seems to have lost any desire to tell me more grisly details, which is a relief. In fact she's gone quiet. I glance sideways at her, and notice that her eyes behind her spectacles are closed, which is a little disconcerting. I take a deep breath in and try to focus on the moment, which is presumably what Meg is doing. The clearing smells earthy and mossy, a reassuring smell. I'm not really sure what Streatham smelt of, but it certainly wasn't fallen leaves. Mainly I tried to avoid taking deep breaths, especially near the High Road, where the pollution was almost tangible. As I breathe out again, I try to empty my mind, like Sasha taught me when she was doing her meditation course. My brain isn't ready to switch off yet though.

'I hope Dolly hasn't been bothering Laura too much? She seems to really like her.'

Meg opens her eyes again.

'I mean, I know Laura's down here for a break. I wouldn't want her to think we're using her as a babysitter or anything.'

'Beth, there's something I want to ask you. It's actually something I wanted to talk to you and Noah about, but this feels like the right moment and I think you might understand.'

At this point Drake shoots off into the wood, barking loudly at something. He's gone in a flash of black and white. Meg calls him back, but he ignores her. Cursing him, she sets off into the undergrowth after him, calling, 'Back in a minute.'

Bluebell looks at me, tongue lolling out of the side of her mouth. She has a smug expression as if she wants me to note how good she's being. I reach down and give her a suitably grateful rub on the head. The grove seems to be having the opposite effect on me to the one intended. I'm filled with sudden happiness. My life has changed so much over the past year, and in such good ways. It's not that I had a bad life before; I loved my friends, my little studio flat and Bluebell – and I didn't even hate my job. I liked testing out other people's recipes, even if I sometimes found it frustrating that they didn't work as well as they should. And although I'd broken up with Pete, that was basically a good thing too, because we'd only have made each other unhappy if we'd stayed together. But now I have Noah, who is the most positive and supportive man, and marrying him didn't feel like a difficult thing at all, so maybe it wasn't ever that I was scared of commitment, but more that I knew on some level that Pete wasn't the right person to be committing to. I have Dolly, too, and although she wasn't what I thought I was looking for, and although most of the time I don't know what to make of her or how to behave around her, I still think that we might be able to make this work. We are a family, and the blending, well, that's happening too: she did actually confide in me yesterday, and she's been fine with me since then. And we're all living in a beautiful, grown-up house, with actual space. And I have a chance to start my own business and perhaps even achieve my dream of getting a book published one day. I wonder if perhaps the disturbing feeling I've had for the past few days is just an unwillingness to trust my own good fortune.

Bluebell is sniffing away over by the rabbit warrens. They're on the far side of the grove, where there's a bank of soil, leading up to a slightly higher level of the surrounding woodland. There are multiple tunnel entrances, some slightly higher than others, so that there's a double-decker effect. I can see why a group of children might seize on them as part of their make-believe about Hannah. They look intriguing. Bluebell certainly thinks so – she's got her whole muzzle in one of the smaller and lower tunnels and appears to be trying to make her body fit down there too. So much for the good behaviour. I go over to try and extract her, memories of reading about a dog that got stuck halfway down a rabbit hole and had to be dug out adding sudden urgency to my mission. Fortunately, Bluebell appears less committed to the task than her fellow canine must have been. When I approach, she stands back, wagging her tail and looking meaningfully at the tunnel, as though she expects me to be just as interested in the contents as she is. One ear is flopping forward over her left eye, the other is standing to attention. I crouch down on the grass next to the tunnel and peer dutifully in, but I can see no sign of whatever was causing such doggy fascination. In the woods, I can hear Drake barking. As I turn to haul myself up again, I catch sight of something in one of the other, higher warrens: a glimpse of white against the dark soil of the tunnel edge. Could it be a piece of chalk? I reach out for it. No, it's not chalk, it's made of cardboard. A little box of some sort. I gently pull it out. It's oblong, about 10 cm long. I hold it in my hands. Bluebell is panting and wagging her tail still. She tries to put her nose to it and I push her away, not wanting to get her slobber on the box. I glance back at what's in my hands, and that's when it occurs to me.

I'm holding a tiny coffin.

Chapter Twenty-Two

Beth

The obvious thing to do would be to show my find to Meg, but instinctively I slip it into my bag as soon as I hear her crashing back through the undergrowth. This means that the first time I get a chance to look at it properly is when I'm back at the house. Noah calls out to me as I open the front door. He's in the library, unpacking yet more boxes of books. I go through to talk to him, but I don't want to show him yet either. I feel like I want to know what it is before I share it with anyone. When he asks where we went, I tell him about the grove, and say that I was a bit underwhelmed, but Meg freaked me out with her tales of Hannah the Teenage Witch.

'Did you really play there when you were kids? And summon Hannah back from the dead?'

'I don't remember doing much summoning. I think the girls got really into it one summer. My sister even wrote a play about Hannah and they performed it in the grove. I think Laura played Hannah.'

I can imagine a teenage Laura being a pretty convincing witch.

'I think Laura's been telling Dolly the stories.'

'She probably already knows most of them. I think my mum told her way back when she was little and we used to come down here to visit.'

'They're pretty grisly.'

'Well Mum would have done it in an age-appropriate way.'

I try to think of what the age-appropriate way would be to describe a teenage girl being condemned to death for witchcraft and then drowned alive by the people she shared a village with.

'I'm going to get changed and then I'll come down and help you.'

Upstairs, I can hear the sound of K-pop coming from Dolly's room. I shut our bedroom door and remove the little box from my ever-capacious Uniqlo bag. Sitting on the end of the bed, I place my find on the duvet beside me. It's been carefully made out of pieces of sturdy white card, joined together very neatly with Sellotape. It's about 10 cm long and 3 cm wide. There's a letter about 1 cm high that I didn't notice before, inked onto one of the short ends of the rectangle: a capital R. I lift the lid of the box on its Sellotape hinges and inside is a tiny figure, shaped out of modelling clay. The hairs on the back of my neck stand up.

The figure is as carefully made as the coffin, and somehow even more disturbing. There's a piece of clay for the body, about the size of my thumb, tiny limbs with hands and feet, and a round ball of a head with a small nose and blank, unseeing eyes. It's a perfect miniature human, lying on a piece of pale yellow fabric. Gently, I reach in to pick it up, my fingers brushing the soft material that's lining the coffin, and something else too. When I look closely, I can see a few strands of ash blonde hair. I abruptly put the figure back in the coffin.

The thought of somebody making all this is unsettling. What should I do with it now I've found it? Who put it there? It was probably just a walker who'd read about Hannah's story and left it there as tribute, maybe even as a joke. As soon as I have this thought I dismiss it. Whatever the doll is, it's not a joke. There's something darkly serious about it. I don't believe in Hannah Fortune's magical powers, but whoever made this does – I'm sure of that much.

I close the cardboard lid, leave the box on the bed and walk over to the window, thinking through what to do with it. I don't want to keep it, but it would feel wrong to throw it away; it means something to someone. I suppose I could simply put it back. From the window, I can see Laura and her parents in the garden of their house. Meg and Stuart are sitting in deckchairs and Laura is stretched out on her back on the grass. She might even be asleep. I hope so – she certainly looked like she needed a good rest. The buggy is beside them in the shade, with a muslin draped across it, and Drake is lying flat out alongside it. There's a low table with a tray and tea stuff on it – mugs, a teapot and a pint of milk. A proper glass milk bottle, not a plastic one from a supermarket. There's something slightly unreal about the whole scene, like it's too perfect to be true. As I watch, Stuart lowers his newspaper and says something to Meg, who gestures back towards the house. I should just have shown Meg the coffin when I found it. Maybe it's not even that unusual and they're always finding offerings – if that's the right word – like this in the grove.

'Where did you get that?'

I didn't hear the door open and Dolly's voice makes me jump. Her eyes are wide and fixed on the object on our bed.

'I found it on my walk with Meg in the grove. Do you want a look?'

Usually I try to avoid asking her direct questions, as it makes it even more obvious when she doesn't answer, but I feel like we're making progress since she confided in me after the incident with Ralph yesterday. Her reply is quick and emphatic.

'No.'

'Do you know what it is? Why someone might have left it, I mean?'

'No.'

'You didn't see anything like it when you were there?'

She shakes her head, her blonde ponytail flicking back and forth.

'Shall we go and find your dad? I promised him I'd help him unload some more boxes.'

'I'm busy.'

'Okay,' I say. It's the kind of borderline rudeness that leaves me uncertain how to respond. Sasha would say I should pull her up on it. My Blended Family would say I should be the adult and respond politely.

'Were you looking for something? When you came in?'

'Dad said I could borrow his iPad.'

'I think it's over there on the bedside table.'

Her eyes flick to the table and then back to the coffin on the duvet. She circles the bed, retrieves the iPad from where it's charging, and then retraces her steps, never taking her eyes off the coffin. I'm increasingly sure she does know something about it, despite her denials.

'Meg was telling me the stories about Hannah Fortune. About how people thought she could commune with the dead.'

Silence. I try again.

'Have you heard those stories too?'

This time she snaps back: 'They're not stories.'

At the door she pauses, and then she turns back to look at me over her shoulder. I'm startled by the anger shining coldly from her eyes.

'You should have left it where you found it.'

'Why?'

'You shouldn't interfere with other people's stuff, that's all.' She turns away again and moves out onto the landing. Her final words are said under her breath, almost to herself. 'You'll regret it.'

Chapter Twenty-Three

Beth

Dolly spits the food out into her bowl.

'That's horrible!'

'Excuse me?' I say.

It's later the same day and we're all sitting round the big scrubbed farmhouse table in what I still think of as Noah's parents' kitchen. It's our first proper sit-down family dinner since we moved in and both Noah and I have gone to quite a lot of effort. He's made his special lasagne, with mascarpone instead of white sauce, and I've made a cherry clafoutis for dessert. It's a new recipe that I've been working on and I'm planning to post it on Instagram later.

'It tastes really gross.'

Her dessert spoon clatters back into her bowl.

'Dolly,' Noah says. 'That's rude. Please don't speak to Beth like that. If you don't like something just say so politely. Why don't you try a bit more?'

'No way.' Her pale eyebrows are knitted together. 'I can't eat it.'

Noah takes a spoonful of his dessert and his face contorts involuntarily.

'It does taste a bit strange, Beth.'

I try some myself, and gag. It's incredibly salty.

'Sorry, Dolly,' Noah says, laying a hand on her arm.

He dips his head down to inspect the clafoutis in his bowl and as he does so I catch sight of the expression that flits across Dolly's face before she can hide it: triumph. I think of what I heard her mutter as she left the bedroom earlier. *You'll regret it.* Is this some kind of silly revenge? Something in me snaps.

'She did something to it.'

'What?'

Noah is looking puzzled. Dolly's head has turned towards me, but her expression is no longer triumphant, it's puzzled too. I know there's still a chance to back down, but I think of Sasha and stick to my guns.

'Dolly did something to the pudding,' I say, and even in my own head I sound petulant so goodness knows how I sound to Noah, who is looking at me as if I've taken leave of my senses. He laughs uncertainly.

'Come on, Beth.'

'I'm not joking.'

'I don't understand then. Did you see Dolly do something?'

'I didn't,' Dolly says at once, her eyes starting to swim with tears. Bluebell, who had been lying beside Noah in the hope of scraps from our plates, has sensed the tension and got to her feet.

'I didn't see her, but I know that's what happened.' I look directly at Dolly, but she doesn't meet my eye. 'She was even hanging around in the kitchen earlier, when I came back from taking Bluebell outside.'

The tears start to spill down Dolly's face. I feel a pang of guilt. What am I doing? I've made my thirteen-year-old stepdaughter cry.

'I didn't do anything Dad, I promise.'

'Okay Dolly, I know,' Noah says. As he turns his head away from her, Dolly's eyes flick towards me and a small victorious smile flits across her face. My guilt vanishes. 'Isn't it possible that you just put some salt in instead of sugar?' Noah asks me gently.

'No,' I say. 'It is not in any way possible. In what world would I mistake a bottle of table salt for a bag of caster sugar?'

I can hear the anger in my voice and I can see Noah consider pointing out that a world in which we're all distracted by the move and unpacking all our stuff and starting a completely new life might be one in which we all occasionally do strange things, and think better of it.

Instead he says, 'I'm sure there's a perfectly rational explanation.' He looks from one to the other of us. Dolly has stopped crying now and is wiping her wet cheeks with her sleeve. 'Let's all just take a moment. It's been a pretty stressful few days. Come on, shall we all just apologise to each other and agree to move on. I'm certainly sorry I've been a bit of a stress monster.'

He clearly thinks apologising for something he hasn't done is going to kick start a train of apologies and he's not wrong.

'I'm sorry I upset you Beth,' Dolly says at once, the hint of a sob still in her voice. 'I didn't mean to be rude. It just tasted weird and I wasn't expecting it. Your puddings are normally amazing. I really didn't put anything in the recipe. I'd never do that.'

I can see the relief on Noah's face. It is the perfect apology – apart from the fact that I don't believe her. But if I hesitate any longer I end up looking like the baddie and besides, I have no proof whatsoever. I'm as sure as I can be that I didn't make a mistake in the recipe, but what does it matter? It's a stupid dessert. I can make another one. If Dolly wants to play silly tricks that's her problem and at some point she'll be caught out. Noah is watching me, his expression worried now. I suddenly wonder if this is exactly what she wants, to sow dissent and doubt between Noah and me.

'I'm sorry too,' I mumble, sounding far less gracious than her. 'I shouldn't have snapped like that. You're right, it does taste strange, Dolly. I don't blame you at all for spitting it out.'

I can't quite bring myself to say I don't think she did it and I wonder if Noah has noticed. But he's clearly decided to take his wins where he can get them.

'Salty clafoutis isn't one for the website then?' he jokes, although his eyes anxiously scan mine to see whether I'm going to laugh.

'I don't think it's a keeper,' I say lightly. 'Pass me your bowls and I'll put it in the bin.'

'I don't think even Bluebell is going to want any,' Dolly says. It's said with the childlike earnestness that sometimes disconcerts me. Thirteen-year-olds are such a mixture of grown-up and kid-like.

'Knowing Bluebell, she'd probably wolf it down anyway,' Noah says, bending down to give her back a rub. 'But I think she'd be drinking a lot of water for the rest of the evening.'

'There's some Häagen-Dazs mango and raspberry sorbet in the freezer. I'll get us some of that instead.'

Noah offers to help me, but I tell him to sit down. I need a moment to myself to process what just happened. As I scrape cherry clafoutis into the big pedal pin, I try to work out why I found the whole thing so upsetting. I think it might be partly because I keep hoping Dolly and

I really have turned a corner before something happens to prove me wrong. She confided in me yesterday and even if she regretted it afterwards, I thought it was a step forward – that we were finally making progress – and perhaps that's why I now feel ridiculously hurt that she'd play such a silly joke on me. But as I reach up to the cupboard to get three fresh bowls, dimly aware that Noah and Dolly are now discussing *Traitors*, which Noah, always late to the party, has just started watching on catch-up, I realise that what's disturbing me most isn't her ruining my pudding – because if Dolly had just come out and admitted it and said she was sorry, I might even have started to find it funny too. It's the fact that she can lie so convincingly to her dad's face. It's the growing feeling that, as Sasha says, she's two entirely different people.

Chapter Twenty-Four

The Grief Counsellor

Can you tell me how this week has been?

I kind of think it's pointless me being here.

You know you can stop any time? These sessions are intended to help you, but I can't force you to attend, and I wouldn't want to. That really would be pointless. You're very much in control here. It's your decision.

No, I need to keep coming. I promised my dad I would.

And that's important to you? The promise you made your dad?

This is the only thing he's asked me to do, so I have to do it.

Why do you think he asked you to do it?

Because he's worried about me, I suppose, and because he loves me. I know I should feel grateful for that. I know I'm lucky to have his love. But I don't really feel anything at all any more. Most of the time, it's like I'm numb and I just pretend to feel things. And, you know what? I think I do okay at it. I think I seem okay to most people – I seem normal. But I know that I'm not. I'm anything but normal.

You've been through a very traumatic experience.

Other people seem like they can cope, or maybe they're just pretending, too.

Everyone experiences grief differently. We're focusing on you and how you feel. It's not about comparisons.

I know what happened that day affected lots of other people too – I really do know that – but it's like I'm seeing them all through this glass wall and I can't reach them. They're all muffled, if you know what I mean? But the thing is, I don't even want to reach them. I don't feel like I can deal with their sadness as well as mine. It's all too much.

Let's not worry about anyone else at the moment. This is about you and helping you to adjust to your grief.

Don't say that. I want people to stop saying things like that. I don't even know what you mean. How can you adjust to grief? It doesn't make sense. I can't imagine not feeling like this.

Well that's why I'm here. To help you find some kind of stability again. Together we can visualise a way through this.

There is no way through. Not unless you've invented a way to travel back in time. It was my fault. That's all I keep thinking: it was my fault.

We talked before about how grief and guilt can go hand in hand.

I know, but this actually *was* my fault – that's the very worst thing about it. You know that, don't you? She's dead because of me.

Chapter Twenty-Five

Beth

'Did you get a chance to ask Dolly about what happened with Ralph yesterday?' I ask.

A couple of hours have passed since the stupid showdown over the salty pudding and I'm still feeling a bit on edge. Dolly has gone to bed and Noah and I are stretched out on the big leather sofa in the library, a half-finished bottle of Cabernet Sauvignon on the table, glasses in hand, and Bluebell gently snoring on the rug beside us. The sofa is the perfect length for us to sit propped up at opposite ends, our legs intertwined. Noah is reading *The New Silk Roads*, which I got him for his birthday a few weeks ago, and I've been scrolling through WhatsApp, catching up with messages. It's weird still being in groups for things I can't do any more; there's a chat about who's going to Bootcamp on Clapham Common tomorrow evening, and another one about whether people can make brunch next Saturday. All these things seem to me as if they're happening not just in another part of the country, but in another world entirely. I should probably just mute the chats, but I'm curiously reluctant to abandon this link to my old life. I've also had a quick peek on Instagram, but there are no more abusive messages, just lots of excited comments about my kitchen pics.

'Yes,' Noah says, putting down his book, 'I think it's all sorted.'

'So what happened? Did she say?'

'I think she was trying to take a shortcut through Ralph's garden to get back to the lane and he overreacted.'

'That's not what she said at the time.'

Noah swings his legs round so that his green-socked feet are on the floor again.

'Beth, did something happen between you and Dolly?'

This is my chance to follow Sasha's advice and tell Noah everything. The trouble is, everything is just a combination of small moments, most of which I can't even dignify with the description of facts. Noah, brown eyes looking troubled behind his glasses, continues probing gently.

'I just wondered what made you say what you said earlier.'

I'm not sure I can do this to him, despite what Sasha says. Whatever is going on between Dolly and me, it's for me to sort out. I don't want to worry him. At least that's what I tell myself. The truth is I'm still scared he's not going to believe me. That he's so convinced of Dolly's perfection that he's going to think I'm the one with the problem. And maybe I am – after all, why is it just me that Dolly seems to have taken against?

'I'm sorry. I shouldn't have snapped like that. It was probably a mistake.'

'But you did really think she'd put something in the pudding? As a joke?'

'Maybe as a joke, yes.' Now I swing my legs round too and start to get up. 'I should take Bluebell out for a last walk.'

'Beth. Please. We've got to tell each other what's going on otherwise this co-parenting thing isn't going to work.'

It's the word co-parenting that stops me short. Noah really does seem to think we're in this together. He regards me as a suitable person to help bring up his daughter, even if I feel like I have no idea what I'm doing. And he's right, this will never work if I don't trust him as he so clearly trusts me. I sit down next to him again and take a breath.

'Well, okay, but it's probably nothing.'

'What is?'

'Sometimes Dolly behaves differently around me to around you.'

His face creases in concern.

'Differently how?'

'She'll ignore me entirely often.'

'Probably she hasn't even heard you. Thirteen-year-olds are pretty oblivious. Half the time she's got head-phones in anyway.'

'You asked me to tell you and I am.' My voice has become ridiculously wobbly and I try to gain control of it again. He's reacted exactly as I thought he would. 'I know she's heard me.'

'Okay.' There's a pause. 'Sorry.' Noah takes my hand in his. I look at him and he squeezes my hand. 'Go on. Tell me.'

'And recently it's got a bit more than that.'

'What's happened?'

Is it me or has his voice become warier?

'Nothing massive, but she's said a few things.'

'Like what?'

'Just small things.' I'm curiously unwilling to go into specifics. 'But sometimes they can be quite mean.'

'I'm so sorry Beth.' But he also sounds a bit relieved and I suddenly wonder if he was expecting me to say something worse. 'Let me have a chat with her.'

'No, I don't think that's going to help. I don't want it to sound like I'm complaining about her. I'm really not. I don't mind for myself so much, but I guess it makes me worry a bit about her, and how she's feeling.'

'I won't say anything if you don't want me to, of course I won't, but I don't want this to escalate.'

'Escalate?'

'You said it was getting worse.'

'It's still minor stuff though.'

'I think we all of us need to sit down as a family and talk this through. I know Dolly really likes you Beth – she's told me she does lots of times.'

It's on the tip of my tongue to say: have you considered that your daughter might be lying to you? That she doesn't like me one little bit and that telling you she does is just part of the game she's playing against me? Have you considered that you don't know Dolly that well at all? But I can't bring myself to say the words out loud so instead I say:

'Okay, I think talking about it all together might not be a bad idea.'

'Great.'

'But I don't want to make a big deal out of it.'

'We can keep it very light. Talk about how we're doing as a family after the move, and how we're all feeling. And then you can bring up some of the things you've just told me so she knows it's all out in the open. It doesn't have to sound like you're accusing her of anything. You can talk about how it's made you feel.' Noah's approach is actually quite similar to Sasha's advice. 'Let's do it tomorrow,' he

125

says. 'We could go on a walk. Take a picnic. Make the most of the end of the summer holidays.'

A walk is a good idea. My Blended Family says that it's often easier to have tricky conversations while you're walking.

'Yes, all right.'

Noah gets up from the sofa and gives me a hug. He smells of sandalwood and shampoo.

'I'm sorry you're having to deal with this stuff with Dolly. I wish it wasn't so complicated.'

'There's no need to apologise. It's not your fault. It's no one's fault,' I say hastily. 'There's just a lot going on right now.'

'Beth, is there something else bothering you?'

'How do you mean?' I hedge. It was hard enough telling Noah that Dolly might not be quite as perfect as he thinks she is; I don't think I can also tell him that something about Fortune's Yard itself makes the hairs on the back of my neck stand up. He's going to think I'm losing it.

'You just don't seem quite like your normal self.'

There is at least one tangible thing I can mention.

'Well, I did find something a bit weird when Meg and I walked to Hannah's Grove earlier.'

I left the tiny coffin upstairs, in the drawer of the bedside table, but I describe it to him. He seems curiously untroubled.

'We used to do stuff like that when we were kids.'

'You used to make cardboard coffins?'

'Not that exactly, but we'd leave gifts for Hannah Fortune. Hoping to harness her magical powers over life and death. It was a bit of fun. This is just someone doing the same.'

'You should see it. Someone took ages making it.'

'Well even if it's someone who really believes in Hannah Fortune's powers, it still seems pretty harmless.'

Again, I feel frustrated that he can't see what I'm seeing.

'I think whoever left it there might be quite troubled.'

I've chosen my words carefully, but he quickly replies.

'You think this has something to do with Dolly?'

'She came into our room earlier and saw the little coffin thing on the bed and she acted a bit weirdly. And she has been a bit fixated on Hannah's Grove ever since she went there with Laura.'

'You took the coffin away from the grove?'

'I think you're missing the point here,' I say, beginning to feel exasperated.

'You're not meant to move the things you leave for Hannah.'

'Are you serious?'

'Sorry.' But he doesn't sound sorry. He sounds annoyed. 'Look, Beth, teenage girls have always loved things like that, haven't they? It's no big deal.'

'I think it's the kind of thing that could get out of hand quite quickly.'

'It seems like pretty harmless make-believe to me.'

'You're the one telling me I shouldn't have moved the coffin.'

'It's just something we used to believe as kids.'

'So you keep saying. It doesn't make it any less weird.'

'I don't understand what's worrying you so much.' His hands are bunched up in the pockets of his jeans and his normally placid face is thunderous. 'Maybe,' he snaps, 'it's because you didn't grow up here.'

127

His words are like a punch in the guts and my face must reveal something of how I'm feeling, because he's instantly contrite.

'I'm so sorry, Beth. I shouldn't have said that. I didn't mean it like that.'

'You think I'm an outsider? That I don't understand this place?'

'Of course not.'

'Because, guess what? I already feel like that, so I don't need you to rub it in thanks very much.'

'I really am sorry.' Noah looks distraught that he's upset me. He pushes his glasses back up his nose and attempts to explain. 'I just meant that if you'd grown up with the Hannah stories like I did you might feel differently about them.'

'Okay, but how do you know that what you feel is right?'

'I'm not saying I'm right and you're wrong. All I was doing was putting forward another perspective.'

'Sometimes an outsider can see things people on the inside can't.'

'You're not an outsider, Beth. I feel terrible that I made you think that. Fortune's Yard is as much your home as it is mine.'

Which isn't true. And never will be. But I return his hug all the same.

Chapter Twenty-Six

Beth

In an attempt to shake off the feeling that I don't belong in Fortune's Yard, and that even my husband thinks so, I decide to take Bluebell out for her evening walk. Noah wants to come with me, but, although I'm glad we've cleared the air, I need some time by myself to calm down. I keep Bluebell on the lead because I'm still worried that she doesn't know the area and might get lost if she runs off. Besides it's dark – properly dark in a way that it never is in London. There are no streetlights here. I suddenly long for the artificial yellowy-orange brightness of Streatham High Road. But I can at least see lights on upstairs in Meg and Stuart's farmhouse, and Ralph and Evelyn's cottage has a faint glow from the hallway. I decide they're probably the kind of people who go to bed early, but just as I'm thinking this, an outdoor light snaps on, the front door opens and a figure that I think must be Ralph emerges. I freeze, not keen for an evening chat. I wonder where he's going. I see him walk to the end of the path and then, still faintly illuminated, take out a packet of cigarettes and light one. Maybe Evelyn won't let him smoke in the house. He and the glow of his cigarette disappear up the lane.

I'd been planning to head that way myself, but I definitely don't want to bump into Ralph, and suddenly walking anywhere at all seems like a bad idea. I'm already wishing I'd taken Noah up on his offer to join me. I know my uneasiness about the dark is irrational. After all, it was broad daylight when I got mugged at the end of our street in Streatham, and I'm probably safer in Fortune's Yard than I ever was there. Despite the unsettled feeling the place gives me, I'm hardly likely to get mugged here: there are literally seven people in the whole place – well nine, I suppose, now that Laura and her baby are here – and none of them strikes me as a chance low-life who wants to nick my bag.

Just thinking about the mugging is making me feel shaky. They were only kids, but it turns out that even kids can be pretty frightening. The image of the ringleader is instantly in my head: short brown hair, big ears and pale blue eyes in a pasty face. The police never found them of course; I'm not even sure they looked. All I got was an email to say that they were sorry to hear I'd been a victim of crime, but they were closing my case because with the evidence available it was unlikely they'd find out who was responsible. They realised I'd be disappointed, they said. I wasn't disappointed so much as wearily resigned. It's the kind of thing that happens dozens of times every day, in London at least. But not here. I push the memory away, wondering why it's come back into my head now – maybe it's because the whole situation with Dolly is making me feel vulnerable.

I decide I'll wander over to the millpond where I saw Laura and her baby standing yesterday morning. It's literally within metres of the front door and there's some-thing reassuring about still being able to see the house – our house – looking all cosy and welcoming, despite the lingering feeling that I'll always be an outsider in this place. I turn on my phone torchlight and cross the lane. Bluebell is snuffling happily on the ground, tail wagging.

I try to work out why I'm still feeling so uneasy. Okay, so Noah doesn't understand why I'm worried about all the Hannah stuff, but maybe I should cut him some slack and try to understand that the stories were part of his childhood. And maybe I *am* making a big deal out of very little. I may have grown up in Stevenage rather than Fortune's Yard, but when I was Dolly's age I remember trying levitation spells at sleepovers and waving sage around my bedroom to cleanse it of evil spirits, so perhaps this isn't that different. And the more important thing is I've actually managed to talk to Noah about how Dolly's been behaving towards me and it went all right. He was defensive of her to start with, just like I'd expected, but I think he did believe me. Now I've got a bit of time to consider what I'm going to say to Dolly tomorrow and although the thought of the whole conversation makes me squirm, I know that getting things out into the open is the right thing to do.

As I gaze out across the millpond, the moon comes out from behind the clouds and the water is illuminated temporarily in an eerie silver light. I try to spot the swans as Bluebell finally squats and has a pee. My phone beeps with an incoming message and I glance down. It's from Sasha.

> Hey! How's everything going? Know you're busy but don't forget what we said about trying to post at least once a day to build followers. It's really going to help when we do the book proposal xx

Feeling guilty, I quickly tap out a reply.

> All good here thanks. Even talked to N
> about the stuff we were discussing. Sorry,
> haven't forgotten what you said – been bit
> full on, like you say, I'll post something
> now.

I hit send and watch as Sasha types her reply. I wonder whether I'm doing the right thing trying to turn my hobby into a business. It's exciting, and it's a chance to finally be my own boss, but the Instagram account has always been a fun thing up until now. I've never felt any pressure; I'd post because I had a new recipe or because I wanted to share a bake that had gone particularly well. Once I launch my baking business it will be my job or part of my job, and I hope that doesn't change how I feel about it. I'd been planning to post the cherry clafoutis recipe from earlier, but I need to know what it actually tastes like before I share it with the world. I open my photos to look for other options and find one of Bluebell that I took just before dinner, fast asleep in her basket, with her head resting on her paws. I've occasionally posted pictures of her before and my followers seem to love them, and Bluebell is a level of personal content I'm certainly happy to share. This one will be a quick fix for today, and I'll post another recipe tomorrow. I've still got the app open from when I was sitting on the sofa just now, so I click into it to upload the photo. I go to type out the caption: *Good night – hope everyone's had a great weekend.* But just as I'm about to do this, I notice a new comment under the kitchen pictures. My heart lurches as I read the words.

Beth Bitch is a liar. No surprise if you know where she came from. Don't trust her business or anything about her. She's devil's spawn.

Chapter Twenty-Seven

Beth

'I'm really sorry Beth, I think I'm going to have to fly out there.'

I already know it's bad news because I've heard Noah's half of the phone call. It's 8:30 a.m. on Monday morning. Dolly is still in bed. Noah and I had been having breakfast when his mobile rang, shattering the early morning calm.

'No, of course.'

'They don't know whether he's going to pull through.'

'Oh God, Noah, I'm so sorry.' I give him a hug and he clutches me tight. The lingering awkwardness from our conversation last night has vanished.

'Amy said they don't know how long he was lying there before mum found him and called 911, and obviously when you have a heart attack time is the crucial thing. Mum and Amy have gone to the hospital, but Amy said they're not being given much information.'

'You've always said your dad's a fighter.'

'I know. I just wish I wasn't so far away. I need to look up flights.'

'I can do that. Why don't you go upstairs and start packing?'

'Thank you, you're the best. Ideally from Stanstead or Luton I guess, but I don't know if you can get flights to

San Francisco from there. I've always gone from Heathrow when I've visited Amy.'

'Don't worry. I'll sort it. Just go.'

'I'll message Amy to say I'll be there as soon as I can.'

'What about Dolly?'

'I'll wake her up and tell her when I've packed.'

'No, I mean should I be getting a flight for her too?'

'I don't think she should come with me. She starts school in three days.'

'But if it could be her last chance to—' I don't finish the sentence because I'm trying to stay positive for him.

'I think it will be too much for her. It might bring back memories of when her mum was in hospital.'

I've always assumed Juliet died shortly after the car hit the tree. I didn't realise she'd been taken to hospital. I wonder how long she'd survived, but now is obviously not the time to ask for more information.

'If this really is the end for my dad,' Noah says, his voice breaking, 'I want Dolly to remember him as he was. I don't want her to see him hooked up to all kinds of machines in a hospital bed.'

I'm worried he's going to cry.

'No, of course, I understand.'

I'm not sure Dolly will, though. She's going to want to go with him.

'Will you be okay, though?' he asks, a different note of anxiety in his voice. 'I mean, just you and Dolly? After what we were talking about yesterday.'

'Don't be silly, I'll be absolutely fine.' I look straight at him as I say it. My hand on his arm. I need to convince him. He has enough to worry about without this too. I've never been on my own with Dolly for more than a couple of hours, but of course we'll be okay. She's a thirteen-year-old child, not my arch nemesis.

'Thanks Beth. I'd be in pieces without you here.'

He heads upstairs and I push the remains of breakfast to one side and jump on my laptop to start finding flights. By the time he comes back, I've found him a flight that afternoon from Heathrow to San Francisco, which I think he can make if he leaves soon. It costs a crazy amount of money, but if ever there was a moment for putting something on a credit card and worrying about it later this is it. Noah's clutching a rucksack and his passport and looking, if possible, even more worried than earlier. As we're booking the flight, Dolly appears in the doorway. Her eyes are red and swollen. She's dressed already, in shorts and a jumper with a lightning bolt on the front.

'I want to come, too.'

'We've talked about this, love,' Noah says. I take his passport from him and start entering passenger details. 'You start your new school very soon. It's best for you to stay here.'

'I want to see granddad. I don't care about school.'

'I know you do. And all being well, you'll see him at Christmas. Remember we said we'd go out there and see them both, and stay with Aunty Amy.'

'Please don't leave me here by myself,' she says piteously.

'Dolly, love, please don't make this any more difficult for me. I'll call as soon as I get there, I promise. And you won't be by yourself. Beth will be here.'

Dolly doesn't miss a beat.

'I'm not staying here with her. I'd rather die.'

136

'Okay that's enough.' It's the first time I've heard Noah ever sound angry with her. 'I know you don't mean it. Apologise to Beth.'

Her eyes dart from his face to mine and back again. Her expression is mutinous.

'It's fine,' I say quickly. 'She's upset.'

'It is not fine. We're all upset – that's no excuse.'

In a way, it actually *is* fine. I mind far less about this outburst, when she's so obviously distressed and frightened, than I did about the under-the-breath insult as we were walking into a roomful of people. This is out in the open, at least. And it feels, if not normal, then at least not unexpected.

'We're going to need to leave in the next ten minutes if you're going to catch that train from Woodbridge. Why don't I go and sort out the car and you two can follow me out?'

I pick Noah's rucksack up off the floor, grab the car keys from the bowl on the worktop and head for the front door. There's a limit to how much the car needs sorting for a half-hour drive to the station, but it seems like a good idea to leave them alone to work things out.

When I get out on the drive, I see Laura is trundling past with the buggy and Drake, who's trotting at her heels.

'Hey!' I call out, relieved to have another person to talk to after the tension in the kitchen. 'How's your break going?'

'Oh hi, Beth.' She looks a bit startled. I guess she, like everyone else in Fortune's Yard, has got used to this house being empty over the past few months. She's dressed again in the muted but expensive leisurewear she was wearing yesterday morning, and her long fair hair is streaking out behind her in the early-morning breeze. 'It's going okay thanks. I feel different here. It's a special place. Are you heading out?'

I explain about Noah's dad and his emergency mission to San Francisco. She leaves the buggy at the end of the drive, with Drake still beside it, and comes over to me, her face creased with sympathy.

'Shit, that's awful. Poor Noah. His dad can't be that old.'

Up close, her eyes still have big dark circles under them.

'He's seventy-two.'

'It's a big deal to move to another country at that age.'

I know we're both thinking that maybe the stress was too much for him.

'Yes, and it makes it even more difficult for Noah being so far away,' I say. 'He's used to being able to pop up to see his parents.' Again, I feel that stab of envy that I can't quite dispel no matter how hard I try; it's like a reflex.

'Is Dolly going too?'

'No, Dolly and I are staying in Fortune's Yard.'

Laura seems much less on edge than the first time I met her and talking to her now, I feel like she might be someone I can confide in, maybe even a potential friend, which would be great if she comes here regularly. Meg and Stuart seem welcoming but I'm struggling to imagine my social life here revolving around them. Laura's the only person in Fortune's Yard apart from Noah who's even roughly my age and she lives and works in London, so at the very least I feel like she inhabits a common world, and although friendship is clearly about much more than this, something about moving to Fortune's Yard has made me crave the familiar. I decide to risk sharing a little of how I'm feeling about the prospect of several days as Dolly's sole carer.

'I'm mildly terrified about the whole thing,' I say, trying to keep my tone light. 'But obviously I can't tell Noah.'

Her eyebrows flicker.

'Is this the first time it's been just the two of you?'

'The first time for more than a few hours, yes.'

'You'll be fine. Dolly's lovely. I get why you're nervous, but it won't be nearly as bad as you're imagining.'

'I don't suppose you fancy coming over this evening?' I say on impulse, relieved that she isn't judging me. 'I can tell you how it's going. We can share a bottle of wine?'

She hesitates; her tired face looking briefly panicked. Instantly, I feel guilty. I'm usually good at judging these things, but I'm so desperate for a new friend here I'm probably being too pushy. Other than a wave from the kitchen window yesterday, this is only the second time I've met her, after all, and the first time wasn't exactly a huge success.

'Don't worry,' I say, backtracking rapidly so she doesn't feel awkward about it. 'It was just an idea. I know it's very short notice and you're probably busy.'

'No, it's just…' She glances over at the buggy. Drake is lying down protectively beside it.

'Of course. I'm so sorry, I didn't think.'

'But you know what,' she says suddenly, 'it's all right. Mum and Dad will babysit.'

'Seriously?'

'Yes. They'd like me to have an evening out, honestly. It's just usually there's nowhere for me to go. A solo trip to the cinema in Aldeburgh doesn't really do it for me.'

'Oh God, Laura, I've just thought you must think I'm a total idiot. I'm so sorry. You solo parent all the time.'

She flushes slightly.

'Don't be silly. I don't think you're an idiot at all. It's not the same thing. You're allowed to be a bit scared about looking after Dolly by yourself. I know you're going to be okay, but I get why it's a big deal.'

Again, I feel relieved that she understands.

'She seems to really like you,' I say, hoping it doesn't come out as resentfully as it sounds in my head. 'You'll have to give me some tips.'

'We've got a lot in common,' she says. Before I can ask her what she means, she adds quickly, 'I could take her for another walk if it helps? We could head up to Hannah's Grove again.'

'There's no need. You're supposed to be having a break,' I say. Maybe I'm overreacting and Noah's right that there's no harm in it, but I still don't want Dolly anywhere near the grove if I can help it. 'Coming over tonight would be brilliant though. I'll cook us something.'

'That sounds good.'

'Let's swap numbers.'

Laura goes over to the buggy and roots around in the bag attached to the front, removing several packs of wet wipes, formula and a rattle before she finds her phone and heads back towards me. As she's entering my number, Noah comes out of the house, with a subdued Dolly trailing in his wake. At the sight of Laura, her face crumples and then she launches herself at her. Laura is nearly knocked over by the force of it.

'Dolly, be careful!' Noah admonishes her. Laura recovers her balance and wraps her arms around Dolly. 'Sorry Laura. We've just had some bad news and we're all feeling a bit emotional.'

'Beth told me. That's awful.' She makes an effort to gently extract herself from Dolly's grip. 'I'm so sorry to hear about your granddad, Dolly. I hope he's going to be okay.'

'I don't like it when people leave me,' Dolly says, so quietly it's hard to make out the words. I'm not sure whether she's talking about her granddad or her dad, but Laura, now released from Dolly's hug, says simply, 'No one does. It's a horrible feeling.'

She clearly has a knack of being able to say the right thing, something I feel I lack, especially where my step-daughter is concerned. Dolly nods solemnly and although she still looks upset, there's hope lighting up her face as she asks, 'Will you come with us to the station, Laura?'

'Laura's busy, Dolly,' Noah says, before she can reply. 'She can't just drop everything.'

Dolly's face clouds over again.

'I'll be here when you get back, though, if you want to talk,' Laura says.

'Why don't you go and say a quick hello to Drake and the baby?' Noah says.

Dolly gives him a look like she knows she's being got out of the way, but she heads down the drive towards the buggy on her long thin legs, like a slightly shaky baby giraffe. Laura watches her go, looking troubled.

'Sorry about that,' Noah says, as soon as Dolly is out of earshot. 'She only found out about half an hour ago and it's really thrown her.'

'Don't worry at all. It's understandable.'

The three of us watch as Dolly bends down to talk to the baby. Then Noah turns back towards Laura, and fills her in on what he knows.

'Your mum must be so worried,' she says when he's finished. 'I'll be thinking about you all.'

She reaches out and gives him a hug. Dolly is now standing upright beside the buggy. The other two aren't looking at her, but she's watching the two of them and even from a distance I can feel the ferocity of her gaze.

Chapter Twenty-Eight

Beth

On the way to the station, Dolly apologises for what she said in the kitchen, so whatever Noah said to her while I was outside with Laura clearly did the trick. It's her second apology in under twenty-four hours, and this one is less polished than the first. I feel sorry for her; she's so clearly frightened and upset about her granddad.

'I'm sorry I was rude to you, Beth,' she says doggedly from the backseat. 'I didn't mean it.'

'I know you didn't,' I say quickly. I glance in the rear-view mirror but she's looking out the window, not at me. 'It's not a problem.'

Noah keeps up a fairly steady stream of upbeat chat about going to see grandma and granddad at Christmas and what Christmas in San Francisco will be like. I know how worried he is himself, and how difficult this must be for him, and I know that he's trying to reassure Dolly, but I can't help worrying that he's overdoing it. If his dad does die now, it's going to be even harder to explain to her. Dolly herself is very subdued, although she makes a bit of an effort for Noah's sake, saying that there's no way she's eating sushi for Christmas lunch and that it's turkey and roasties or she's not going.

The goodbyes pulled up outside the station are hurried and a bit chaotic. There are only seven minutes until Noah's train is due, and at the last moment he can't find his passport, and I realise it's still in the pocket of my jeans. Bluebell adds to the general sense of panic by barking enthusiastically from the car. Dolly makes Noah promise to call as soon as he lands and again once he's seen her granddad. He gives her a final kiss on the forehead and envelops me in a quick but fierce hug. And then he's gone, running in the direction of platform two. Dolly and I stand forlornly beside the car in the dropping off area and I'm seized with a sudden and almost overwhelming desire to run after him. I take a deep breath to steady myself. This is hardly an impossible task. I'm looking after my stepdaughter for a few days, not working as a trauma surgeon in a war zone, or trying to save starving children in a famine, or any of the other terrible things I read about people doing and wonder how they find the strength to go on.

'Do you want to pick up a hot chocolate for the journey back or shall we head straight off?'

There's a small cafe just outside the station entrance.

'I don't want anything.'

She climbs into the passenger seat in the front. Well at least she's sitting next to me. I get back in the driver's side and Bluebell leans over the seat to lick my ear enthusiastically. The day stretches ahead of us. In a tiny hamlet.

'Or we don't have to go home straight away. Is there anything you'd like to do? We could go into Ipswich.' I've been away from London for three whole days and I'm already craving the distractions of a city. 'We could see if there's anything on at the cinema?' I picture us buying popcorn and vast fizzy drinks, and sitting through some chick flick together, maybe going for burgers afterwards. 'Or look round the shops. Is there anything you need for school?'

She shakes her head. I wait for more but that's it. A dismissal of it all. I put my seatbelt on and turn the key in the ignition.

'We could go for a walk or something when we get back.' I'm not quite sure what the 'or something' is, but I have a whole car journey to think of it. Thirty minutes that I'm already sensing is going to feel like four hours. 'And there's a new recipe I want to try out for peanut butter cookies. I could really do with some help with the photos.'

This time nothing at all, not even a shake of the head. I'm probably trying too hard. Dolly clearly wants to be left in peace, and that's fair enough given the news she's just had. My Blended Family gets pretty specific sometimes, but I haven't come across a scenario in which you're looking after your traumatised young stepdaughter, who's previously lost her mum and is now faced with the imminent loss of her grandfather, so I don't know exactly what it would say. The theme of overcompensating because you're anxious you're not doing it right comes up again and again though.

'We can decide later.'

I start the engine. And then, because I'm not sure I can face thirty minutes of silence, I add brightly, 'Let's turn the radio on, shall we, and have some tunes on our way back.'

It's on Radio 4 because I hardly ever listen to music stations any more, tending to just put my phone on Spotify. But I don't want to subject Dolly to my music choices and I'm not sure I can face a one-sided conversation about what she'd like to listen to. I flick between stations until I find a local one playing something poppy that I think is Taylor Swift. To me, Taylor Swift feels current; to her, it's probably old person's music. But it's hard to tell whether she even recognises it because her face doesn't change.

Even with the music playing, the lack of conversation starts to feel oppressive after about fifteen minutes, which is ridiculous because I can drive happily in silence for far longer with other people in the car. What's the phrase? A companionable silence. Well it's probably all in my head but this feels the very opposite of that. I also start to fear that if I don't say something soon, I'll cease to be able to say anything at all and we'll spend the next however long it is – I'm deliberately not thinking about how long Noah is going to be gone – in mute incomprehension.

'Have you stayed with your Aunt Amy many times?' I don't know why I keep asking her questions. I leap in before it's obvious that she's not going to reply. 'I've never been to San Francisco, but I hear it's beautiful. I haven't even been to the States before.'

I babble on for a while longer, outlining where I most want to go and why and then eventually, mercifully, I trail off.

'Try not to worry too much,' I say at last, turning down whatever nonsense the DJ is currently splurging. We're winding our way down the narrow country lanes that lead to Fortune's Yard. Almost home. 'Your dad will call as soon as he gets there and your granddad is in the best possible place. I know they'll be taking really good care of him.'

It's exactly what I should have said all along. As if to confirm this, Bluebell suddenly sits up in the back seat and barks loudly. Dolly turns to me. She's going to say something.

'You should have a harness for Bluebell.'

'Sorry?'

'It's dangerous for her to be loose in the back like that.'

She has a point; I'm just disconcerted by the change of subject.

'Oh, okay. I mean that's a good thought. We can get one.'

'Anything could happen.'

I'm suddenly very conscious that the 'anything' we're talking about is a car crash and that Dolly has been in one and lost her mum in one.

'You're right. I'm sorry. I don't know why I haven't thought about it before. I'll get her a harness, I promise.'

She is still regarding me intently. Somehow this is even more disconcerting than when she was staring fixedly out of the window. Her deep blue eyes are full of hostility. Fortune's Yard is drawing closer and the feeling of oppressiveness – of something being very wrong – has returned sharper than ever. But is the feeling the place or Dolly herself? Or somehow the combination of them both? I try to push this thought aside and focus on the conversation. I'm being ridiculous and the more I indulge myself the more I'm likely to have that on-edge feeling.

'You know it only takes a second to lose control, don't you?'

We're on a relatively straight stretch of the lane, and I'm doing about 40 mph, because for once I can see a decent distance ahead. There's something about the way she says it that makes it sound almost like a threat. Involuntarily, I slow down. Surely what I can hear in her voice is fear, nothing more. She's had a terrible experience and she's the one who's scared. I try to make my voice as soothing as possible:

'I'm not going to lose control Dolly, I promise.'

I glance over at her again, looking for confirmation that she's seeking reassurance. Her eyes flick to the steering wheel.

'You can't know that,' she says very deliberately. 'You might swerve going round that next corner and drive straight into a tree.'

Again, her eyes flick to the steering wheel. And suddenly there's no mistaking who's the most frightened person in this car, and it's definitely not Dolly. My hands have gone clammy and my heart is thudding against my ribs, but I don't want her to know just how much she's scared me. I try to keep my voice steady.

'I know this is a really difficult time for you, but we'll get through it, I promise.'

Suddenly she twists away from me and opens the car door. I slam on the brakes and we stop dead in the middle of the country lane.

'Shit! What are you doing?'

'I'm going to walk the rest of the way.'

'That was really dangerous! We were still moving.'

'Barely,' she retorts. Her tone is scornful and this is somehow comforting. Normal teenage contempt is preferable to the chill that had been in her voice when she'd talked about driving into a tree.

'Please don't go Dolly.'

'It's only five minutes. There's a footpath, Laura showed me.'

'Okay,' I say weakly, because she's already out of the car, and short of abandoning it here and following her there's not much more I can do. She slams the door. 'Come straight home!' I call plaintively after her.

I should drive off. It's not safe to stay stopped here in the middle of a narrow country lane. I try to reach down to put the car in gear, but my hand refuses to obey my instructions. It's shaking too much.

Chapter Twenty-Nine

Beth

When I finally pull up in front of the Old Watermill, I'm so eager to get out of the car that I get tangled up in my seatbelt and end up half-falling onto the drive. I sit there on the gravel for a few moments, trying not to give in to the tears that have been threatening to overwhelm me, but then the disconcerting thought that Dolly might already be back and watching me from one of the windows makes me scramble to my feet. I know I should go and check on her, but I really, really don't want to see her again just yet. I have no clue what I'm going to say to her. How do you possibly follow what just happened in the car? And what exactly *did* happen in the car? I need to make sense of it before I'm ready to talk about it.

Instead, I let Bluebell out of the back, my hands slightly steadier now. I make a show of patting her and standing waiting while she squats for a wee. I seem incapable of a single rational thought. My mind is a blank. Finally, there's no putting it off any longer and I turn towards the house. It's an indication of how incoherently I'm thinking that it's only as I take out the key and unlock the front door that it occurs to me that Dolly couldn't be inside the house as she hasn't got a front door key – unless she took one with her? But why would she do that? It's hardly like she could have planned this. I call out her name just in case, my voice sounding way more shaky than I would like. There's no answer. That doesn't mean she's not here though. The thought of being in the house and not being sure whether she's also here somewhere is unbearable, so I go from room to room to make sure. I start in her bedroom, the obvious place. The door's not even closed and she's definitely not there. But somehow the room itself is reassuring; the fairy lights she's already put up around the bed, the pink-and-purple tie-dye duvet, and propped up against the wall the canvas print with the slogan 'Girls rule the world'. It's all so normal. I take a deep breath. I call her name again, this time sounding more confident; there's still no answer, and when I've checked all the rooms, and I'm as sure as I can be she's not there, I slump down at the scrubbed wooden table in the kitchen and try to make a plan. She could be back at any moment, and I need to know what I'm going to say to her.

The big old-fashioned kitchen clock ticks away in the background.

It's now more than half an hour since I got home. My apprehension about encountering Dolly again is rapidly giving way to panic at the thought she might not be coming back at all. Didn't she say it only took five minutes by the footpath? When I stopped the car we were less than a mile from Fortune's Yard. Even if the footpath isn't the most direct route, it can't possibly have taken this long to get back. I try her mobile several times, but it just rings out. Where is she? Has something happened to her? What am I going to say to Noah? I should have done more to stop her. She was so upset, she wasn't thinking straight – she tried to jump from a moving car, for God's sake. I should go and look for her, but I don't even know what footpath she was talking about. In my head, I hear Noah say 'You didn't grow up here.' If I had, I'd know where she might be.

Shit, this is a disaster. Why have I wasted all this time sitting at the kitchen table? I push my chair back so abruptly that I make Bluebell jump and she gives a sharp bark and gets to her feet too. Seeing her steadies me. And I have my first sensible thought. Maybe Dolly is at Meg and Stuart's, with Laura. Laura even offered to talk to Dolly when she got back from the station. Why didn't I think of that before? What is wrong with my brain right now? I'll head over there now.

–

'Is Dolly here?' I blurt out as soon as Meg opens the front door.

'Beth.' She reaches out and touches my arm. 'Laura told us about Noah's dad. We're all so very sorry.'

Her sharp eyes behind her burgundy glasses are full of sympathy.

'Thanks,' I say. Why isn't she answering me? 'Is Dolly here?' I repeat.

'No, I thought Laura said she went with you to the station?'

'She did.' I hesitate. 'It's just I haven't seen her since we got back and I'm starting to get a bit worried about her.'

Meg shoots me a look that suggests she realises that 'a bit worried' might be something of an understatement.

'Come in.'

'Where's Laura? Could Dolly be with her?'

'She's in the garden, but Dolly's not there.'

My heart sinks and I realise how badly I've been counting on her being here.

'I don't know where else to look.'

Meg takes my arm and ushers me into the dark kitchen. The other night it had seemed a bit oppressive, but today it's a haven from the baking heat of the day. My head is throbbing with a tension headache. I lean back against the worktop, the chaos of the other night now augmented with a bottle steriliser, several multi-packs of formula and a pile of bibs.

'When did you last see her?' Meg asks calmly.

'Nearly an hour ago,' I say, fighting not to let the panic overwhelm me. There's no way I can tell her about the exchange in the car, and anyway it's already becoming fuzzier in my head, replaced by the almost overwhelming anxiety of where Dolly might be now. 'I dropped her off in the lane on the way back from the station because she said she wanted to walk the last bit. She said there was a footpath,' I add anxiously. I wonder again if I should have done something more to stop her, but I can't think what I could have actually done, short of a physical fight.

'There is. Did you drop her by that field with the two bay ponies in it? It's a nice walk back over the fields. I sometimes take Drake out that way.'

'How long does it take?'

'About ten minutes.'

Meg sees my face.

'I'm sure she's just decided to go a bit further. It's a beautiful morning. She's probably lost track of time. It's never a strong point for teenagers in my experience.'

I long to have Meg's experience, or any experience at all, so I can cope with this a bit better than I'm currently managing.

'Stay for a coffee and I'm sure she'll be back by the time you've finished it.'

'You don't think I should call the police?'

'The police?' Meg echoes.

Ralph suddenly appears in the doorway from the house, making me jump.

'Ah Ralph, can I get you a coffee? I'm just making one for Beth.'

'Not for me, thanks,' Ralph says, primly.

'Did you find it?' Meg asks. She turns to me to explain. 'Evelyn thinks she might have lost an earring the other night. I was helping Ralph look for it when the door went.'

'No sign.'

'What a shame. Especially if they're her favourites. I'll keep an eye out, I'm sure it will turn up at some point.' Ralph is staring at me. 'Beth is looking for Dolly. You haven't seen her have you?'

Ralph shakes his head. The expression on his face is very odd indeed – a curious mix of triumphant and almost fearful. In my head I suddenly have a picture of him and Dolly as I saw them the day before yesterday on the footpath above his cottage, his face contorted with fury. And the various nebulous scenarios of something terrible happening to Dolly are now replaced with a very specific one in which Dolly met Ralph on the way home over the fields. This is clearly ridiculous. I try to dismiss it, but somehow it won't shift. Now all I can see is Ralph with his hands around Dolly's throat. I remind myself that Ralph is an elderly man; he must be eighty at least. And he hardly looks like a physical threat – he stoops slightly and he's no taller than me, five foot six at most. But then Dolly is a child and although she's quite tall for her age, it probably wouldn't take a huge amount of strength to attack her. Again, moments from my own mugging a few months ago come hurtling to the front of my mind. My pasty-faced attacker with the pale blue eyes jumped out at me from behind a garage wall and it made no difference that I was bigger than him: I was still frightened. I know from experience that if you're taken by surprise, strength doesn't necessarily matter. I'm conscious that Meg is saying something, but I'm not following. Ralph is edging towards the door. Why is he so keen to get away from me?

At that moment the door opens, almost into Ralph, and Stuart comes in.

'Look who I found outside.'

Chapter Thirty

Beth

I feel like I have been punched in the stomach. All the tension of the past hour is expelled in one big breath. Dolly is just behind Stuart. Thank God. I glance at Ralph, mentally apologising for categorising him as a deranged killer. What is wrong with me? Ralph nods at Stuart, averts his gaze from Dolly as if she's somehow unclean, and then sidles off out of the open door, mumbling something about Evelyn wondering where he is. I'm still finding it hard to like him, but at that moment he's not my main concern. Now that the initial overwhelming relief has passed, my next impulse is to yell at Dolly for what she's just put me through, but even a crash course in parenthood has taught me that this would be a very bad idea, so I manage to say instead, 'Dolly, thank goodness! I was wondering where you'd got to.'

Her eyes had followed Ralph as he left, her expression watchful, but they snap back to me as soon as I speak, and her face changes to something softer and more neutral. She's back in perfect child mode. She didn't have the chance to put on her usual mascara and lip gloss this morning, which makes her look younger than normal. Her natural lashes are white gold like her hair.

'Sorry, Beth. I meant to come straight back, but I saw Drake running loose in the fields and I knew he must have got out, so I tried to catch him.'

Drake, who has been standing at Stuart's heels, slinks over to his basket.

'That dog!' Meg says, handing Stuart a mug of coffee. 'I don't know how he does it. I thought we'd already blocked up all his escape routes.'

'He's like Steve McQueen,' Stuart agrees.

Judging by Dolly's mystified expression, it's not a cultural reference she's familiar with.

'Thank you so much Dolly,' Meg says. 'We're always worried that he's going to chase the sheep when he gets out.'

'I know, because he's got sheepdog blood. Laura told me.'

'He certainly looks suitably sheepish at the moment,' Stuart says.

Dolly giggles. It's hard to compute that she's the same child who just over an hour ago sat in chilly silence next to me in the car and then talked about car crashes in a way that made me feel so uncomfortable I wanted to stop driving. It's a relief to hear her laugh, although increasingly what I'm finding most disconcerting about Dolly is not any one of her moods, but how easily she seems to be able to switch between them. It makes me wonder if any of it is true, or if she's just an extremely proficient actor and the real Dolly is in there somewhere, buried too deep to reach.

'After I first saw him, he disappeared – you know in that field with the barn at the top of the hill? Well, he just vanished over the hill and when I got up there I couldn't see him at all, even though I'd run all the way.' The enthusiasm in her voice as she tells the story is endearing, and it must be genuine surely? She is describing what happened and she didn't just stay out because I'd asked her to come straight home. 'It took a while to find him again, and then he really didn't want to come with me.'

'Would you like a hot chocolate Dolly?' Meg asks. 'I can do cream and marshmallows.'

'Yes please,' comes the instant response and it's ridiculous to think the alacrity with which she accepts is in any way linked to my own offer of a hot chocolate earlier.

'Laura was telling me about your granddad,' Meg says as she boils the kettle and fetches a bottle of squirty cream from the fridge. 'You must be so worried about him.'

Dolly's eyes fill with tears. I feel terrible that I could even for one moment have thought that any of this was an act. Meg goes over and puts an arm around her, and the tears spill down her ivory cheeks.

'Try not to think the worst. I know your granddad, and I know that he's not going to give up without a fight. He'd want you to stay positive for him – you know that don't you?'

She nods.

'I'm scared,' she whispers. 'I'm scared that he's going to die.'

'We all have to die some time, sweetheart,' Meg says, her voice serious with an edge of some rawer emotion, as if she has particular reason to be conscious of this. 'But I don't think this is your granddad's time.'

I feel the same misgivings I felt when Noah said something similar earlier. Supposing he actually does die. But maybe that doesn't matter at the moment. Maybe all that matters right now is giving Dolly some comfort that it's all going to turn out okay, even if it isn't. She wipes her eyes with the old-fashioned handkerchief Meg has given her.

'How do you know when it's someone's time?' she asks, with that curious childlike simplicity she sometimes has.

'It's just a feeling,' Meg says.

Dolly nods, solemnly this time, as though she's turning the idea over in her mind. She sits at the table between Stuart and me, and starts spooning up the cream from her hot chocolate.

'What are you going to do with your day now your dog rescuing duties are done, young Dolly?' Stuart asks. Her next answer comes with the same ease as her acceptance of the hot chocolate.

'Beth is making peanut butter cookies and I'm going to help her take the photos.'

So she *was* listening to me earlier. I wonder if this is just for Meg and Stuart's benefit, but I allow myself to hope that it isn't. When Noah does call, in what I've already worked out is going to be the small hours of the morning, I badly want to be able to tell him, truthfully, that there's nothing for him to worry about.

'It's for Instagram.'

'I'm never totally sure what Instagram is,' Stuart says.

Dolly looks at him pityingly.

'I'll show you. Can I borrow your phone Beth?'

I hesitate fractionally, and then reach quickly into my bag – after all, what harm could there be in her having my phone while I'm sitting next to her? I unlock it and hand it to her with Instagram open and she starts tapping. Stuart glances at me and winks. I suspect he knows perfectly well what Instagram is, but has judged rightly that professing ignorance and getting Dolly to explain it will be a good distraction.

'This is Beth's account. She posts photos of what she's making and then she links to a recipe on her website. See? She clicks on this plus sign here and then she can add pictures from her camera reel.'

I glance at the screen to check she's not actually posting anything, but she's already clicked away and back onto a coffee and walnut cake recipe in my feed.

'So I could just go on and look at Beth's photos myself?' Stuart says, peering over her shoulder.

'You can't just "go on", you need an account and then you follow people. Hang on a minute, I'll show you.' She drops my phone on the table and whips her own from the back pocket of her shorts to demonstrate. I remember the calls I made earlier, which she didn't pick up. She clicks onto Instagram and then almost instantly dismisses the screen. She's quick, but not quite quick enough. Before it disappears, I have time to see that it's not Dolly's own account at all. My heart plummets.

Chapter Thirty-One

Beth

Dolly and I walk back to the Old Watermill. She's just in front of me, eyes fixed on her phone. I'm trying to work out what to do. She's clearly not going to mention it and I can't even be certain whether she knows I saw or not. I remind myself not for the first time that the fact that she had @TruthTeller1001's account open doesn't necessarily mean she's the troll. @TruthTeller1001 first posted about me three years ago, when I started my account, way before I'd even met Noah and Dolly. Maybe she just came across the comments and clicked through to the account out of curiosity. All the same, it makes me feel uncomfortable that she was looking at it, particularly now I've also told her about my parents. I wonder if she can see what I see every time I look at those messages: someone who knows what my parents did. I know I should bring it up, but I'm not sure I can face the possibility of another clash. I need to talk to her about it – of course I do – but I don't have to do it right now. I'd love the chance to build some positive moments before I risk any further conflict. While I search for the front door keys in my bag, I try to decide how Noah would handle this.

Just then she asks, 'When do you think Dad will ring?'

'He's only just taken off and it's an eleven-hour flight so not until about one a.m.'

'Can I stay up?'

'I'll wake you up when he calls.' As exchanges go, it's hardly profound, or extensive, but it's at least relatively normal and she accepts my answer with a nod. It seems like a sign of how I should approach this. Keep it calm, keep it straightforward. Tackle the difficult conversations when you've had a chance to build some trust. I open the front door and we both step into the hallway. Emboldened by my temporary success as a step-parent, and with Dolly's surprise announcement at Meg and Stuart's still running through my head, I decide to take the plunge.

'Would you like to help with the peanut butter cookies?'

'Can I take the photos?' she asks. 'My phone's got a better camera than yours.'

'Sure.' Her photographer dad has picked her the best camera phone out there; it's even fancier than the one I invested in when my Instagram account started to take off. 'You can decide which ones to post.'

'Okay,' she says simply, and heads into the kitchen.

Almost holding my breath, I follow her. She sits at the scrubbed wooden table tapping away at her phone while I get out the ingredients. I realise I'm hurrying because I'm worried that she's going to change her mind. I make a conscious effort to relax. I should try to enjoy this. I don't quite trust it, but it could, perhaps, be actual progress. Maybe what happened in the car was some kind of watershed moment. I fight the urge to put the radio on. We're just going to talk.

'It's a real pain not being able to remember where anything is yet,' I say.

She glances up from her phone.

'The first photo's all the stuff that goes in it, right? Can I start setting it up?'

'Go for it. You just need to make sure that we can see all the ingredients. And then we need a couple of action shots as I make them. I thought one where I show the consistency of the mixture would be good. It needs to be nice and thick, otherwise there's a danger the cookies will be too dry.'

'I'll take loads and then we can pick the best.'

I notice her use of the word *we* and feel a frisson of validation, like the cool kid at school has included me in her gang.

'Good idea. I don't usually take that many when it's just me as it's such a big faff so it will be lovely to have lots to choose from.'

The next half hour is almost like the scene the interview for the Suffolk Life blog described, with Dolly helping me set up the shots. She's great at it too. She has a real eye for what will make a good picture and issues instructions about colours and composition.

'We have to be careful with this one,' I say, 'because some people are allergic to peanuts. I'll pop a warning up front on the recipe. You think the clue would be in the name, but there's no way you can be too careful with allergies. It's such a real danger.' She's holding her phone up towards me and something about the angle makes me ask: 'Are you filming?'

'I thought it was a good idea,' she says, almost shyly. 'I thought we could post a few reels.'

'I just use photos.'

'I was thinking just photos is a bit basic though. You should get on TikTok and YouTube too, Beth. There's a much bigger audience out there.'

'Maybe,' I say. I don't want to crush her idea, but I don't want to change my format right now either. I remember Stuart asking her about Instagram earlier. 'You'll have to show me how TikTok works.'

She pulls a face.

'I think you can work it out.'

'I meant how to make good videos.'

'I can show you some of the best ones,' she says, 'so you can see what works.'

'Let's stick to photos for this one though.'

'Okay,' she says amicably enough. 'Can you move the tea towel so that it's underneath the tray, and then kind of hold the tray up a bit, tilting it towards me? You should get your nails done a bright colour for shots like this.'

'You haven't got me in it have you? There's no way I want to feature.'

'I can crop it so it's just your hands like you have usually.' She's clearly been studying my posts. 'Why don't you want to be in it?'

I remember how panicked I felt about spending time with Dolly when I saw Laura earlier, and during the car journey it seemed like all my worst fears were coming true. But actually, I allow myself to think cautiously, the day's turned out okay despite all the drama. I still don't feel ready to tell her that I'm paranoid my parents might be able to track me down, though.

'I guess I don't want to be too attention-seeking about it. I want it to be all about the bakes.' I try to think of a new subject to talk about. 'Laura's coming over this evening for some dinner.'

The change in Dolly is almost tangible. She's quivering with energy again.

'Laura from next door?' Her voice is different, too – sharper, more suspicious.

'Yes.' *Literally the only Laura I know in the whole of Suffolk. The Laura you've been obsessed with for the past three days. The Laura your dad went out with, briefly.* 'You like Laura don't you?'

'What about Rosie?'

'Meg and Stuart are looking after her. Will you join us for some food?'

'I didn't know you and Laura were friends.' It comes out as an accusation, and I feel confused about the shift in mood.

'Well we only just met, but she seems really nice.' Even to my own ears my voice sounds ridiculously upbeat. Nice is not the right word to describe Laura at all: intense, interesting, perhaps even damaged.

'Laura's special,' Dolly says. And I wonder again what it is that draws the two of them together.

'Do you want to do some more photos of me putting the cookies in the oven?' I say, hoping to recapture the relaxed atmosphere.

She shakes her head.

'I'm going up to my room.'

'Right.'

At the door she pauses.

'Laura's mine. No one can take her away from me.'

Chapter Thirty-Two

Beth

'I brought wine.'

Laura is standing on the doorstep, looking slightly awkward. The hot weather broke in a giant thunderstorm that finished about half an hour ago and the ground behind her is wet and glinting in the sun.

'Thank God!' I say, with feeling.

She smiles, and her face is briefly transformed.

'Good thing Evelyn can't see me,' she says, stepping past me into the hallway.

'She probably can. Have you noticed the slightly creepy way that all the houses seem to overlook each other, even though there's hardly any of them and acres of space?'

Something in Laura's smile shifts slightly, and I remember too late that, unlike me, she did grow up here and she seems just as attached to the place as Noah.

'Sorry creepy is probably the wrong word.'

'No, you're right, that is creepy. I'd just never really thought of it like that.'

She's wearing a pair of cargo pants and an impressively clean white shirt for a woman with a seven-month-old baby. Her long fair hair is pulled back in a ponytail. She's very well-groomed. She even smells nice: a citrusy perfume that I don't recognise. There are signs of strain on her face though, furrows running across her forehead and big dark circles under her eyes like she hasn't slept properly in months – and from what I remember of friends with babies, she probably hasn't. Despite, or perhaps because of, the stress, she still has that slightly manic energy about her that I remember from Meg's drinks party on the first night. I wonder if this is what draws Dolly to her. *Laura's special.* It's strange that Dolly clearly wanted me to worry about Noah's relationship with Laura, whereas what I've actually ended up fretting over is Dolly's own fixation with her.

'Come through to the kitchen,' I say. 'Get down Bluebell, leave her alone.'

'Oh, don't worry.'

She bends down and makes a fuss of Bluebell, who's ecstatic.

'Dolly's going to be joining us. She's upstairs watching YouTube I think. I'll shout up in a minute and let her know you're here.'

I'm hunting around in the drawer for a corkscrew for the bottle of Pinot Grigio that Laura brought with her.

'How's it been going?'

'Better than I thought,' I say cautiously. I'm pretty sure Dolly is still in her bedroom, but I keep my voice low and go over to shut the kitchen door just in case. I don't want her to discover that the motivation for dinner with Laura was partly a debrief about her. She'd never forgive me. 'We had a bit of a weird drive back from the station.' I reach up to the shelf where we've put the glasses and then pour us each a generous glug of white. 'But then we spent the afternoon making biscuits.'

An activity which came to an abrupt end after I mentioned you were coming round to dinner, I think. But although the baking had ended awkwardly, it had gone well up until that point and later, Dolly WhatsApped me a series of perfect photos: the set-up ingredients shot, and five great mid-recipe pictures. And a yellow heart emoji. This is also a first. She hardly ever messages me, only basic information when she can't get hold of Noah and wants me to tell him something, and the only emoji I've ever received before today is a thumbs up. I'd spent far too long thinking about how to reply, eventually discarding emojis altogether and settling for a simple 'Thanks so much — these look fab! X'

Laura takes a big swig of her wine and says, 'What happened on the journey from the station?' I hesitate. It's a natural question and I invited Laura round because she feels like a person I might be able to confide in one day, but I'm not sure I'm ready to share the precise details of what happened in the car with anyone, let alone someone I only met a few days ago. As I sip my own wine, I try to decide how much I'm comfortable sharing, but before I can say anything, Laura continues. 'Did Dolly talk about her mum?'

I stare at her.

'How did you know that?'

'So she did?'

'Not exactly. But well, she talked about the car crashing.'

'It's such an awful thing for her to lose her mum like that.'

'She's talked to you about it?'

I remember Noah saying Dolly hardly ever mentions Juliet. I feel my heart beating faster.

'A bit, when I was down last weekend.'

'What did she say?'

She looks awkward again.

'It was just about how much she misses her. It must bring it back every time she gets in a car.'

I nod. I'm not sure how to explain that what happened felt less like Dolly was scared there was going to be a car crash, and more like she was threatening to cause one. And I'm already doubting my interpretation anyway. The kitchen door opens, and the conversation comes to an abrupt end as the subject of it enters the room.

'Laura!' There it is again, her face lighting up in Laura's presence.

'Hey Dolly,' Laura says. 'Great outfit.'

Dolly has changed and is wearing a black jumpsuit with giraffes all over it and her hair is loose over her shoulders. It's one of the disconcerting moments when she looks much older than her years.

'It's from Urban Outfitters,' she says, smiling at Laura with something like adoration. It's her favourite store.

'Would you mind laying the table, Dolly?'

I wouldn't normally ask her anything like this, but I'm buoyed by the success of the afternoon and by the presence of Laura. Somehow I don't think she's going to be rude to me in front of Laura, and sure enough, Dolly agrees readily and with every sign of enthusiasm.

The meal itself goes well – almost without a hitch in fact. Laura is really nice about the quiche I've made, which tastes fine, despite my sudden fear that there was going to be something off about it. We start by exchanging celebrity gossip and then somehow move onto *Friends*. Laura turns out to be a huge fan, and can quote most of the episodes. Dolly – bizarrely, to my mind – started watching it recently on Netflix and raves about it, so they spend ages exchanging catchphrases from seasons one and two. It's hard to join in much as I haven't watched an episode of *Friends* since about 2002.

'It's so cringe when Rachel's mum and dad both turn up at her birthday party and they have to keep them separate. And Monica makes this minging flan instead of cake.'

'"It's a festive custard Mexican dessert,"' Laura quotes instantly.

Dolly bursts out laughing.

I fix a smile on my face, feeling momentarily shut out. It's like I've created a new group of three in which I don't quite belong. First Noah, Dolly and me, and now Laura, Dolly and me. But I know I'm being ridiculous; it's just a TV show, after all. What I should be feeling is relief that their bond seems to be as simple as a shared interest in sitcoms.

Laura looks more relaxed as the meal goes on, and the only strange moment comes when we've almost finished eating and Dolly asks Laura if she's been to Hannah's Grove again. But Laura shuts her down quickly, saying she hasn't had time. Maybe Laura picked up on my uneasiness about the place when she suggested it earlier in the day and knows I don't want Dolly going there. If so, I'm grateful to her. I wonder if Dolly will be upset, but to my surprise she looks relieved.

When we've finished eating, Dolly asks politely if she can head upstairs to message her friends. I'm so taken aback – both that she's voluntarily leaving Laura's company and that she's asked my permission – that I gabble my answer.

'Sure. Of course. Remember no more phone after ten.'

It's the kind of thing Noah usually says to her, and I feel for a brief moment like I'm a proper parent.

'Night Beth, Bye Laura,' she calls as she goes up the stairs.

I stare after her, wondering if there's more to this, wondering if I should be worried. When I look back, Laura is checking her phone.

'Have you heard from your mum and dad?' I ask Laura.

'Yes, all's fine.'

'Is she a pretty good sleeper?'

She takes a gulp of wine and shakes her head.

'No, Rosie's never been the kind of baby who sleeps through.'

'God, that must be so difficult, especially when it's just you.'

'Yeah,' she says, draining the remains of the glass in one go. 'I can't really remember what it's like to actually be able to sleep through an entire night.'

Her voice is shaking ever so slightly.

'Do you get any help from Rosie's dad?' I probe cautiously.

I'm curious about what happened with Laura's ex. Noah said he was a bit of an idiot, but even so, what kind of person leaves their partner with a seven-month-old baby?

'Ewan's not really in the picture any more.'

She doesn't sound like she wants to expand on that and I don't push her. We take a new bottle of wine into the library, where there's still some evening sun coming in through the big glass doors. We sit either end of the brown leather sofa.

'Thank you for this, Beth. I needed this.'

'Oh God no, you're the one doing me a favour. I really need distracting tonight.'

'Nothing from Noah yet?'

'He sent me a message as he was boarding, so at least I know he made his flight, but he didn't have any more news.'

'I'm so glad for Noah that he's found you,' she says. She sounds concerned about him as an old friend, but nothing more – much as he sounded when he talked about her. 'I know my mum and dad were really worried about him after Juliet died. But you're good for him. I can tell that just seeing you with him.'

'Thanks. He's good for me, too. I feel like my life's transformed over the past six months, and most of that is due to Noah. Not that I had a bad life before, or anything, it's just that there were certain things that needed to change. When I look back at how I was feeling this time last year and compare it with now, it's crazy.' I push down a nagging feeling that I've just changed one set of problems for another. And besides Noah is definitely not one of those problems.

'What was so wrong with this time last year?'

'Well, for a start, I was stuck in a relationship I knew wasn't working, and then I wanted to move out of London, but I was too scared to actually do it because I'd lived there ever since I'd left home and it had become this kind of safety blanket for me.'

'What wasn't working? With the relationship, I mean.'

I take a mouthful of wine. It's a while since I've talked about Pete.

'In lots of ways it was good. Pete was a lovely guy – he *is* a lovely guy. Not as lovely as Noah obviously,' I add hastily. This makes her laugh. Her face looks different when she laughs: momentarily carefree. I get the sense she doesn't laugh much at the moment. Encouraged by this,

I continue, 'But the truth is we just weren't right for each other.'

Laura isn't going to be satisfied with the clichés.

'What did this lovely guy do wrong?'

'When we first started getting serious, we had this big conversation about what we both wanted from a relationship. You know, marriage, kids, where we wanted to live, that type of thing, and it really seemed like we were on the same page. I was very clear right from the start that I didn't want children. I was a bit apprehensive about telling him. I was worried it might be a deal-breaker for him, but he agreed straight away. He said he wasn't interested in having kids either, and I remember at the time I felt so relieved. We didn't really talk about it again and maybe that was a mistake because I just assumed he'd carry on feeling like that.'

'And he didn't?' she prompts, when I fall silent, remembering *the* conversation.

'No. We'd been down visiting some of Pete's uni friends in Brighton. They'd just had their first baby, Lola. She was asleep most of the time and I didn't really see much of her until the end when she woke up and I held her for a while after she'd been fed. Babies terrify me a bit if I'm honest – they seem so fragile, even though I know they're not. Anyway, on the train home, Pete said something about how his mate Jonny didn't like the name Lola and it had been his partner Angela's choice, and then Pete said, "When we have ours, we're agreeing on the names together, right?" And I knew straight away that he was serious.'

'Did you talk to him about it?'

'Yes, right there and then in the middle of the train carriage.'

Her eyes widen.

'I'd had a couple of beers and it seemed like a good idea. First he said he was only joking and that I was making a big deal out of nothing, and then when I stuck to my guns he got really defensive. He told me he'd always wanted kids and he thought I would just change my mind about it one day. He said, and I quote, "Because everyone wants kids ultimately. Why wouldn't you?" Anyway, it's possible neither of us were entirely sober at this point and that we weren't making the best sense in the world, and eventually we shouted ourselves out and the train carriage had to go back to staring at their phones for entertainment.'

'Did you break up straight away?'

'No, it took months. We kept trying to find a way through, but the truth was, there really wasn't one.'

'Do you mind if I ask you something? It's something very personal so tell me if you'd rather not answer.'

I nod, already knowing what she's going to ask.

'Why did you decide you didn't want children?'

I don't mind her asking, and I even have a sense that she might understand at least some of what I feel, but I start by answering in a roundabout way.

'I mean, obviously I worry about what kind of world I'd be bringing a child into – it's pretty bleak right now. It's got to the point where I almost can't bear to listen to the news any more. And I also get the whole fear that some people have of somehow losing your own identity.'

'God, I get that too,' she says quietly. 'Your life is subsumed – to start with at least.'

'Even that isn't really it though,' I say, trying to articulate feelings that I've had ever since I was old enough to have children, but which won't form into coherent thoughts. Parenthood has long been a difficult subject for me. 'I think what I really don't want is the responsibility.' She flinches, and I wonder if I'm right that she'll understand what I'm talking about. Pete certainly never did, and I'm not sure Noah does either. When I told him, he went very quiet for the rest of the day, like I'd said something he couldn't quite get his head around. I really want Laura to understand what I mean, so I try again to explain. 'I mean, I know I'm responsible for Dolly now, but that's different. Dolly's already a person. It's the idea of shaping a human life right from the start that scares me. All the decisions you make, everything you screw up, that has an impact on that individual. And that individual is going to grow up and judge you.'

Just as I judge my parents. I'm not sure I'm ready to tell Laura about them yet, however good a listener she is. Laura gets up and goes over to the doors out into the garden. Her back is to me, and she looks out into the growing darkness.

'Sorry,' I say to the back of her head. I've probably gone way too far. I barely know Laura and she's a mother to a seven-month-old baby. Both of these are good reasons why I shouldn't have picked her as the person I'm trying to explain my very far from cogent thoughts on motherhood to. 'That's obviously just how I feel, and I don't even know it's exactly what I mean anyway. Everyone's going to think about it differently, and I get why for lots of people having children is the most important thing. It just isn't for me.'

I get up too, and start turning some more lights on, so that the room is flooded with warmth and brightness. Bluebell raises her head to watch me and thumps her tail a few times. Laura turns back towards me.

'You shouldn't apologise,' she says. And I'm relieved that her voice still sounds friendly, although her gaze on me is intent, and I think there might be tears in her eyes. 'You're right. It *is* terrifying. And as a parent, that terror is always there, just under the surface.' She comes over to stand right next to me. 'I understand why you don't want that, I really do.'

'What about you? Did you always know you wanted kids?'

It's not the kind of question I would normally feel I could ask but, after all, she's quizzed me on pretty much exactly the same thing and I think this gives me licence to ask her in return. She answers without hesitation.

'For as long as I can remember. I was the one who'd babysit younger siblings when friends came over. I always knew I would be a mother.' I love that Laura and I disprove all the clichés. I think that most people hearing about us – the slickly-dressed hotshot city lawyer and the baking influencer living in the country – would probably assume that I was the maternal one. 'But Ewan and I tried for a baby for a long time before Rosie came along. We'd even started thinking about IVF. And then one day I woke up, and I just knew. I did a pregnancy test, and there it was for the first time: the double line.'

'And is it how you imagined being a mother would be?'

'Sometimes,' she says quietly. 'Sometimes it's perfect.' And as she says it her face is so transported with joy that I feel almost envious.

Chapter Thirty-Three

Beth

'You need to look online – *now*.'

I'm feeling way too mellow for this late-night phone call. Laura left about twenty minutes ago and I've been dozing on the sofa ever since. I woke up abruptly when my mobile rang, thinking it might be Noah, but it wasn't.

'Hey Sasha. What happened to "how are you doing"?'

'I'm serious Beth, you need to open Instagram.'

Suddenly my slightly alcohol-induced feeling of chilled relaxation is replaced with trepidation. I put Sasha on speakerphone and open Instagram. At first I can't work out what she's talking about. My peanut butter cookie posts are the first thing I see and the photos look great. There are also loads of comments, which is surely a good sign.

'Go into the comments,' Sasha says.

Shit. These are not good comments.

> You selfish bitch.

> I hope you die a slow painful death so you know what it feels like.

> People like you are evil. I hope you get cancer.

My heart races.

'I don't understand. It's just a cookie recipe.'

'You need to look up Truth Teller 1001. Some really weird shit is going on.'

My finger shakes slightly as I type the account into the search bar. For the first time, Truth Teller 1001 has posted something. A video. I can already see it's a video of me. Taken in our new kitchen, about six hours ago, as I made the cookies. Which makes sense. Because, although Sasha doesn't know it yet, and although I still don't know how she did it, Dolly must be the person trolling me, an inconvenient fact I've done my best to ignore all afternoon and evening. But what could be so terrible about a video of me making cookies? So terrible in fact that people want me to die? I try to remember exactly what I was doing when Dolly was filming. Maybe it's enough that she's posted a video of me talking to the camera and people have recognised me and connected me to my parents.

A lump of fear in my throat, I press play on the video. It's a short clip. Ten seconds at most. I'm not facing the camera, other than briefly at the start. I'm wearing the bright red apron with 'Beth Loves 2 Bake' on it that Noah bought me, and my long brown bob is looking particularly messy. I turn to get a bowl out of the cupboard and that's when I start talking: '*It's a real pain some people are allergic to peanuts. I'll pop a warning up front on the recipe. You think the clue would be in the name, but people are thick. It's such a big faff. There's no real danger — people with allergies are just attention-seeking.*'

My heart plummets.

'I didn't say that. Sasha, I would never say that.'

And yet obviously I did say those things: it's my voice. They are all words I must have spoken while Dolly was filming.

'I know that, hun,' she says. 'But what the fuck is going on here? That is 100 per cent you in the video and I'm guessing that really is your new kitchen – it looks like the photos you posted the other day. And it *sounds* like you. You can even see your lips say "it's a real pain" before you turn around.'

'It *is* me. I mean, I literally used all those words. I must have done, I guess. But not to say those things. Oh God, I feel sick.'

'Were you filming yourself? How has someone managed to get hold of a video of you?'

'Sasha, there's something I need to tell you. I only realised for sure when I saw the video.' I take a deep breath. 'Dolly's the troll.'

There's a shocked silence and then Sasha says: 'Dolly? As in your stepdaughter, Dolly? What the actual fuck? She was filming you?'

'She was helping me make the cookies,' I say, and for a moment I feel sad rather than furious. Nothing about making the cookies was real. Dolly hadn't said yes because she wanted to spend time with me, but because she'd seen a chance to get at me.

'She must have been recording me for most of the time, and she's edited together bits of what I said.'

I'm playing the video again.

'She's done a great job of it,' Sasha says grudgingly. 'Top editing skills.'

We both laugh uneasily. I feel like I might cry.

'You need to get her to take it down, Beth.'

'I know.'

'Like now.'

'Yes, okay. I'll go straight up there.'

'Then I'll help you deal with the fallout. I've done it for clients in the past. We can think of something to post on your account explaining it wasn't you.'

'How are we going to explain that exactly?'

'I don't know.'

'I don't want to mention Dolly. I don't want the trolls turning on her.' I try to imagine explaining all of this to Noah.

'What the fuck did she think she was doing?'

'She's going through a lot right now.'

'Stop making excuses for her.'

'No, seriously.' I explain about Noah's dad.

'Shit, Beth. You've had quite a day. So the two of you are there by yourselves?'

'Yeah, I was just waiting up for Noah to call when you rang.'

'Okay, I think you should delete your cookie post right now and then tell Dolly to delete that video. The whole account in fact.'

'Yes, okay, okay, I'm deleting my post now.'

'Good. Go talk to Dolly.'

'She'll be asleep.'

'I don't care. Wake her up. This can't wait.'

'Yes, you're right, okay.'

'And keep it calm, right?'

'I am calm.'

'You don't exactly sound it.'

'A few minutes ago you were the one telling me to stop making excuses for her!'

'You can be as mad as you like later. Right now you just need her to get rid of that video.'

'I know. I get it.' But as I'm agreeing, I think even if she does delete it, she could always post it again. Or something worse.

'You can save this. It doesn't have to be the end of your account.'

'Thanks Sasha. I'll call you later.'

Before I go upstairs, I watch the video one more time. It really is very well done. Even though I know it's edited together from a whole load of different things I said, it's still hard to spot the joins. A lot of time's gone into it. A lot of painstaking effort. At that moment, I don't really care about my account. I care about my relationship with my thirteen-year-old stepdaughter, who must hate me so much to have done what she's just done. And I wonder if I can, in fact, save this.

My legs feel heavy and unwilling to obey me, like they belong to someone else. But there's no avoiding this confrontation. I force myself out into the hallway, and then up the wide staircase towards her room. The house is still and dark. I can hear my own breathing, the tread of my footsteps. As I go, I try to work out how it must have happened. Dolly can't be the original troll, but she must have found the comments from way back and reused the account name. Again, I'm hit by how much time and research must have gone into this plan. I remind myself of Sasha's instructions: the priority right now is to keep calm and get her to take the video down. Then I can decide what to do next. I pause outside her room and raise my hand to knock. A sharp rap and I push open the door.

There's no sign of Dolly.

Chapter Thirty-Four

Beth

My brain slowly takes in the details. Dolly's room is perfect. Preternaturally tidy for a teenager – it was in London, too. The fairy lights above her bed are alight, but the bed is empty. The duvet is pristine, neat. She hasn't been lying on it, then. But she's been in her room all night hasn't she? Ever since she said good night to Laura and me at about half eight? And it's now, what? I glance at my watch. Midnight. Oh shit. Where on earth is she? It's like earlier, but so much worse.

I don't care about the video; I don't care about anything. I just want to know where she is. God, I should have checked on her earlier. Isn't that what a normal parent would have done? A *real* parent. I've screwed this up again, and any minute now Noah is going to call and I'm going to have to tell him it's the middle of the night and I don't know where his daughter is.

My thoughts are racing. She knows Noah is going to call about now. Surely she wouldn't miss the chance to talk to her dad. I take a deep breath. Maybe she's just gone to the bathroom, or maybe she went to the kitchen to get a snack and I somehow missed her on the way up. God knows this house is big enough. And if she had gone downstairs, she might have overheard me on the phone with Sasha and realised that I knew. I'm back to thinking she's left. I rush out onto the landing and quickly check the bathroom. No sign. I'm shouting her name now. Double checking she's not in any of the other rooms upstairs. I come out of our en suite and stop dead in my tracks, the shock smacking into me with almost physical force.

Dolly is standing facing me at the top of the stairs, still and silent like she's been there all the time; a beautiful ghost or a statue.

'Where the hell have you been?'

So much for calm. I'm dimly aware that I'm crying. At least I seem to have astonished her into speech.

'I went downstairs to get some water.' She waves a glass in my direction. 'And then I ended up reading one of the magazines. I thought it was almost time for my dad to call.'

It's just about plausible. She wouldn't have had to go past the library to get to the kitchen, so I might not have heard her. She's wearing pyjamas and she's barefoot. Where after all do I think she's been? It's not like Fortune's Yard has much to offer in the way of late-night entertainment.

'Sorry I yelled,' I say tightly. 'I couldn't find you and I was worried.'

'Right,' she says, in an offhand way that manages to convey that she thinks I'm totally mad. 'Did my dad call?' A fresh wave of anger overtakes me.

'No, he did not. Dolly I know about the video.' Her eyes widen slightly, but otherwise her expression doesn't alter. 'I can't believe you did that to me.' I'm aware this is coming out all wrong, but there's nothing I can do about it. I'm almost scared by how furious I am.

She shrugs. She doesn't seem particularly moved by any of it, but then she must have known I'd find out. Once the video was posted, @TruthTeller1001 could only possibly be one person. She just probably didn't think I'd find out tonight.

'Haven't you got anything to say?' Her silence is infuriating.

'I thought it would be funny.'

'How is it funny? There are people online who are threatening to kill me.'

'It's not people online you need to worry about.'

'What does that mean?'

She drops her gaze.

'Just that trolls are always threatening things like that.'

'You should know, you're one of them.'

'You're taking this way too seriously.'

'Do you think your dad's going to think so?'

A flush of colour spreads over her face. I'm not proud of resorting to Noah but it's a relief to have got some kind of reaction, and it helps me to let go of part of my anger. I take a deep breath.

'Dolly, you've really hurt me. I thought we were having a good time working on that recipe. You betrayed my trust.'

'It was a joke,' she mutters. She's contemplating her feet, the lilac polish on her toe nails. 'It's obvious it's not serious.'

'I need you to delete the account.' She's still looking at the floor. 'Did you hear me?'

'Why should I?' She sounds disconcertingly young. I try to keep my voice steady. I don't want this to turn into any more of a shouting match than it already is – not that Dolly has done any of the shouting.

'Because it's hurting me and I'm asking you to.'

'It's only a stupid video.'

'Please don't make this into a battle.'

Silence. Broken abruptly by the ringing of a phone. Mine. It's on the hall table. We both run downstairs. She's first, but I'm close on her heels and I know exactly where I left the phone, so I manage to grab it before she does. We stand facing each other in the hallway. I'm holding the phone just out of her reach.

'It's your dad,' I say, hating myself for the implied threat, but it works at once.

'Okay, whatever, you can delete it all!' she says. 'Look, here's my phone.' She reaches in the pocket of her pyjamas for her mobile and thrusts it at me.

'Thank you.' The words stick in my throat, but I have to try to salvage something from this.

'Please will you answer it.'

'Let me do this first.'

I delete the Truth Teller account, and close the window on her phone. Behind it, a Safari page flashes before my eyes and I can see she's been googling Roxeter Investments – my dad's company. I glance up at her. Dolly is still focused on the other phone in my hand – the one that has her dad on the end of it.

'It'll stop ringing.'

Perhaps it's not that surprising that she's been doing her own research. I should never have told her about my parents in the first place if I didn't want her to know. I hand her back her phone and then I slide to answer mine.

'Noah. It's good to hear your voice.' My own voice sounds forced and I hope that he's too distracted to notice. 'What's the news?'

As Noah starts to fill me in, I take the phone into the library, almost automatically. Dolly follows close behind, practically treading on my heels. Noah explains that Amy picked him up from the airport and now he's in her car, heading towards her house in San Francisco. She's given him all the latest news, but there isn't that much of it. Their dad's stable, but he's had a pretty massive heart attack and he's not out of the woods yet. The next twenty-four hours are going to be critical. I'm sitting on the arm of the big leather sofa and Dolly is standing right in front of me, her face creased with worry, her eyes pleading. I don't know if she can hear any of Noah's side of the conversation, but I try to make encouraging noises on my end for her sake as well as his.

'Noah, Dolly's right beside me. I'm going to hand you over now.'

She snatches the phone out of my hand so quickly that I feel a slight scratch from her nails. As she listens, I see her face relax fractionally. I'm guessing Noah is making the picture seem as positive as he can.

'So there's no way he's going to die?' she asks intently at one point. Whatever he says in reply to that, it produces something that's almost a smile in Dolly. I wander over to the French doors and look out onto the darkened garden. There's only a sliver of a moon. Something with eyes runs across the lawn – a fox maybe. I hear her describing her day.

'Beth and I made cookies.' I turn around but she doesn't look at me. 'They were really yummy, and then Laura came over to dinner. We're doing okay, Dad.'

The narrative already established. When she hands me back the phone a few minutes later she still doesn't meet my eye. She slips from the library and I hear her heading up the stairs to her room. Noah is saying, 'Sounds like everything's going well there.'

There's a slight question in his voice and it's not too late to unpick the story Dolly's told, but I'm not going to. Noah sounds exhausted; he's got more than enough to worry about already without me adding to it. I'll tell him when he's back, when this is all sorted out. He promises to call again when he has more news. He and Amy are going to head to the hospital once he's had a shower. I hear Amy sending her love in the background. I only met her once, when she came over for our wedding, but I got on with her really well. She has the same sense of humour as her brother. I wish I was in the car with them, somewhere in the San Francisco sunshine, rather than here in this big old house, in the darkness of a Suffolk hamlet, alone with Dolly. I very much don't want Noah to hang up. I hear myself tell him I love him. Then he's gone.

It's nearly one in the morning. I message Sasha to let her know I've deleted the account. Posting the video means that for the first time I have tangible proof of how Dolly's been behaving towards me and I wonder whether she thought this through when she did it. Everything else she's done has been deniable. This isn't. It's her first mistake and I wonder if she knows it. She certainly knows things about me – it makes me uncomfortable that she's been looking up my father's company – but now I know things about her, too. Things I can prove. Things I need to discuss with Noah when he returns.

Wearily, I pick up the empty glasses Laura and I left on the low table in the library and carry them out to the kitchen. Bluebell's not in her basket and, despite my now almost overwhelming tiredness, I feel a stab of apprehension. She's a big sleeper and it's not like her to be up and about at this time. I go in search of her, the expanse of the darkened house with its shadows stretching out all around me. As I stand in the hallway, wondering where to start, I notice that the door to the posh sitting room is ajar. In the three days we've lived here we've hardly used it at all except to unpack things. We've been keeping the door shut, but maybe it wasn't latched properly. I think – I'm almost sure – it was shut when I said goodbye to Laura, though. I don't know why, but suddenly I'm frightened about what could be behind it. Telling myself firmly to get a grip, I push it open.

The first thing I see is Bluebell, curled up on one of the slightly over-stuffed Victorian sofas. She lifts her head and gives a few guilty wags of her tail. Then I look down, and there are Dolly's black Converse on the carpet just by the door. Exactly where you might put them if you came in the front door and needed a quick place to hide them so that you could pretend you'd been in the kitchen. I pick them up and look at the soles. They're slightly damp to the touch and there's a leaf on one of them.

Chapter Thirty-Five

The Grief Counsellor

So how's this week been?

Horrible. They're all horrible. Horrible doesn't really cover it actually. I feel like I'm playing a part the whole time – you know, when I'm with other people. And they think I'm okay. They can't see anything wrong, so I must be good at it. They believe me. But it's exhausting and I don't know how much longer I can go on doing it.

Are you still having the feeling of detachment you described in our last session?

Sometimes it's hard for me to know what's real and what isn't, if that's what you mean. Actually, a lot of the time it's hard to tell. I'm not even sure it matters any more.

When someone suffers a sudden bereavement they can often experience a sense of disbelief. It can help to talk about the person you lost.

You said that before.

Do you ever talk about her?

No.

Do you think it might help to try?

No. Don't make me. I don't think I can bear it.

I'm not going to make you do anything. I'm here to help you. It was just a suggestion. It's important to find a lasting connection with the person who died. *That's one of the things that will help you to start to build a new life.*

I've told you before, that's not what I want. I don't want a new life.

Are you still having flashbacks?

Every night when I go to sleep – if I can sleep – it's what I dream about. It's the *only* thing I dream about. But the worst is during the day. Something will make me remember and then it's like I'm living it again for the first time. I keep going over and over it in my head. I have this weird idea that remembering all the details is somehow going to make it turn out differently.

Have you been trying to use some of the coping mechanisms we talked about before?

None of them make any difference.

Okay. Well maybe we can talk through some other techniques today. It's important that you find something that works for you. Is there anything at all that helps?

Only one thing. And I really don't want to talk about that.

Chapter Thirty-Six

Beth

Despite not going to bed until nearly two a.m., I wake early and with a dull ache at the front of my skull. The digital clock on the bedside table says it's 5:34 a.m. I listen to the water rushing past and slowly re-familiarise myself with all the things that are responsible for the gnawing uneasiness I'm feeling. It's not even properly light yet – dawn is very much still breaking – but I decide to go downstairs and do some baking. I'll make something simple with whatever ingredients I have and maybe I'll take some pictures so I have something new to post on my account. I don't know what Sasha is going to come up with by way of an explanation for the peanut video, but I'm sure she'll think of something, and although that's not my main concern right now, at least it's a distraction. I slide my feet into the furry slippers Noah got me for our move to the country, go to the toilet and then pad out onto the landing.

Dolly's door is closed and, in light of what happened last night, I wonder if I should check whether she is actually there. I would never usually go in her room without knocking – My Blended Family has several articles about respecting your teenager's privacy, but surely safety trumps that. I turn the old brass handle and it squeaks, but as I push the door, it glides smoothly over the carpet and when I peer in, Dolly is fast asleep, her white-gold hair spread over the pillow, the fairy lights still on. Even after the events of last night, there's something comforting about the sight. She's safe. She looks almost shockingly young. It's a reminder, once again, that she's a child in my care. A reminder of how important it is for me to keep on trying.

Gently I close the door again and retrace my footsteps along the landing to the stairs. The curtains on the landing window are open and outside it's beginning to get light. I pause to look out over the pond, searching for the swans, wondering if they're sleeping. If they are, it's somewhere out of sight. As I'm about to move away, I catch a glimpse of a movement in the lane immediately outside the house, and in the eerie glow of the dawn, I make out Drake, Meg and Stuart's dog. He must have escaped again. I feel suddenly energised. First good deed of the day: rescue Drake. Meg and Stuart mentioned how much they worried about him running off chasing the sheep and it's horrible to think of a farmer shooting at him. I rush downstairs, grab my waterproof from the hook as a cover-up and exchange my slippers for trainers. Then I pick up the front door key from the hall table and slip outside, closing the door quietly behind me so as not to wake Dolly.

It's then that I see it, attached to the front gate. A glimmer of sliver. I know at once what it is: the scarf that went missing from the scarecrow – like the one I was wearing the day I got mugged. The sight of it makes the hairs on the back of my neck stand up and for a moment I stand frozen on the path. But then reason reasserts itself. It must have blown off the scarecrow and someone – probably a walker – found it and tied it on the gate in the hope of reuniting it with its owner. I force myself to keep walking down the path. I untie the scarf with shaking fingers and stuff it in my pocket, trying to push it out of sight and out of mind. I'll throw it away as soon as I get back from taking Drake home. I cross the lane, trying to enjoy the dawn and the beauty of my surroundings, to where Drake is busy exploring by the edge of the millpond.

I'd imagined grabbing Drake's collar and him trotting straight over to Meg and Stuart's with me, but although he gives a brief flick of his long black-and-white tail when he sees me, he bounds off straight away. I follow him, thinking he might be heading home anyway, but wanting to make sure. When he reaches the crossroads though, he heads left, towards the pub, rather than right towards the old farmhouse. He's probably making for the woods. I jog to try and catch up, calling his name, but softly so as not to wake Ralph and Evelyn. Right outside the Fortune's Arms, he slows down again and I'm able to grab hold of him. He reacts docilely enough, looking up at me with his brown, slightly frantic eyes and giving me the full benefit of his panting doggy breath. I pull his collar and he walks a few paces, but then he sits in the middle of the lane and refuses to go any further. I tug, but it makes no difference and short of pulling him along the ground, he's clearly not budging. I crouch down and reason with him, hoping the sound of my voice will reassure him. His ears prick up, but he still won't move. I look around me, wondering what to do next. I should probably just go and tell Meg and Stuart where he is, but this seems a bit pathetic and maybe he won't stay put once I leave. It's hardly the neighbourly rescue mission I was envisaging.

It's almost completely light now and the old pub looks marginally less sinister than last time I saw it – or maybe I'm just getting used to it. If you squint slightly in the early morning sunlight, it's possible to picture it as it must have been four or five years ago: a welcoming spot for a lunchtime pint after a long walk. You can imagine pushing open the door and stepping into the refreshing coolness of the little bar. It's at that point that I notice that the front door is slightly open. I'm almost certain it wasn't like that on Saturday, when I last stood here inspecting it. Still feeling community-minded, I decide I'll pull it shut.

I leave Drake sitting in the lane, watching me. Maybe this was a Lassie moment, and he was trying to tell me about the open door all along. It's when I notice that there are keys still in the door that I start to feel vaguely uneasy. I don't know why though; probably one of the neighbours is in there right now. Stuart most likely, and that's why Drake is out here. Maybe he and Meg noticed something wrong and he's come over to investigate, but somehow this perfectly logical explanation doesn't satisfy me. Somehow, I know Stuart and Meg are both still tucked up in bed in the farmhouse. I push open the door, and, just as I imagined, step into the cool darkness within.

'Hello? Anybody here?'

It's extremely gloomy inside, thanks to the metal shutters on the downstairs windows. The only light is coming in through the open front door. I feel in my pockets, but all that's in there is the stupid scarf. I must have left my phone somewhere in the Old Watermill, so I can't even use that for a torch. I edge forward into the unknown, holding my hands out in front of me, and abruptly encounter first a bar stool, soft and velvety to the touch, and then the bar itself, looming out of the blackness. I call out again, although this time more to hear my own voice than because I have much expectation of someone replying.

The whole place smells of stale beer and toilets – it's familiar and almost reassuring. Cautiously, I edge along the length of the bar, keeping hold of it, and when it ends, I grope blindly forward, my arms stretched out in front of me, hands held up like stop signals, my feet taking small shuffling steps. I should probably just give up now, it's obvious there's no one here. My hand touches the edge of a banister rail and, a second later, my left foot touches what must be the edge of a bottom stair. Then, immediately, my right foot touches something else and I recoil.

Chapter Thirty-Seven

Beth

My first instinct is to flee, and come back with a torch, a phone and reinforcements, but I manage to get control of myself. I grip onto the banister for support, my heart thumping. I can't leave. Not yet. I think I know what I just touched, but I need to make sure. Slowly, I bend down and, gently, reach out, trying to stop my hand shaking. I make contact with flesh and my hand shoots back, and deep inside me my stomach clenches.

There's someone lying at the bottom of the stairs.

I know I should check for signs of life, but I can no longer get my hand to obey the instruction I'm giving it. It's refusing to move. I can feel vomit rising in my throat and I'm worried that I'm going to throw up right here in the bar. From my crouching position, I tip backwards so that I'm now sitting on the thin carpet of the pub floor. I wrap my arms around my knees, take some steadying gulps, and then I try again. I edge my hand forward so that my fingertips are touching the flesh of the person lying at the bottom of the stairs. I make contact with their palm and nausea threatens once more. The skin feels papery and cold. I slide my fingers up to the wrist. Slowly, agonisingly, I make myself feel for a pulse. Nothing.

Once I'm certain, I can't get out of there fast enough. I scrabble to my feet and stumble across the bar towards the open door, knocking bar stools over and crashing into tables as I go. I burst out into the cool fresh morning, hunch over and throw up on the tarmac of the pub car park. As I straighten up, wiping my mouth on the sleeve of my waterproof, I can see the chimneys of Meg and Stuart's farmhouse, like a beacon of normality and I flee down the lane towards it as though all the demons of Fortune's Yard are pursuing me. They'll have a phone. They'll know what to do.

I'm ready to hammer on the door, but it's open before I've even got there.

'Beth? I saw you through the window. What's wrong?'

Meg stands back to let me in. She and Stuart are already dressed and in the kitchen having breakfast. It takes them a frustratingly long time to work out what I'm trying to tell them, so I know I can't be making much sense, but as soon as they understand, they leap into action.

'I'll call an ambulance,' Meg says.

'I don't think an ambulance is going to be much use.'

Meg looks at me sharply and then turns away to find her phone.

'The police then.'

'Did you recognise the person?' Stuart asks.

'No.' I really don't want to think about the body again. 'It was too dark to see properly. I didn't have a torch.'

'It could be a stranger,' Meg says. 'Someone who broke in to spend the night there.'

'I'll go up there now and have a look,' Stuart says. 'Make sure there's nothing we can do.'

Meg is on the phone, but when she's done she shepherds me over to the kitchen table and helps me into a chair. She hands me a glass.

'Whisky. For the shock.' I hate whisky but I can still taste the vomit in my mouth and anything is better than that, so I sip at it anyway, feeling the burning sensation as I swallow. 'The police are on their way.'

We sit in stunned silence until Stuart returns. He's out of breath – he must have run all the way and back – and his face is bone-white. It's a few moments before he can speak.

'It's Ralph.'

Meg picks up my glass with the whisky and finishes it. I try to work out if I'm surprised. My brain doesn't seem to be functioning properly. On some level, I think I'd already guessed who it was. I couldn't see him properly, but I think I saw and felt enough to know it was somebody old and male.

'Oh God, poor Evelyn,' Meg says. 'This is going to destroy her.'

'I don't understand,' I manage at last. 'What was he doing in there?'

Neither of them answers me, both preoccupied with their own thoughts.

'It's going to take the police at least half an hour to get here from Ipswich,' Meg says. 'I'm going to go and sit with Evelyn. It should be someone she knows who tells her, not the police.'

'Take the spare key,' Stuart says, 'in case she doesn't hear the door.'

'Oh shit,' I say, rocketing to my feet.

'What's the matter?' Meg asks, a new note of fear in her voice.

'Dolly. I need to tell Dolly.'

Chapter Thirty-Eight

Beth

'There's been an accident.'

As soon as the words leave my mouth, I realise it's the worst possible thing I could have said. Dolly's startling blue eyes dilate and go blank.

'It's all right,' I say quickly, 'it's not your dad, or your granddad. Or anyone else you know.' Not exactly true, but I'm keen to undo the damage I've just done as quickly as I can. She sinks down onto the floor, her back against the kitchen cupboard. I sit down beside her and push Bluebell out of the way.

'I thought,' she manages and then trails off, unable to say it out loud. She rests her head on her knees, her white-gold hair almost covering her face.

'I know, I'm sorry, I should have realised.'

I reach out and take her hand. It's cold. It reminds me of touching the flesh of the body on the pub floor, forcing myself to feel for a pulse, and it's all I can do not to drop it at once.

'Who?'

'It's Ralph.' She goes very still, like she's temporarily paralysed. 'You remember?' I ask stupidly. 'Our new neighbour.'

Slowly, she lifts her head, the sheet of hair parting to reveal a face with eyes that are still huge and sunken into her head.

'Is he dead?'

I can see why her mind would go straight there. After all, she has personal experience of this.

'Well, he was already quite frail,' I begin.

'But is he dead?' she interrupts, those eyes boring into me.

'I'm afraid he is, yes.'

She flops forward, covering her face again.

'It would have been very quick,' I say. 'He wouldn't have known anything about it.' I'm far from sure this is true. In my own head I'm imagining Ralph lying at the bottom of those stairs for hours, perhaps crying out for help and then becoming too weak and dying a slow and agonising death, as his neighbours lie sleeping around him.

'What happened to him?'

I take a moment to decide how to reply, unsure how much to tell her.

'It looks like he fell down some stairs.'

'Did Evelyn find him?'

'I found him.'

'When?'

'About half an hour ago. I didn't have my phone with me so I had to go to Meg and Stuart's.'

'I woke up and I couldn't find you.' She sounds distraught. 'I thought you'd left me.'

'I'm really sorry,' I say, feeling terrible. Why didn't I come straight back? I could have phoned the police myself from the Old Watermill. I wasn't thinking straight. Meg and Stuart's house seemed like a sanctuary, and the truth is that in those terrible moments after finding the body

I didn't even think about Dolly. If I was her real mother, would it have been different? Would some kind of instinct have clicked in? 'I didn't mean to be that long. I needed to call the police.'

'The police?'

'They'll be here soon. Why don't you go upstairs and get dressed, and I'll make us some breakfast.'

She hesitates.

'The police always get called when there's a sudden death,' I tell her, trying to sound like I know about these things. 'It's nothing to worry about.'

'I know,' Dolly says, looking at me steadily now, but without the same intensity, and I'm reminded again that she really does know.

Chapter Thirty-Nine

Beth

The police officer who takes my statement is a brisk, effi-
cient woman in her late twenties, wearing navy trousers
and a jade blouse buttoned up to her neck. Her dark hair
is pulled back into a bun, which can't entirely disguise that
it's been dyed blue at the tips. She has petite features and
a round, flat face. I think she said her name was DS Lee.
We're both sitting at the scrubbed wooden table in our
kitchen. Bluebell is sitting beside me, her muzzle in my
lap. There have been blue lights flashing past the kitchen
window for the past half hour or so, as the emergency
services finally turned up en masse, with the arrival of an
unnecessary ambulance and three police cars shattering
the early morning stillness of Fortune's Yard.

'Do you live here by yourself, Mrs James?'

I'm not used to being called this; it's only been a few
months, and I still mainly use Beth Montgomery. Not
that Montgomery is my real name either. I changed it
two years after I left home – just after my mother made
contact again. I explain about Noah and Dolly, and DS
Lee scribbles in the small notebook she's holding. Her
colleague is prowling round the kitchen, as if he's in a
showroom seeking design inspiration. He's a tall, skinny
guy of about the same age as DS Lee. I didn't catch his

name or rank but I definitely get the impression that she's the boss.

'How long has your husband been away?'

It feels like for ever, I want to say. It's probably the shock still, but I'm finding it hard to concentrate on this interview. More than anything, I want to talk to Noah. I've heard nothing since his one a.m. phone call. Surely he must have seen his dad by now. I can feel myself starting to worry that something might have happened to him. Dolly's fear is contagious. DS Lee is writing down Noah's movements.

'And where's your daughter?'

It's strange hearing the words 'your daughter'. I don't think anyone's ever described Dolly as that before. I'd deliberately left our relationship vague, talking about my husband and Dolly, and DS Lee has made the obvious assumption.

'Upstairs in her room watching YouTube.'

I hope. Because, after all, the last time I thought she was doing that, she was actually piecing together a seamless video that she knew would get me trolled.

'She wasn't with you when you found Mr Kettering?'

For a moment, I can't think who they're talking about. I don't think I ever even knew Ralph and Evelyn's surname.

'She was still asleep.'

'Do you often leave her alone in the house?'

The guilt comes hurtling back. And I wonder if they can see it on my face. I wonder if they can smell the whisky on my breath.

'Hardly ever.' I look back at DS Lee, trying to keep my voice steady. 'I was just popping out.'

'To a disused pub?' says the male police officer, who has finished inspecting Noah's parents' state-of-the art appliances and kitchen cabinets. 'At six in the morning?'

His tone is just the right side of scornful. I don't think it's that he suspects my story exactly; it's more that he suspects me of being a bad parent. With good reason. It's not illegal to leave a thirteen-year-old child alone in a house in the early hours of the morning, but it's not exactly responsible behaviour either.

'I didn't set out to go to the pub.' I explain about seeing Drake. 'I just thought I'd be a couple of minutes. I didn't even think about Dolly.' The words are out of my mouth before I can stop them. Both police officers are regarding me steadily. I feel their judgement boring into me. What kind of a parent says that? 'Because I thought I'd be so quick,' I add. I'm just making it worse.

'I see,' DS Lee says. 'What made you go to the pub?'

'I could see the door was open and there were keys in it, and I was worried something had happened.'

'Why did you think that?'

Well it had, hadn't it? I want to retort. But they already think I'm a terrible parent and I don't want them to decide I'm a horrible person too.

'I just thought it was odd, I suppose, that someone would leave their keys in the door like that.'

I look down, wishing they'd agreed to the tea I offered so that I'd have something to do with my hands.

'How well did you know Mr Kettering?'

'Hardly at all. We only moved down here a few days ago. I've met him a couple of time since then.'

'Is there anyone you can think of who would wish him harm?'

'No, of course not,' I say, almost as a reflex. The implications of the question sink in. 'Why are you even asking me that? It was an accident, wasn't it?'

'We have to check every possibility when there's a sudden death,' DS Lee says, unmoved. It's pretty much exactly what I said to Dolly earlier. Dolly who had a blazing row with Ralph three days ago.

'So no arguments or neighbourly tensions that you're aware of?'

I feel a flush of heat creep up my face and wonder if it's visible to DS Lee. There's no way she can know about the row Dolly and Ralph had on the footpath. Even if someone other than me had witnessed it, I'm the first person DS Lee has spoken to; she told me that when she arrived.

'Nothing. Like I said, we haven't lived here long, but it seems a very friendly place.'

'And what sort of man would you say Mr Kettering was?'

'He was just an ordinary old man.' They wait. I try to sum up my impressions of Ralph without sounding too uncharitable. 'Quite old-fashioned. Religious. Protective of his wife – she's an invalid. Maybe a bit nosy.'

It doesn't seem much, but DS Lee looks pleased and makes a note.

'The sort of person who might go looking round an old pub by himself?'

'I suppose so,' I say doubtfully. 'I mean if he saw something that caught his attention.'

'What do you think he saw?'

'I don't know. I was just trying to work out why he went in there. Something must have made him get out his keys.'

'How do you know they were his keys?'

'I was just assuming. We all have keys,' I explain, feeling briefly like a proper Fortune's Yard resident rather than an interloper. 'In case we need to check on anything.'

'That's a bit odd, isn't it?' says the male police officer. He's now leaning languidly against one of the worktops.

'It's a very small place. The owners of the pub live quite a way away. Apparently they thought it made sense,' I say, sounding defensive. 'As a safety precaution.'

'So you have a set of keys too?' DS Lee asks.

'I believe so, yes.'

'Where are they now?'

'I'm not sure.'

'You've lost them?'

'They're probably in the drawer of the dresser in the hall,' I say, remembering that's where Noah said his parents kept all the spare keys.

'Could you go and look please?'

'I'll come with you,' says the male police officer.

'I'm not even sure I'll know what they look like.'

'Maybe they'll have a label on. As a safety precaution.'

I get up from the table and, without looking at either of them, head out into the hallway. I pull open the central drawer on the old-fashioned dresser that stands to the left of the front door. If this had been my house – really my house, not just the one it feels like I'm pretending to live in – the drawer would have been full of a tangle of keys, cables, old batteries and receipts, but because this is Noah's parents', everything is beautifully ordered. The police officer is right: the keys even have little labels on, with what they're for typewritten and inserted inside a plastic display on the keyring. I know from what Noah's told me about his parents that it will have been his dad who did this and, although I don't know Noah's parents well, it makes my heart ache to think of his dad, lying in a hospital bed halfway across the world, fighting for his life, while we search through his carefully labelled keys.

'Are you all right?' asks the police officer, sounding human for the first time.

'I'm fine.' I take a steadying breath. 'It was just a shock that's all.'

'Have you found them?'

'No. They don't seem to be here.'

'I see. Is there anywhere else they could be?'

I turn away from him, as if looking for other places in the house they might be found, and as I do I catch sight of a flash of white-gold hair. Dolly is watching us through the banisters. I quickly turn back towards him, shaking my head.

'When did you last see them?'

'I don't think I've ever seen them. I was just assuming we had some because apparently all the neighbours do. Maybe Noah's parents accidentally took the keys to the States with them?'

'Why would they do that?'

I explain about the whole moving into their house thing. When I've finished, the police officer says, 'Very nice.' His tone belies his words.

'We're buying the house,' I say defensively. 'They didn't give it to us.'

'And you think they took the keys to America with them?'

'I don't know. Maybe. All I know is I can't find them.'

'If you could come back into the kitchen. We've got a few more questions.'

As I head back into the kitchen, I risk another glance up at the banisters on the landing. Dolly has gone.

Chapter Forty

Beth

When Noah finally calls, I'm so relieved to hear his voice, my eyes well up with tears.

'Sorry, I meant to call sooner. When we got back from the hospital it was four a.m. your time and I didn't want to wake you up again, so I thought I'd have a quick nap and give you a call in a few hours, but the quick nap turned into a long sleep.' I can already tell from his voice that the news must be good and his next words confirm it. 'Things are looking so much better. Dad's doing well. He's out of danger, Beth.'

I feel a wave of relief. I hadn't realised how much tension I'd been carrying on his behalf until then. I sink down onto the sofa.

'That's great. Really great.'

'Are you okay?'

'I'm fine. Tell me more about your dad.'

I listen to him explaining about visiting him in hospital and what the doctors said, and when he's talked himself out I say, 'I'm so relieved he's okay.'

'Beth, something is definitely wrong. Please tell me what it is.'

'Okay, but it's not a big deal. I mean it *is* a big deal, but we're all fine, so you're not to worry about us.'

'What's happened?'

'Ralph's died.'

'Ralph?' For a few seconds he just sounds confused. His head is very firmly on the other side of the Atlantic.

'Next-door neighbour Ralph. Ralph and Evelyn.'

'Of course, I'm sorry. That's so sad, especially for Evelyn. I don't know what she'll do without him. It must have been very sudden – he seemed fine when we saw him the other night.'

'He fell down the stairs in the Fortune's Arms and I found his body,' I blurt out. And now I'm actually crying.

'Oh God, Beth, that's awful, I'm so sorry.'

'It was pretty horrible. He was all cold, and it was dark, and I had to touch him and—'

'Are you by yourself?'

'Dolly's here somewhere.'

'She wasn't with you when you found him?' His voice is sharp with fresh worry.

'No, it was just me.'

'Does she know about it?'

'Of course she knows about it,' I say, feeling childishly annoyed that he seems focused on Dolly. 'The place has been full of police cars all morning. It's been chaos.'

'Sorry.' Noah sounds contrite. 'I wasn't thinking straight. I feel terrible you're having such an awful experience and I'm 5,000 miles away.' He hesitates and then: 'How's Dolly taken it?'

'She was very upset to start with.' Feeling momentarily pissed off with him has at least stopped me crying. 'But I think that was partly because I screwed up telling her.'

There's a pause and I imagine him choosing his reply.

'I'm sure you didn't Beth,' he says, but I can hear the concern behind his reassurance. 'There's no right way to do this stuff. I'm sorry I wasn't there to help you.'

'She seemed calmer once I'd explained properly and she knew what had happened.'

'Good. That's good, isn't it? I suppose it's not like she knew Ralph. She only met him briefly at the drinks thing.'

'Apart from the argument they had,' I say before I can stop myself.

'What?'

'On Saturday. Remember I told you about it?'

'Of course I remember. What's the argument got to do with it?'

'Nothing. I was just thinking the drinks party wasn't the only time she'd met him that's all.'

There's no way I will ever be able to articulate my half-formed fears to Noah and that is probably just as well. I need those fears to stay half-formed. Anything else is unthinkable.

'Well yes, I suppose that's true, but it's still not the same as someone she knew. Sorry Beth, I'm only going on about it because of what happened before, you know with Juliet.'

'Of course,' I say, feeling like a terrible person again. Even without the trauma in Dolly's past, it would hardly be surprising that a dad thousands of miles away is concerned about his daughter's reaction to a sudden death. It would be a worry if he wasn't concerned. I don't want to turn into one of those people who are jealous of their partner's affection for their stepchild – My Blended Family has a scathing article on this subject. 'You don't have to explain. It's completely understandable.'

'It must have been a huge shock for you finding him like that. I'll get the first flight back.'

'There's no need. I'm okay, honestly, I'm just a bit shaken up by it all. Stay out there a bit longer now you're there. At least until your dad gets out of hospital.'

A bit of me hopes that he'll insist, but instead he says, 'Okay if you're sure, but I don't think you should be by yourself. Can you go round to Stuart and Meg's? Is Laura still there?'

'I haven't seen her since last night but I guess so. Maybe I'll go round a bit later. It's been a shock for them, too.'

'What was Ralph doing in the pub in the first place?'

'I don't know. I guess he saw something, or someone. His keys were in the door, that's what made me go in.'

At the mention of the keys, I feel vaguely uneasy again.

'Noah, you didn't move your parents' keys, did you?'

'The keys to the pub? They should be in the drawer of the dresser.'

'They're not there.'

'Have you pulled it right out? Sometimes things slip down the back of that drawer when you put them back in. My mum always used to complain about it.'

I'm again conscious of his innate familiarity with this place. This really is his home – always has been.

'Who are you talking to?'

I whip round and find Dolly standing just behind me. My stepdaughter not only looks like a beautiful ghost, she seems to be able to move about the house with the stealth of one. I wonder how long she's been there.

'It's your dad,' I say brightly. 'I'll pass you over. He's got good news.' She shoots a look at me, a mixture of hope and suspicion that makes me feel a rush of sympathy for her.

I go out into the hallway to give them some privacy. I can hear her questioning him, her voice low, so it's hard to make out what she's saying at first and then faster and more excited.

Outside, I hear several cars drive past, heading out of Fortune's Yard – there's probably a limit to how many police they need here and there must be plenty of other things for them to do. Plenty of actual crimes. I walk over to the dresser and pull out the drawer with the keys in it. This time, I feel right to the back and my fingers close around metal. When I retrieve my find, the typed label tells me it's the spare key to the Fortune's Arms. It was probably there all along.

Out of the corner of my eye, I see the silver scarf hanging out of the pocket of my waterproof on the hook by the front door. In the shock of finding Ralph's body, I'd forgotten all about it. Determined to banish one set of demons for good, I march over and pull it out, but as I hold it in my hands, two things occur to me: if a walker tied it to our front gate, they must have done so between the time Laura arrived last night, when I'm sure I'd have seen it, and 5:45 a.m. this morning when I left the house. Which doesn't seem terribly likely. And it's not just *like* the scarf I was wearing when I was mugged; it actually *is* the same scarf. There's a small red felt-tip dot on the label, which is because I bought it in the sale. When I got home that evening, I'd wanted to get rid of everything I associated with the mugging, and I'd shoved the scarf and the dress I'd been wearing to the bottom of my wardrobe, meaning to take them to the charity shop. I can't remember whether I ever did. I certainly don't remember packing them up with my other things when we moved. As if it's suddenly burning hot, I practically run into the kitchen and throw the scarf in the bin, in the hope I can simply bury it and all it signifies.

Chapter Forty-One

Beth

'Why can't I just stay here?'

'I don't want you to be by yourself.'

'Why?'

'Laura will be there. You can play with the baby.'

Dolly looks up from lacing up her Converse.

'Did she say that?'

'She said she'd be happy to see you.'

'I want to see her too,' she says. Although she's complained a bit, it feels more for form's sake than anything else and she seems basically content with the idea of going to Meg and Stuart's while I go and visit Evelyn. When she came off the phone with Noah she was elated, her eyes shining with relief and happiness.

'Are we taking Bluebell?'

'Let's leave her here.'

I don't think Evelyn's going to be up to Bluebell's ministrations.

'Laura and I could take Bluebell to Hannah's Grove.'

'No,' I say quickly. 'I don't want you going there.'

'Why not?'

Because you're becoming fixated on it. I know I need to have this conversation with Dolly but I don't want to spoil her joy at her grandfather's recovery.

'It's a long way and Laura's supposed to be resting.'

We shut the front door on a crestfallen Bluebell and make our way out into the lane. I'm clutching some freshly baked biscuits to give to Evelyn – I needed to bake something to calm my racing thoughts. Dolly is on her phone typing at lightning speed and managing to navigate around the car parked in the drive at the same time.

'It's good news about your granddad, isn't it?'

She looks up from the phone. Slides it into the back pocket of her denim shorts.

'The best,' she says simply, and again I feel a rush of affection, even love for her. She's so earnest in her pleasure.

'Your dad says he's going to be home from hospital in a few days.'

'I know. He said I could go and visit him at half-term.'

'That's great,' I say, wondering if Noah actually did say this. I'm not against the idea of going to visit Noah's parents in October, but we've literally only just arrived in Fortune's Yard. If we're going to settle in as a family we need to spend some time here.

'Everything's coming right,' she says. Now she's walking beside me, rather than slightly behind or in front like she does normally, as if she's not really with me at all. Her long limbs are loose and swinging. 'Just like I asked for.'

At first the words don't register. I'm looking at the two swans on the millpond, way out on the far side; they've got their heads together, making a heart shape, something I've only ever seen in photos. Then the oddness of what she's just said hits me. Does she mean she prayed for her granddad to get better? Dolly has never seemed at all religious in the time I've known her. In fact, I remember

Noah saying that her mum's accident has left her suspicious of organised religion.

'Like you asked for?' I echo. 'Who did you ask?'

'Hannah,' she says simply. For a moment I don't understand and my confusion must be apparent because she adds, 'Hannah Fortune. The girl who used to live here.'

I feel a chill creep over me.

'You asked Hannah for your granddad to get better?'

'Yes,' she says, her shining face turned towards me. 'And now he is.'

I don't know where to start, but perhaps I shouldn't start at all. Maybe it doesn't matter that she believes that praying to the ghost of a dead child saved the life of her grandfather. It's absurd, and there's something disturbing about her complete conviction, but perhaps all that matters right now is that she's happy.

'But not just that,' says Dolly, her face still radiant. 'She dealt with *him*.'

We're almost outside Meg and Stuart's now, but I can't let this go. I stop walking and turn to her.

'What do you mean?'

A flush spreads over her pale face. She looks almost embarrassed.

'He was horrible and now he's dead.'

'Do you mean Ralph?'

She nods, the beatific smile creeping back onto her face.

'Hannah made it all work out.'

I'm standing in the late August sunshine next to Meg's state-of-the-art Range Rover, clutching my iPhone, a symbol of twenty-first-century technology and connectivity. I try to focus on these external things because Dolly herself is behaving like someone from a far more primitive time.

'Dolly,' my voice comes out sharper than I'd intended. 'That's nonsense. You can't say things like that. This isn't a story or a game. Ralph really is dead.'

'He was my enemy.'

'How was he your enemy?'

'It doesn't matter.'

'I want to know.'

She turns away and walks up the path towards Meg and Stuart's front door.

'Dolly!'

She stops. Hesitates. Turns around.

'What were you two arguing about when I saw you on the path?'

'Don't get in my way.' She says it levelly, without emotion.

'I'm sorry?'

'You've seen what Hannah can do.'

She takes a few steps forward and rings the front door-bell.

Chapter Forty-Two

School report for Dolly James
Lord Lane Primary School, Battersea
22 July 2019

*Dolly is an enthusiastic member of Team Pegasus
and shows a particular aptitude for drama and
sciences. We have noticed one slight cause for
concern which we discussed with you both on
parents' day. When Dolly makes friends, they
tend to be quite intense attachments, and she
becomes very protective of the other child. While
this loyalty is admirable in itself, and shows Dolly's
good intentions, we worry that she may be taking
it too far on occasion. As we mentioned in our
email to you last week, there was an incident
involving Dolly's friend Alice that illustrates this
point. Alice had accidentally seen the answers to
a history test on the teacher's desk and was telling
the other children about it. One of the boys said
that he would tell the teacher that Alice had been
cheating. Dolly pushed him and he fell backwards
onto the desk. Luckily he was unhurt, but the
incident could have been much more serious. We've
talked to Dolly about her behaviour and she agrees
that it is never acceptable to use physical force in*

*these situations, but we think it would be helpful
if she could be encouraged to widen her friendship
group and become less focused on one individual.*

Chapter Forty-Three

Beth

It's Laura who opens the door. Even with Dolly's words about not getting in her way ringing in my ears, I notice that although Laura looks a·bit less fraught every time I see her, she still has dark shadows like bruises around her eyes. Stuart and Meg are just behind her, as though the whole family has been waiting for our arrival. Even Drake is there, weaving round us, like a silky fish. I'd forgotten all about him this morning, but he must have come home at some point. Dolly is swallowed up in a huddle of friendly greetings.

'Can I see Rosie?' she asks, already at the door that leads from the kitchen into the main house.

'I think she's asleep,' Laura says. 'We can go and look.' Stuart follows behind and disappears into the house with them, his anxious expression belying his cheerful greeting of a few moments earlier. I turn down the offer of a cup of coffee before I head over to Evelyn's because all I want is to be by myself for a few minutes to process what just happened outside with Dolly. Meg wants to talk to me about Evelyn, though.

'I'm worried about her, Beth. I sat with her for a couple of hours this morning. I saw the mortuary van come and collect Ralph's body, but I think I managed to distract her. And then the police came and wanted to take a statement, so I stayed while they did that. They were kind, but of course it was very upsetting, and then Evelyn said she wanted to have a lie down and would I leave her. She got even more upset when I tried to stay, so in the end I just did as she asked. I gave her a call about half an hour ago, though, to let her know you were coming round. She wants to see you because you found him.'

'I know.' Meg had relayed this to me in a phone call earlier. It's the main reason I'm going at all. I'm dreading it, and I'm also worried that I'm not going to be able to give Evelyn what she's hoping for. What can I say? That he looked peaceful? That I'm sure it must have been quick? I can say all of that I suppose, but I'm convinced she's somehow going to know that it's not true. Meg is still talking, this time something about Evelyn being in shock.

'I'm not sure she's completely taken it in. She's even more confused than usual. When the police rang the doorbell she said something about Ralph coming back.'

I'm only half listening, but the idea of Ralph coming back, following on from Dolly talking about Hannah, is somehow so disturbing that a shadow of it must cross my face.

'Are you all right Beth? You've gone white as a sheet. I know it was a massive shock for you, too.'

'I'm fine. I should get over to Evelyn's.'

'I worry about her being on her own, even for a short time. Ralph did everything for her. There are the children of course, their two sons. One of them lives in Hong Kong and I've never even met him, but we see the Cambridge one sometimes. I gave his number to the police, but I might give him a call myself too. Cambridge isn't that far away, is it? We can't leave her by herself overnight. Will you let me know how you get on? I'll pop over again at lunchtime with some food for her.'

Somehow, I extricate myself. Back in the lane, I stand in the shade of a big horse chestnut tree in front of Meg and Stuart's house and try to make sense of what just happened. Already the memory has faded slightly – the edge taken off it by Meg's disquisition about Evelyn. Did Dolly really just threaten me or did I misunderstand? It was said in such a neutral voice, it seems hard to believe. And yet, the Hannah stuff was real enough; I mean Dolly thought it was real. That was the most chilling thing about the conversation. She really did think a young girl condemned to death for witchcraft 400 years ago had saved her grandfather and cursed an elderly neighbour who'd taken a dislike to her. Where has all of this come from? We've lived in Fortune's Yard precisely five days. How can Dolly have come to believe the local folklore so thoroughly?

My phone vibrates in my hand making me jump. It's Sasha. She's sent me multiple messages this morning, none of which I've had a chance to reply to. I've been so caught up in Ralph's death, the events of last night seem like they took place about a decade ago. That silly video about the peanut cookies couldn't seem less important now. So what if it damages my Instagram following? Ever since I touched Ralph's cold skin, I haven't given it a thought. I literally couldn't care less. But Sasha doesn't know any of this. It's not fair on her to keep ignoring her; she'll be really worried about me now. Besides, I suddenly urgently want to hear her voice.

'Sasha. I'm so sorry I haven't got back to you.'

Sasha is pissed off at first and I can't blame her, but when I explain about Ralph's death and finding his body, all her anger evaporates.

'Oh God, Beth, that sounds horrendous. It's like the place is cursed or something.'

'Don't be ridiculous!'

This must come out wrong, because instantly her voice is soothing.

'Hey, it's okay. I only meant you've had a lot of bad luck over the past few days, but shit happens, we both know that, and it tends to all happen at the same time. You'll get through this.'

'I didn't mean to snap, sorry. It's just that this place is seriously getting to me now. I thought it had a strange atmosphere right from the start.' But as I say this, I realise it's not even true. When I first came to visit with Noah a couple of months ago, I'd really liked Fortune's Yard. It had seemed serene, beautiful and full of possibilities for our new life together. It was only when I'd come back with Noah and Dolly, when the house was ours, that I'd experienced that same serenity as an almost unnatural stillness: stifling and oppressive. It was then that I'd started to think there was something wrong here. For a moment, I think back to what Sasha suggested when I first mentioned my bad feelings about the place to her, and I wonder: could the wrong feeling actually be Dolly, or some weird combination of Dolly and this place?

'Beth, are you still there?'

I've missed everything Sasha just said and I apologise again.

'I was asking what the police think happened.'

'It's hard to know. They didn't really tell me anything. I guess they think he fell down the stairs. It's the obvious explanation.'

'But that's not what you think?' I don't answer her at first, but she persists. 'I can tell from your voice.'

'I'm not sure.'

It's the first time I've acknowledged it, even to myself.

'Why not?'

'The police asked if Ralph had any enemies.'

'Isn't that just a thing they have to ask?'

'Maybe.'

'And did he?'

'I barely knew him. I didn't like him very much the few times I met him, but that's not the same as having people who'd want to kill you.'

'So why aren't you sure?'

I take a deep breath. And then I tell her about the argument Dolly had with Ralph. When I finish my account there's silence for a few seconds before Sasha says, 'I'm not getting why this is bothering you so much.' But before I can reply, she continues, 'I mean obviously I get why the whole thing is upsetting you. You found his body – that's horrible. But what's with the Dolly thing?'

I realise I'd been hoping that Sasha would get what I was trying to say without me having to say it at all. Because I very much don't want to say it out loud. I want someone else to put the half-formed thoughts into a fully formed sentence for me.

'I guess it's just left me a bit unsettled,' I hedge.

'Come on, Beth. Tell me what you're thinking.'

I still can't quite bring myself to say it.

'When we were talking just now, Dolly made this weird speech. It started okay. All about how she was so relieved her granddad is better.'

'Noah's dad's okay? That's great news.'

So much has happened since last night, I'd forgotten I hadn't even told her this bit.

'Yeah,' I say impatiently, 'yeah it is. The thing is, Sasha, once Dolly had finished talking about her granddad, she started talking about Ralph and she basically said something about – about how he deserved to die. She's got really into this local story that Laura told her about a young girl who used to live here hundreds of years ago and how she was a witch. Anyway, Dolly basically implied that Ralph's death was somehow the result of witchcraft.'

I wait for her reaction.

'That's a bit creepy.'

I wait some more.

'Beth?' Silence. I need her to get there herself. I really do. 'Hang on a minute, you don't believe her, do you?'

'No,' I say quickly. 'No, I mean, not literally.'

'Not literally?'

'I don't believe a witch from 400 years ago killed Ralph.'

'You think Dolly had something to do with it don't you? You think Dolly is involved somehow in this man's death?'

I can't speak.

'Beth, that's crazy.' Sasha's voice is even more deliberately soothing than it was when I'd first mentioned finding Ralph's body. 'I mean I know you two don't get on, but I think you might be letting this place, the move, get to you. You've had a horrible experience and you're by yourself in a new place—'

'I'm not by myself,' I protest. 'There are people here, you know. It's a proper community.'

'A pretty strange-sounding one. Take a step back for a moment and think about what you're saying. There is no way Dolly has anything to do with this. She's a thirteen-year-old child, Beth. And yeah, she's a giant pain in the arse, and she's basically screwed up your Insta feed for the foreseeable – it's still full of people calling you vile names and telling other people to stop following you – but there's a huge difference between being a teenage dickhead and being a killer.'

'I never said that,' I say rapidly backtracking. 'I would never say that.' If even Sasha, who's been on Dolly's case since the first peculiar thing she did, thinks that I've lost it, I really must have done. 'You're the one who calls her the wicked stepdaughter,' I say defensively.

'Beth, however vile she sometimes is, she's hardly going to go out and kill an old man because he shouted at her.'

'I know that, of course I do. That wasn't what I meant.'

'Okay good.'

'It just creeped me out a bit that's all. I can't explain it properly. I think it's one of those things where you had to be there, and hear the way she said it. I'm worried that she's becoming obsessed with this witch thing and now it's going to get even worse because she's tying it all up with Ralph's death as well. I have literally no idea what I'm doing, Sash. This is all way beyond my experience. I feel like if Dolly had her actual mum here – or if Noah was here – they'd know what to do.'

As I say this, I feel a wave of relief. Maybe, deep down, this is really what's bothering me. I'm terrible at this and no matter how often I read My Blended Family and the other websites, I don't seem to be getting any better. Dolly needs a parent right now, and I'm all she's got and I'm failing her.

'Oh Beth,' Sasha says. 'Of course they wouldn't. They'd be as confused as you are. No parent ever knows what to do. We're all just making it up as we go along. And it's hardly like this is an everyday parenting challenge. You've got a disturbed teenager who's dealing with traumatic grief from the death of her mum, her granddad having a heart attack, and now the violent death of a neighbour. None of us would know how to handle that.'

'Noah would,' I say. 'She's so different with him.'

'He's had thirteen years to get to know her. You've had a few months. It's not going to happen by magic. You need something to bring you together. You'll both get through this, believe me, and you and Dolly will be closer because of it.'

'I can't really imagine it.'

'Hey. I wish I was there to give you a hug.'

'I wish you were, too. Sash? What do you think I should do? About Dolly I mean.'

'Well what would you do if I was in a bad place?'

'I'd probably sit you down in front of an old movie, and give you a giant plate of brownies.'

'Do that, then. Just don't let her help you make the brownies.'

I give a gulping laugh.

When I hang up, I realise I never told Sasha about Dolly threatening me. Before I head towards Evelyn's cottage, I glance up at Meg and Stuart's farmhouse, in front of me. Framed in the window on the first floor, Dolly's pale face surrounded by white-gold hair is looking right back at me. Abruptly I turn away and start walking along the lane. I try not to run.

Chapter Forty-Four

Beth

Standing beside the low iron gate that bears the sign *Workshop Cottage* stamped in gothic gold letters on a granite background, I hesitate. I have no idea what I'm going to say to Evelyn. I barely know her. Besides, I'm not sure I'm in a fit state to offer comfort to anyone. The shortbread biscuits I made and brought with me seem suddenly crass; crumbling the butter, flour and sugar together in my fingers helped to steady my shattered nerves earlier, but perhaps I should have left the finished product behind. *You've lost your husband, so I've brought you baked goods.* I cringe at the thought. Meg says that Evelyn wants to see me, but now that I'm here, all my instincts are telling me to turn around and escape while I still can.

A small figure appears silhouetted against the latticed glass of one of the downstairs windows. Evelyn. She raises a hand, and I raise one in return, giving a slightly manic wave like I'm delighted to be here. Committed now, I lift the latch on the gate and make my way down the path. Then I wait for a few seconds by the front door, expecting Evelyn to come and open it. It's slightly disconcerting when this doesn't happen. I place my finger on the porcelain doorbell and hear it ring out inside. Still nothing. Oh God, supposing she's had a fall or something.

This is exactly what Meg was worried about. I press the bell again, and then step off the path onto the pristine lawn and over to the window where I saw Evelyn a few minutes ago. The sun is shining brightly on the little diamond-shaped panes of glass, making it hard to see anything inside. I cup my hands around my face to shade my eyes, and as I do so, the room comes into focus. Suddenly there are other eyes looking back at me. I take several rapid steps backwards, my heart thumping.

A few deep breaths and I'm back for a second look. It's Evelyn, of course. Who else did I think it would be? She's just standing there, in the living room, staring at me. And while it's a relief to discover she's not lying injured on the floor somewhere, it's disturbing in an entirely different way that she appears somehow frozen to the spot, seeing and yet not seeing me. She's about three feet back from the window, and I suppose she must have moved there after she waved at me, but I've no idea what stopped her going any further. At a loss for what to do next, I try tapping gently on the glass. She looks to the side first, as if she thinks the noise might be coming from inside the cottage, and then she turns her head very slowly back towards me. This time when she locks eyes with me, something happens: her face becomes less mask-like, it crumples. She looks confused. I smile back as reassuringly as I can manage and point in the direction of the front door. She hesitates, but then to my relief, turns and moves towards what I assume is the door to the hallway. I wait at the front door again, and eventually it opens.

'Hi, Evelyn,' I say brightly. She stares back at me, her cloudy eyes perplexed. 'It's Beth. From the Old Water-mill.'

'Beth?'

'We met the other night, at Meg and Stuart's. I'm Noah's wife. One of your neighbours.'

She's smartly dressed again, this time in a cream blouse, with a tweed skirt and deep magenta cardigan, and her white hair is pulled back in a bun at the nape of her neck, but the deterioration from when I last saw her a few days ago is marked. She'd seemed frail then, but now she's more hunched and clinging onto the front door frame for support. I suppose it's hardly surprising, she's had a big shock.

'Beth,' she says, still sounding uncertain. Then her face breaks into a smile. 'One of the neighbours, yes, I remember.'

And she looks so relieved I think she actually might.

'I came to say how very sorry I was about Ralph.'

'He's out somewhere I'm afraid.'

I take this in slowly. My smile falters, but hers is unwavering.

'I saw him in the garden just now,' she says. 'So I'm sure he won't be long.'

'You saw him?' I echo.

'He waved to me from the end of the path.'

'Evelyn, can I come in?'

'Of course you may, my dear. It's very rude of me to keep you standing on the doorstep, and I'm sure Ralph will be back soon.' She turns and I follow her inside, stooping because the front door is so low. Once I'm standing in the floral-papered hallway, my head is only a few centimetres from the ceiling. 'Would you like a cup of coffee while we wait? We normally have ours at half past eleven and Ralph does the crossword, but I'm sure he won't mind if we make a start a bit earlier.'

'A coffee would be lovely thanks,' I say automatically, my brain grasping at normality at the same time as it desperately tries to work out the best thing to do.

'The sitting room is just through here.' She gestures to the room where I saw her through the window.

'Let me help you with the coffee.'

I follow her down the hallway to the kitchen, which is at the back of the cottage. It's newer than Meg and Stuart's 1980s pine version, but nothing like as swish as the one Noah's parents had installed. There are bland wooden cabinets and a pale grey fake marble worktop. A pair of yellow washing-up gloves are a splash of colour on the otherwise empty drainer. It's all very clean and neat. I still can't think what to say. It even occurs to me that perhaps I can say nothing. Drink my coffee, talk politely to Evelyn and then make my exit. But I know deep down that I won't be able to face Meg if I do this. Or myself.

'I brought you some shortbread.'

'How kind of you.'

She's filling up the kettle from the tap. It's one of the old-fashioned sort that you have to boil on a hob, rather than plug in. It seems to be a tremendous effort for her to hold the kettle as it fills with water. She's using both hands and I don't know how she's going to manage to keep hold of it and turn off the tap. I reach over and do it for her.

'Thank you my dear.'

Even her voice is shakier than when I last saw her.

'Evelyn, do you remember Meg coming round earlier?'

She's trying to light the gas under the kettle, but it keeps flickering and then dying.

'Stupid thing,' she says querulously, turning it up higher and lowering her face to peer at it more closely. 'Why won't you light? Ralph knows the trick. He always says I don't have the knack.'

I'm worried she's going to take her eyebrows off if she carries on like this.

'Shall I try? Why don't you take a seat?'

There's a small round table in the corner of the kitchen with two chairs.

'That's not right at all.' She sounds quite put out. 'You're the guest.'

'You could find a plate for the shortbread,' I suggest.

This seems to placate her. I manage to light the gas and, while she searches for a suitable plate, I find matching rose-patterned bone china mugs in the cupboard, and put a spoonful of Carte Noire in two. All the time, I'm thinking. It seems so cruel to have to break the news to her again, but crueller still to leave her waiting for the return of a man who's never going to come home, no matter how long she stares out the window. Meg is right: Evelyn can't stay by herself. Now I've seen her again, I'm not sure she should be left alone even for a few hours, let alone a few days. I wonder what we're going to do. The kettle shrieks, and I remove it from the hob, remembering just in time to use a tea towel to avoid burning my hand. Evelyn is laying out the biscuits.

'These look homemade.'

'Yes, fresh out of the oven,' I say, putting our mugs of coffee down on the coasters already waiting on the table. Maybe the biscuits weren't such a bad idea after all.

'Clever girl.' I take the seat opposite Evelyn at the table. 'We'd better put the kettle on again for when Ralph comes in.' She avoids my gaze as she says it.

'Evelyn, about Ralph.' She takes a shortbread biscuit from the plate, but makes no move to eat it. 'Do you remember what happened earlier this morning?' Her thumb and forefinger crumble the biscuit. 'Do you remember the police coming to see you?' Her eyes fill with tears. I feel, ridiculously, almost relieved. So she does remember.

'He's not coming back, is he?'

'I'm very sorry.'

'I could have sworn I saw him just now in the garden, as plainly as I see you sitting there.'

'I think your brain was playing tricks on you,' I say gently. 'It happens. When we want a thing to be true.'

The tears spill over and run down her cheeks. She drops the uneaten biscuit and fumbles in the sleeve of her cardigan for a handkerchief.

'I'm sorry,' she says, her voice muffled.

'There's no need to apologise.' I reach out and touch her hand. Her skin is paper-thin.

'It was you who found him, wasn't it?' For all her confusion, she is still capable of moments of lucidity. 'I remember now. Meg told me.'

'Yes. I really think it must have been very quick,' I say, the lie coming easily now that I'm confronted with Evelyn's stricken face. 'He wouldn't have known anything about it.'

'Meg said you found him in the pub.'

'Yes. I think he must have fallen.'

'But what was he doing in there?'

Her voice is querulous again. It's a very good question.

'I don't know. He didn't say anything to you about going there?' I probe.

She shakes her head.

'When did you last see him?'

She looks down at her fingers, plaiting the handkerchief around them.

'I can't remember.'

'Was it last night?' Because surely she'd have noticed if he'd gone missing before then.

'He was reading the newspaper,' she says with sudden conviction. 'He always finishes off *The Times* in the evening after I've gone up to bed, and then usually he goes out for a cigarette. He thinks I don't know but I hear the front door go.'

'What time do you go to bed?'

'Always before nine,' she says. 'Ralph says I get very tired if I don't go to bed early.' Evelyn's cloudy eyes briefly light up as another idea occurs to her. 'Maybe he went to the pub to do his thinking.'

'His thinking?'

'He says he can't think properly in the cottage because I crowd him.'

Ralph may be dead, but he's proving no easier to warm to. Also, I notice she's slipped into talking about him in the present tense, but I'm hoping this is just a verbal slip-up, rather than an indication that she's forgotten again.

'Sometimes,' she says, 'when he's got a lot on his mind, he'll go and find somewhere quiet to sit and think things through.'

I want to point out that Fortune's Yard must offer many more suitable spots for contemplation than the upstairs of a disused pub, but the explanation Evelyn's come up with seems to be giving her some comfort so I ask instead, 'Did he have a lot on his mind at the moment?'

'He was very angry.'

My heart beats faster.

'Really? Did he tell you why?'

'Oh yes, he told me all about it when he came home.'

'When was this, Evelyn?'

'Yesterday.' I feel a wave of relief. Ralph's argument with Dolly was three days ago, so if Ralph was angry on Monday it must surely have been about something else. Almost at once, though, the doubt creeps in. It's hard to know how much reliance to place on what Evelyn tells me. 'He'd been out for a walk, you see, and when he came in, I could tell at once that something was wrong. He gets very tense when he's angry, and his eyes were all sparkling too. He'd found something out. I guessed that straight away.'

'What had he found out?'

'It was about a doll.'

My hand, which was lifting the mug of coffee, freezes.

'A doll? You're sure?' Does Evelyn even remember what my stepdaughter is called? 'Could it have been Dolly?'

'A doll or a dolly. I can't remember exactly what he said now.' She's starting to sound flustered. 'My memory isn't always very good any more, I'm afraid.'

'It's okay. Honestly. Is there anything else you *do* remember about what Ralph said?'

'He said it was a disgusting thing to do. I tried to calm him down, but he said I didn't know what I was talking about.'

She's becoming more and more upset, and I don't want to push her too far, but I also need to know what it was that made Ralph so angry.

'Can you remember anything else he said?'

'He said it was wicked and it oughtn't to be allowed to go on. It was against God.'

In my head, I hear what Dolly said: *He said that I would go to hell.*

'Evelyn, did you tell the police about any of this?'

She looks at me blankly. The front doorbell shatters the silence and I jump, shooting some of the coffee in the mug I'm still holding out over the table.

Chapter Forty-Five

Beth

For a moment, I think I'm losing it – just like Evelyn. Ralph is standing on the doorstep, illuminated by the glare of the midday sun. I gape at him.

'Hi, err, I'm Simon, Ralph and Evelyn's eldest.'

He takes a step towards me and, without the light behind him, it's easier to see his face. He does look uncannily like his father: the same sharp, pinched features and hard grey eyes. The thick hair is sandy, not grey though, and he's casually dressed in a T-shirt and jeans – items I'm willing to bet Ralph never possessed. I stand back to let him enter and he ducks and steps into the hallway, then turns back towards me.

'Are you from the police?' he asks, understandably puzzled to find a total stranger in his parents' house – and one who appears incapable of speech.

'Oh no, sorry.' I attempt to pull myself to together and explain who I am and that I've been sitting with his mum for a while.

'Well, thank you, Beth,' he says. 'That's really kind of you.'

'It's no trouble at all.' Now that I've started talking again, familiar social phrases trip off my tongue. 'And I'm so sorry,' I add, 'about your dad.'

239

'Thank you. He was old of course, but it was still a bit of a surprise.' I don't detect much grief for his father in Simon's words. I feel my familiar fascination about other people's relationships with their parents temporarily taking over. Meg said Simon came up to visit sometimes, but maybe he and his father weren't close. And, after all, who am I to judge? I don't even know if my father's dead or alive, and that's the way I intend to keep it.

'It's Mum I'm worried about,' he says. 'She'll be lost without him.'

I take him down the hallway to the kitchen, where Evelyn is still sitting, staring straight ahead of her. When she sees Simon though, it's as though a warm glow spreads over her face, bringing it back to life again. He bends down to envelop her and she clings to him tightly. This is the point at which I should almost certainly leave them to it, but something about the pull of this moment of parental love, combined with Evelyn's jumbled revelations, means I don't want to go just yet. Instead, I busy myself making Simon a coffee he almost certainly doesn't want, while he talks to Evelyn about what to do next. He takes charge of the situation with compassion, so clearly he hasn't inherited his father's personality along with his looks. When Evelyn protests that she can't possibly leave, he's insistent but kind, explaining that she can't be in the cottage by herself and must come and stay with him and Carly for a few days in Cambridge.

'In Cambridge? Oh, but it's such a long way.'

'I've got the car outside. We'll be there in no time. The boys can't wait to see you.'

'I'd love to see them, but another time, Simon. This is all too sudden.'

'We've just been through this, Mum. You can't stay here by yourself, and Carly and I can't get away at the moment.'

'But I haven't had a chance to pack.'

'I'll help you to pack some things now. It won't take long.'

'I haven't done any washing. I haven't got anything clean. I need Ralph to help me.'

She looks bewildered. Over the top of Evelyn's head, Simon and I exchange glances.

'You just stay there, Mum. I'll go upstairs and sort a few things out for you.'

I follow him out into the hallway and close the kitchen door behind me.

'Do you mind hanging on a bit longer while I pack some things for her?'

'Of course not.'

'Thank you. I won't be long.'

'Just so you know,' I say, speaking softly in case Evelyn can still hear us, 'your mum seems quite confused. In fact, when I first got here she seemed to have forgotten what had happened entirely. She was expecting your dad to walk back through the door.'

I decide not to mention that for a few seconds when I first saw him that's exactly what I thought too.

'Mum's been confused for a long time now,' Simon says, sounding suddenly weary. 'She was almost completely reliant on Dad. He took care of everything. Now he's gone she's really going to struggle to cope.'

'It's good she's got you.'

He gives me a wry smile.

'I'm not sure how long Carly is going to want her living with us, to be honest, but we can sort out a home once we've got her back with us.'

He pads up the tiny staircase, which is steep and flanked by white wooden banisters. It seems an unsuitable thing to have in the house of an elderly couple, but if Ralph was used to going up and down these stairs, it's strange he tumbled down the ones in the Fortune's Arms. I suppose it was dark though, and less familiar territory – which brings me right back to the question of what he was doing in there in the first place. Back in the kitchen, Evelyn is still sitting at the table, staring at the pile of shortbread crumbs from the biscuit she picked up earlier. She looks exhausted with shock and grief, but I realise that this is probably my last chance to ask her anything.

'Evelyn,' I say in a low urgent voice, not quite sure why I don't want Simon to overhear. She looks up from the biscuit, her eyes cloudy again.

'What dear?'

'Last night. When Ralph went out, did he take the keys to the pub with him, do you know?'

She stares at me blankly.

'What keys?'

'The keys to the Fortune's Arms. Meg said everyone has some.'

'Meg?'

She repeats it like she's never heard the name before.

'You know, Meg and Stuart, from down the road? With Laura and the baby.'

'Laura doesn't have a baby.'

She sounds worried and frightened. I try one more time, although I'm not sure I'm going to get much sense out of her.

'Do you remember what you were telling me before? Just before Simon got here. About Ralph going out last night?'

'Simon's my eldest,' she says, more confidently.

'I know.'

'He's in Cambridge.'

'He's upstairs, Evelyn, packing some things for you. You're going to stay with him for a few days.' *Longer if Carly will have you*, I hope.

She begins to cry again and I feel terrible.

'It's all right. It's going to be all right. Let me make you another coffee.'

By the time Simon comes back downstairs, the two of us are sitting on the sofa in the living room, fresh mugs of coffee – destined to remain undrunk – on the coffee table in front of us. I'm holding Evelyn's hand and she's clutching onto me like I'm a life raft. I've given up trying to ask her anything more about last night. She seems confused by my questions and I don't want to make her any more upset than she is already. *Mum's been confused for a long time now.* I wish I knew how much of what she's already told me could be relied on.

'All right Mum?' Simon appears in the doorway. 'I think we're all done now.'

She turns to me, looking bewildered again.

'Simon will take good care of you,' I say. 'You're going to stay with him.'

'But I need to pack.'

'I've packed for you, Mum. That's what I've just been doing.' There are two suitcases in the hall, the old-fashioned kind, without wheels, which Simon picks up. I wonder if Evelyn realises she might never come back here.

I take her arm and she clings to me. We shuffle slowly down the path, following in Simon's wake. Simon's Audi is parked behind his dad's Fiesta on the gravel driveway – at least I assume it's Ralph's, it's hard to imagine Evelyn driving anywhere. I help Evelyn into the front seat, while Simon packs the boot. It's full of football gear and he's having trouble fitting the two suitcases in. As I lean over to help Evelyn fasten her seatbelt, she clutches at my hand, her grip vice-like.

'I didn't tell the police,' she whispers, sounding frightened, 'because I didn't want to get *her* in trouble.'

'We'll be off then,' Simon says from behind me. 'Sorry I didn't mean to make you jump.'

I rub my head where I hit it on the roof of the car. Evelyn's words are still ringing in my ears.

'No problem,' I manage. 'I think we're all just a bit on edge, that's all.'

'Thanks for all your help.' He shuts the passenger door and lowers his voice. 'I went to have a quick look when I got here.' He gestures in the direction of the Fortune's Arms. I notice that all you can see from Ralph and Evelyn's driveway is the upper storey of the pub. 'I can't think what Dad was doing in there.'

'No one knows,' I say. Although I wonder if Evelyn does, without even being aware of it; if the answer is in something she's already told me, and I haven't realised. Now Simon is about to drive her off to Cambridge, taking the solution with her, and it says something about my state of mind that what I mainly feel at this thought is relief. My head is churning with all that's been going on and I'm not sure I can deal with anything else right now. On autopilot, I say my goodbyes and seconds later, they're gone, the brake lights of the Audi showing at the corner before Simon turns right and out of sight, whisking Evelyn away.

My last memory of her is of the confusion in her cloudy eyes as she waved at me from the passenger seat, and the fear in her voice as she told me she didn't want to get Dolly into trouble.

Chapter Forty-Six

Beth

What I should do now is go and pick Dolly up from Meg and Stuart's. What I badly need to do instead is bake. I'm so wired I can't think straight, and it's the only thing I know that will calm me down and help me put the thoughts that are whirling round in my head in some kind of order. I walk down the hill, turning to the right, rather than heading straight on to Meg and Stuart's farmhouse. I think of Sasha's advice from earlier. I'll bake some brownies. A big batch of them. I'm not sure I can imagine Dolly and I watching a movie together while we eat them, but at least making them will delay the moment when I have to face her again.

Bluebell greets me with wild enthusiasm when I open the door. A bit of me wants to scoop her up and head out of here as fast as I can, to follow Simon and Evelyn in the direction of the A12. To drive and keep on driving until I get back to London. What's stopping me? Dolly's in safe hands. Meg and Stuart will take good care of her and she adores Laura and the baby. I could call them from somewhere on the road and explain I've suddenly been called away. I don't know whether it's a desire to get out of Fortune's Yard that's driving me, or a desire to get away from Dolly, or some kind of twisted combination of the two things, but I do know that if I go, I'll never be able to explain this to Noah and that it will be over between us. So instead, I walk into the kitchen in a daze and start taking down ingredients from the cupboard: cocoa powder, dark chocolate, plain flour, unsalted butter, eggs. Just handling these items makes me feel safer, calmer.

I light the oven, put the chocolate in a bain-marie to melt, and start weighing out the flour and cocoa powder, doing all of this automatically. Meanwhile, I try to sort through my thoughts. What's really going on here? What do I know for sure?

There's one thing I saw with my own eyes: Ralph and Dolly arguing. And I know exactly when the argument happened, three days ago – the day after we arrived. Evelyn said that Ralph was angry yesterday, but, the more I think about it, the less certain I am I can rely on that – she could just have been remembering a conversation they had earlier in the week. Or maybe – a worrying new thought – Ralph and Dolly had another argument yesterday. Dolly was missing for nearly an hour after she got out of the car, and although Ralph was at Meg and Stuart's when I got there, he could have met Dolly earlier. There had certainly been something exultant about Ralph when I'd seen him briefly in Meg and Stuart's kitchen yesterday.

I go over again what Dolly told me about that first argument: Ralph said that she would go to hell and she believed him because she felt guilty about her mum's death. *I killed my mum.* For the first time I think about the literal meaning of her words. I think about Noah saying *Dolly didn't always have an easy relationship with Juliet.* In my head, I can hear Sasha telling me I'm losing it. Dolly was nine years old when her mum died. Even supposing she wanted to, could a nine-year-old kill her mother? The answer comes almost at once. *She could if she was driving in a car with her.*

I turn up the mixer, as if the whirring sound can drown out the sheer horror of what I've just thought. It's ludicrous. Unbidden, I remember the moment in the car when I'd wondered if Dolly meant to harm me. She could have killed us both if she'd tried to take the steering wheel, but maybe she didn't care about that. After all, she tried to leap from a moving car only moments later.

Okay, I think, brushing the excess cocoa dust from the worktop into my hand, let's run with it. These are just thoughts and no one else need ever know I've even had them. Let's suppose Dolly did kill her mother four years ago and somehow Ralph found out. That would make sense of what Evelyn said Ralph had uncovered. A wicked thing that went against God. I'm struggling to think how he could possibly have found out – the accident happened in Surrey and Dolly and Juliet were the only people in the car – but the rest of it fits. He confronts Dolly and I witness the aftermath. But if he did find out such an awful thing, why did he choose to go to Dolly about it, rather than come and tell me or Noah? I think of Evelyn's description of him when he returned from his walk – she made him sound almost triumphant. In our brief acquaintance, Ralph struck me as the kind of man who'd enjoy having power over another individual, especially a child. He might actually take pleasure in tormenting Dolly, threatening to reveal what he knew to us, to the police.

So what happened last night? All I have is more supposition. If Evelyn can be believed at all, Ralph went out last night sometime after nine o'clock, after she'd gone to bed. I'm practically certain that Dolly slipped out last night too, while I was talking to Laura in the library. She said goodnight to us at half-eight. Here at least I'm sure; I remember glancing up at the clock in the kitchen when we all got up after dinner, and then Laura and I stacked the dishwasher for a few minutes and went into the library with a bottle of wine. I didn't see Dolly again until I went to look for her after the call from Sasha. It was gone midnight, so she could have left at any point over more than three hours. At the time, I couldn't work out what she could have been doing wandering around Fortune's Yard late at night – it's hardly Streatham. But now I have a theory for exactly what she could have been doing. Because now I know Ralph was out that night, too. Did the two of them arrange to meet?

As I tip the brownie batter from the bowl into the cake tin, I try to remember whether there was anything unusual about the Converse she hid near the front door. Anything that might tell me where she'd worn them. I hadn't paid much attention at the time, though. I'd just felt indignant that she'd lied to me. Again. All I can remember is the leaf and that hardly narrows it down. Anyway, what am I expecting? A piece of fibre from the old pub carpet? Ralph's blood? I slam the oven door on the brownies, feeling sick. I'm not sure giving free rein to my worst imaginings was a good idea at all. Because thinking things makes them more real, even if you don't share those thoughts with anyone.

Bluebell has her front paws up on the worktop, trying to lick some spilled brownie mix and as I go to shoo her away, I catch the edge of the mixing basin and it shatters on the stone floor. It feels like some kind of judgement. I ferry Bluebell out of the room, and as I bend to pick up the shards, I try to remember exactly what Evelyn told me Ralph said. I freeze, my grip tight on the broken glass. Maybe Ralph really did say doll, not Dolly, because suddenly I realise what he might have been talking about: the doll I found in the grove, in the tiny coffin. I'm aware of a sharp pain, and when I look down there's blood starting to drip onto the tiles from the cut on my hand.

And that's when I remember something else, too. The letter drawn on the end of the coffin. R for Ralph.

Chapter Forty-Seven

Beth

I'm sure I left the little cardboard coffin and its modelling-clay figure in the drawer of the bedside table, but it's not there now. I remove both drawers and take everything out of them just to be certain. There's already a surprising amount of crap given the short time we've lived here: tissues, bookmarks, biros. Down the back of one of the drawers I even find a packet of hearing aid batteries, which must belong to one of Noah's parents. It strikes me as odd suddenly that I don't know which one. I've only met them a handful of times. As a family, I know so little about them all. I suppose it's just about possible that the little coffin is somewhere else in our bedroom – that Noah moved it for some reason and didn't mention it to me – but I'm not going to waste time looking, because I think I've got a better explanation. Other than Noah, Dolly is the only person who knows I found it, so if it's gone missing, she must have it.

Her bedroom door is shut, but I don't even hesitate. It's an invasion of privacy, but I think we're way beyond that now. I'm in the kind of territory where My Blended Family can't help me. Bluebell follows me in, and lies down bang in the middle of Dolly's sheepskin rug, looking at me with sad eyes, as though she at least still thinks I shouldn't be doing this. I sit on the pink-and-purple tie-dye duvet and look around me. As well as the bed, there's a white painted chest of drawers over by the window, a matching dressing table with an oval-shaped mirror and a set of bookshelves with a few books and some neatly stacked board games. There's no real clutter anywhere. She's a teenager without random stuff, or at least without stuff that she displays on every surface, and even with my limited experience of parenting I know that this is very strange indeed. If she has the coffin, it's going to be shut away somewhere. I get up and move over to the chest of drawers. My hand is throbbing from where I cut it on the glass and blood is starting to seep through the make-shift bandage of kitchen towels I wrapped around it. I pull open the top drawer. Bluebell lets out a small grunt of disapproval. It's full of underwear: Primark pants and padded bras. I make myself sort through them, because after all, I was a teenager once, and my underwear drawer was definitely where I kept the things I didn't want anyone else to find. Dolly, though, seems to keep only underwear in hers. In fact, when I've been through the entire chest of drawers, I have to conclude that either she has nothing to hide, or she doesn't hide it in here. The dressing table drawers are similarly ordered and unrevealing: nail varnishes in one, make-up in another. I sink to the floor, sitting beside Bluebell, who's now decided I'm so lost to shame that the only way she can cope with it is by going to sleep.

I type 'Where do teenagers hide things?' into Google. Internet to the rescue, as always. I click on an article called 'Ten ways to hide things from parents' and quickly scan down the list. Most of the suggestions are places I've tried already. Number seven suggests hollowing out a book, and hiding things inside it: I look up at the shelves. In the end, it's not in a book at all, though. I find what I'm looking for in the box of one of the board games. Disney Villains Monopoly, as it happens. There's no tiny coffin, but there is a figure. I know at once that it's different. It's bigger for a start and much more crudely made, out of Blu-Tack rather than modelling clay. The other figure had a few strands of human hair attached to it – I shiver slightly at the memory – whereas this one has a long Blu-Tack bob framing its face.

The figure is still small enough to hold in the palm of my hand and for a long time this is what I do. It grimaces back at me with the mouth that's been carved into its Blu-Tack face. Only when the fire alarm shrieks into life do I finally remember the brownies I put in the oven. Even then I don't move. I'm wondering if the doll is meant to be me.

Chapter Forty-Eight

Beth

'Thanks for making time for this.' Laura gives me a tense nod, and I wonder if I've made the right decision. I confided in her quite a lot last night, but this is taking it to a whole new level. Plus, last night we'd drunk two bottles of wine and now it's two thirty in the afternoon and we're both awkwardly sober. If I don't tell someone though, I think I might go mad. Maybe I've already gone mad. In fact, could I be sane and think some of the things I've thought over the past few hours?

'Will Rosie be okay without you?'

'It's fine,' Laura says, after a pause that makes me wonder if even my attempt at making conversation came out weirdly. Can she already tell I'm falling apart? 'She's sleeping.'

'I hope your mum and dad won't mind keeping an eye on Dolly for a while longer.' I know I'm babbling. 'I just really need to talk this through with someone. I tried talking to Noah, but he's so far away and he's worried about his dad, and anyway I can't talk to him about this over the phone, it's too complicated. It's the same with my friend Sasha. I thought I could explain, but I ended up sounding like a crazy woman. I need to speak with someone who's physically here if that makes sense.'

As I say this, I'm suddenly conscious of how much the world of Fortune's Yard – never expansive – has shrunk over the past few days. First Noah, then Ralph and now Evelyn. The people who are physically here are literally me, Dolly, Meg, Stuart and Laura.

'Where do you want to go?' Laura asks.

We've reached the junction in the lane. The sun is still beating down on us; it hasn't lost any of its heat yet.

'I don't mind. Anywhere. Not further into the woods,' I say suddenly, remembering Hannah's Grove.

'Let's go out across the marsh,' Laura says, turning left back towards the Old Watermill. 'Have you been that way?'

'I don't think so.' I'm reminded again how little I know this place that I now call home. Laura opens a small wooden gate beside a footpath sign, further down from our house, on the opposite side of the lane. Bluebell and Drake have already bounded through and set off ahead of us. The first few metres of the path are narrow, forcing Laura to walk ahead of me, but then it widens out into a grassy track, with rushes either side, and I move next to her.

'It's so beautiful here,' she says, and for the first time since we came outside she sounds almost relaxed, more like the Laura I shared dinner and confidences with last night. 'In London, I feel like I'm trapped – by people, by the buildings, even by the sky pressing down on me. But here I feel free. I can be anyone. Anything is possible.' She turns to me, her face eager, almost childlike. 'Do you know what I mean?'

This is so exactly the opposite of how I feel about Fortune's Yard that for a moment I can't think of how to reply. I wonder again whether this conversation with

Laura is such a good idea. So much of where I've ended up is to do with the bad feeling this place gives me. How can I begin to explain that to a person who so clearly loves it? But before I can change my mind, Laura says, 'So what is it you want to talk to me about?'

'It's kind of hard to explain.' Okay, here goes. 'So, please don't laugh at me, but ever since we got here, I've had this strange feeling that something's wrong.'

'Wrong?' she asks sharply. It's not the most encouraging start, but she's definitely not laughing at me, at least. I plough on, already half committed. 'I thought at first it was the place. That there was something wrong with Fortune's Yard, or something wrong going on here.' There's a deep frown line in the centre of Laura's forehead. Like Noah, she's very defensive of her childhood home, so I say quickly, 'But then I started to think it isn't really the place at all. It's Dolly's reaction to it.'

'I thought Dolly loved it here?'

'She does.' Up ahead, Bluebell has caught sight of a bird or small animal in the rushes and is barking loudly and running up and down; Drake is watching, his body quivering with excitement. I call Bluebell and eventually she trots back towards us looking contrite. Laura is waiting for me to continue. 'Okay, this is going to sound ridiculous, but hear me out. Do you think Dolly might be a bit *too* into Fortune's Yard? Into the history of it, I mean?' I don't want Laura to think I'm blaming her, so I add quickly, 'I know you were just telling her a story when you told her all about Hannah Fortune and what happened to her, but she's taken it like it's the literal truth.'

'It *is* the truth. It's well documented.'

'The historical facts, yes, sure,' I say, 'but I mean the stuff about Hannah's powers and everything. The idea that her spirit's still here, in Fortune's Yard.'

'Lots of people do believe that, Beth. Not just the locals – visitors, too. That's why people come here to see Hannah's Grove.'

'I get that. Some people love those kinds of stories. I'm just not sure it's a very healthy thing for Dolly to believe.'

'What exactly are you worried about?'

'I found a clay figure. In the grove. I think Dolly might have put it there.'

We walk for a few moments in silence.

'Would that be such a terrible thing?'

'Dolly's been through a lot. I know Noah and everyone else thinks she's recovered, but I'm not sure she has at all. She's not my child,' I feel the familiar uncertainty, 'and maybe I'm wrong, but I think she's still quite damaged by what happened. She's at an age when the borders between truth and fantasy are still quite blurred. I don't think it's healthy for her to spend her days obsessing about a teenage witch who has the power over life and death.'

'Maybe the stories help Dolly. Hannah can help you reconnect with the people you've lost.'

'Dolly told me Hannah killed Ralph.'

I think I say it so abruptly because I want to jolt Laura out of her childhood faith in all this Hannah nonsense. I want to provoke a reaction. In this, at least, I succeed.

'Why would she say that?' For the first time, Laura sounds shaken.

'I don't know. The thing is, Laura, I've even started to think that maybe, okay I don't know if I can say this…' In front of us the land stretches out flat and vast, the sky and the water of the marshland the same blue so that it's hard to tell where one ends and the other begins. The rushes are golden brown. Seagulls circle overhead. Again, I have that contradictory feeling of oppressive, claustrophobic *space*.

'Go on.'

'I'm starting to think that maybe she somehow knows something about his death.'

This is as far as I can go.

'That's quite a leap. I know you're worried about her interest in Hannah's Grove, but why would she have anything to do with what happened to Ralph?'

I can't answer this because it's the *why* I don't understand. Instead, I explain about Dolly leaving the house last night.

'You think she was in the pub?'

'I don't know what to think. I keep going over and over it in my head. I really don't want to believe what I'm thinking, but I can't stop thinking it, and I don't know what I should do.' We've come to a halt at a viewpoint and we lean on the fence, gazing out across the marshland. 'I told you you'd think I was a crazy lady.' I mean it to come out as a joke, but even I can hear my voice wobbling. Laura puts her hand on my arm.

'Hey, you've had a tough few days.'

'So, you do think it's all in my head?'

'I think you're right to be worried about Dolly. Grief like that doesn't just go away. When she came down here with Noah the other weekend, she was really upset about her mum. I found her sobbing her heart out. I was going to say something to Noah, but she begged me not to. I told her the stories because I thought they might help. I'm sorry that they've just caused more problems.'

'It's really not your fault. What do you think I should do?'

'I think you should talk to Dolly. Ask her where she was last night.'

'As simple as that?'

'You might be surprised. She might even want to tell you.'

'You don't think I should wait for Noah to come back?'

'You're worried about her now aren't you?'

I nod.

'Then talk to her. She's just a child Beth, and just because she's hiding stuff it doesn't mean that it's bad stuff or that she's a bad person. Don't wait for Noah. You can do this as well as he can.'

'He's her dad, though.'

'You'll just do it differently.'

Laura's right. It's obviously the sensible thing to do rather than going over and over it in my head and coming to a worse conclusion every time.

'Beth,' Laura says, suddenly. 'What did you do with the figure you found in the grove?'

Chapter Forty-Nine

Beth

My Blended Family has lots of advice about difficult conversations with your stepchildren and I'm frantically cramming it as though my upcoming chat with Dolly is an exam that I can revise for and that I'll pass as long as I put in enough work. As I scroll, I wonder about the endless variety of other difficult conversations that must be taking place. I can't imagine anyone's had one quite along these lines, though. Where the articles give examples, they're usually mundane things like rudeness or step-siblings not getting on. I find myself longing for the days when all I was worrying about was Dolly being rude to me. We seem to have escalated pretty quickly over the past few days from pretending she can't hear me to threatening to invoke witchcraft to have me killed. And probably one is as petty and silly and ultimately unthreatening as the other. Laura is right: Dolly's just a child, and she's clearly a damaged one, but that doesn't make her a bad person. She's lashing out. This place has made things worse, not better, but that's not Dolly's fault. She needs our help – mine and Noah's – and right now, with Noah thousands of miles away, I'm all she's got. I can't screw this up.

The articles are all pretty similar, but I keep reading in the hope that the next one will contain some morsel of advice I haven't come across yet and that will make this turn out okay. Everything I've read so far emphasises the importance of active listening. The assumption here is that Dolly will say something that I can actively listen to, whereas my main fear is that she'll simply refuse to talk to me and nothing I read explains what to do if that happens. Apparently, I should also pick a neutral space. A car journey can be good, suggests one article, because the pressure of making eye contact all the time is removed. There is no way I'm having this conversation with Dolly in a car. There is no way I'm even getting in a car with her. As I think this, I remember how genuinely frightened I was of her on the journey back from the station, and doubt starts to creep in again. If Dolly actually has something to do with Ralph's death and genuinely means me harm, shouldn't I be doing something rather more about it than encouraging her to confide in me? Shouldn't I be talking to the police? I think of DS Lee and her colleague, and I wonder what they would make of all of this if I tried to share any of it with them. Then I try to imagine how Noah would react when he found out what I'd done.

Behind me, the kitchen door opens and, wraith-like, Dolly enters. She glides over to the cupboards by the sink, neither speaking nor acknowledging me. She's been in her room since I picked her up from Meg and Stuart's an hour ago and God knows what she's been doing while she's been up there. Maybe more research on my parents. But then I'm hardly in a position to talk; I've been searching through her personal possessions.

My Blended Family is adamant that difficult conversations should be planned; you shouldn't just launch into them. But this one can't wait. I need to do it now before I lose my nerve.

'Hey,' I say, aiming for friendly. My heart is thumping. Her back is to me, as she stands on tiptoe searching for something in the cupboard. Her white-gold hair is loose and cascading over her shoulders. 'Looking for something in particular?'

I sound inane even to my own ears. She doesn't reply. I take a deep breath. My opening line is lifted from an article called 'Eight ways to start your tough conversation'.

'Dolly, I'd like us to have a bit of a chat about what's happened over the past few days.'

'I'm busy.'

Be persistent but patient. Don't let the situation escalate.

'When would be a good time to talk about it?'

She doesn't reply. Her back says never.

'Dolly, please don't ignore me.'

She sighs theatrically and spins round.

'What do you mean "what's happened"?'

'Shall we go for a walk?'

'No. If you want to talk, we can talk here.'

I don't think the kitchen counts as a neutral space. It's firmly my territory, but My Blended Family is silent on what to do if the other half of the conversation refuses to budge.

'I just wanted to ask you how you're feeling about what happened.'

'Why do you keep saying that? "What happened"?'

'Okay, about Ralph's death then.'

'I'm glad he's dead. He was a horrible person,' she says defiantly, but with a hint of childishness that makes me hope again that this really is all teenage bravado.

'I agree with you,' I say, and have the momentary satisfaction of both disconcerting her and getting her full attention. 'I didn't like him much either, but nobody deserves to die, Dolly.'

She's silent, but she is at least listening to me now.

'Why don't you sit down?'

To my surprise, she does. She regards me warily across the table, but her eyes are less hostile now. She even asks me a question.

'Evelyn's gone away, hasn't she? Aunty Meg said.'

'Yes, one of her sons came to pick her up.'

'Was she sad? When you saw her?'

'Very sad, and quite confused. She saw me waving from the end of the path and she thought it was Ralph.'

Dolly looks down, picking at the primrose-yellow polish on her nails.

'Poor Evelyn,' she says. 'I mean, I guess she thought that if she wishes enough, he'll come back.'

'I guess she did.'

She looks up again, holds my gaze.

'Do you think he will?'

'Oh Dolly. I don't think he'll come back, but he'll live on through Evelyn's memories of him.'

Her eyes fill with tears and she pushes her chair back.

'Please don't go.'

'I've told you.' She wipes her eyes with her sleeve and sniffs. 'I'm sorry about Evelyn. I don't care much about *him*, but I'm sorry about her.'

'There are some questions I still need answers to.'

'What do you mean? What questions?'

'Did you see anything when you went outside last night?'

Instantly, she tenses up again.

'I don't know what you're talking about. I didn't go outside last night.'

'I found your shoes.'

A red flush creeps over her face.

'That doesn't mean anything. I was in my room last night.'

'I don't think you were. I need to know where you went.'

'Are you saying I'm lying?'

Stay calm. Avoid direct confrontation.

'Yes.'

She's biting her lip so hard that it starts to bleed. She doesn't answer, but she doesn't get up from the table either, and this gives me some hope.

'Please Dolly, just tell me about it.'

'I hate you. I'm not going to tell you anything.'

This at least is according to the script. 'I hate you' is a staple of the difficult conversation according to My Blended Family, and it doesn't mean anything, it's just a way of showing fear and frustration. Again, the hope kindles. Even the way she says it sounds almost perfunctory. There's no real venom to it.

'It's important. You might have seen something that could help the police.'

'I didn't see anything.'

'So you *were* outside?'

She raises startled eyes to mine and then snaps back, 'I didn't see anything because I wasn't outside.'

For a moment, we stare at each other across the table. A stand-off in our duel. Bluebell is on her feet, her gaze travelling anxiously between us, sensing the tension.

'Tell me about the doll.'

All the colour leaves her face.

'What?'

'The Blu-Tack doll. I found it in your room.'

She gets up so suddenly her chair goes flying.

'You went through my things! Those are private!'

I get up too, and move behind my own chair. The ferocity of the response is frightening.

'Just tell me, please.' I hope my voice doesn't sound as wobbly as I feel.

'I'm not telling you anything.' Her voice is low now, and steadier, but no less intense.

'Was the first doll you made supposed to be Ralph?'

'What? No! Why would I make a doll of Ralph?'

I can't quite bring myself to say *Because you wanted him dead*. What I do say is almost as bad though.

'Because you argued with him. Because he knew about your mum.'

And as soon as it's out of my mouth I know I've made a mistake. She turns a stricken face to me.

'What about my mum?'

Now I've started this, I realise I have to see it through.

'You told me before it was your fault your mum was dead.'

She reacts as if I'd punched her. She literally crumples in front of me, sinking to the floor, her knees up against her chest, her head buried in her hands, like a ball – a sobbing and shaking ball. Bluebell goes over to her. After a moment's frozen horror at what I've done, I do the same. I crouch beside her. She's distraught and I want to put my arms around her, but I'm not sure how she'll react if I do.

'You think I killed my mum?' she sobs.

'Oh Dolly, of course I don't.' And right now, in this moment, I mean it: it seems ludicrous that I could ever have thought that.

'It was my fault though,' she wails. 'It was all my fault.'

The sobs that wrack her slight body are almost unbearable to watch. This time I do put an arm around her, and she doesn't flinch. She clings to me. I hold her tightly and with my free hand, I stroke her hair. Gradually, the sobs subside. I'm still holding her in my arms and I squeeze her tight. My urge to ask her more questions is almost overwhelming.

'Let's get you up and find you some tissues.' I help her to her feet and then leave her standing, forlorn, by the kitchen table, Bluebell panting and looking up at her, willing her to be Dolly again. I pick up the kitchen roll and bring it over to her. Gently I dry her face. And, miraculously, in the moment – a moment no article could ever have prepared me for – I find I do actually know what to say.

'Would it help to tell me about it?'

'I don't know if I can. I've never told anybody.'

She sinks into one of the chairs, and I sit down beside her. Still acting on the intuition I didn't know I possessed, I take her hand, and she doesn't attempt to pull away. Her fingers close around mine and, in spite of the fact that I don't know what exactly she's about to tell me, I feel something close to elation.

'We were in the car together.' Her voice is so quiet that it's quite hard to make out the words. 'Mum and me. She was driving me back from my friend Alice's birthday and I was annoyed with her because she'd come earlier than all the other parents, and I didn't want to be the first to leave. Alice was my best friend and I wanted to be there until the end. I should have been there.' This seems really important to her and I nod in an attempt to reassure her that I get it. 'Mum and me had an argument about it before we got in the car. We stood on the pavement in the rain shouting –

I was shouting anyway, I think she was just annoyed at me. She said it wasn't her purpose in life to be a taxi service for me and I should be grateful I was getting a lift at all.'

She isn't looking at me any more. Instead, she's staring straight ahead, her eyes slightly glazed, as though she's seeing what she's describing. She is still holding my hand, though, and her grip is so tight I think she might cut off my circulation.

'I said, actually it kind of was her purpose in life to be a taxi service for me. She'd given birth to me, hadn't she? I hadn't asked to be here. I said she owed me. It was silly stuff to start with. I was just a kid,' she says, in a voice that suggests she has aged decades since then. She's silent for a while, but I sense that talking at this point, saying anything at all, could ruin everything, so instead I give a murmur of acknowledgement and it's enough for her to continue. 'Mum got in the car, and I remember thinking that maybe I'd go back inside – that I'd go back to Alice's party – but when I turned to look back at the house I could see Alice's mum, watching us from the living room window. I think she'd been there the whole time and she'd seen me yelling, and so I got in the car.'

I shift my position slightly and the grip on my hand tightens. I still don't dare say anything in case it breaks the spell. With unseeing eyes staring straight ahead, she continues.

'As we pulled away, my mum said the worst thing of all.' Her voice catches. 'She said she'd been talking to Alice's mum about me behind my back, and that they both thought that Alice and I were too close, and that I should try to make other friends. She said the school were worried about me, that I was too friendly with her. It was all because of some stupid thing that happened in class before the summer holidays. How can you be too friendly with someone?

'I told Mum that if she tried to separate me and Alice I'd die, and she said if I was going to say such ridiculous things she was going to stop talking to me. She used to do that sometimes, when she was angry with me. She'd go totally silent and refuse to speak to me. I hated it. It made me feel like I didn't exist. It would go on for hours sometimes.'

This time she does look at me, her eyes beseeching.

'Oh Dolly, I'm sorry. That sounds very difficult.'

She looks away again.

'So, I started saying things to her. Horrible things. I didn't mean them. I just wanted to get a reaction out of her.' She pauses and in the silence I'm conscious of the kitchen clock ticking. The whole space seems even more still than usual. Then Bluebell comes over and pushes her head onto Dolly's lap, and with her free hand Dolly starts stroking Bluebell's ears. 'I told her that I wished she wasn't my mum and that I'd never loved her. You can't even imagine the things I said.'

The strange thing is, I can. They're the things I thought about my own parents when I first found out the details of what they'd done – when the true horror of the lives they'd destroyed, and the lies they'd told, became apparent. I'd never said any of them; I'd just fled. And now, all these years later, I wonder if it might have been better if I had. If I'd yelled and screamed, would it actually have helped me to move on, rather than having that resentment festering inside me? Then I imagine Juliet sitting in the driver's seat listening to her daughter shout insults at her. I think about how that must have felt and how that might have distracted her from the road in front of her. Noah said that it had been torrential rain on the day of the accident, so driving conditions must already have been tricky, and with the addition of a furious Dolly, I can see how Juliet's reactions might have been slower than usual. I can see also how Dolly blames herself for what happened. What a terrible, terrible guilt to have to live with.

'When I started saying that stuff, we were going round this big bend in the road, and Mum looked over at me – just for a few seconds – and then,' Dolly's voice speeds up, as though she needs to get through this bit as quickly as possible, 'the car skidded a bit and then there was a lorry coming towards us and she swerved back, but too hard and then we swerved off the road altogether and there was a tree and I knew we were going to slam into it, and it was slippy and they said it was the rain, but it wasn't, it was me.' She drops my hand suddenly, like it's scalding her, and turns her head away. 'That's why I'm a terrible person.'

This time I fill the silence straight away.

'Your mum would have known you didn't mean any of the things you said. I promise. She loved you. You would have made it up later.'

'I know,' she whispers. 'I know that. But we never got a chance.'

'It wasn't your fault. Dolly, look at me. It was an accident. No one would blame you.'

'I want to talk to Mum again. I need to talk to her.'

I hear Laura saying *Hannah can help you reconnect with the people you've lost*. And suddenly I get it, or at least part of it.

'Dolly, is that why you're so interested in Hannah's Grove?' I try to keep my voice as neutral as possible. 'You think that Hannah Fortune can bring your mum back?'

'Laura told me it can happen,' she says doggedly. 'You leave a figure there to represent the person you've lost, and Hannah can bring them back to you. But it takes time and you can't move the figure or the magic doesn't work. It explains all about it in the book at Aunty Meg's.'

A whole series of thoughts are tumbling into place like dominoes falling.

'That's where you went last night, isn't it? You took the figure I found back to Hannah's Grove.' She hesitates. Her eyes are wary again, but I'm sure I'm right. 'That's why I can't find it anywhere in the house – you took it back because it represents your mum.'

Her expression clears slightly. She sounds almost relieved when she replies.

'I knew you had her in your room,' she says. The pronoun is more than a little creepy, but I hope my face doesn't betray me. 'I saw you put her in the drawer by your bed, so when you were downstairs with Laura, I thought it was the perfect time.' This certainly makes sense of her early exit last night. 'I knew you'd be in there for ages because you had a bottle of wine and everything, so I went into your bedroom and I found her there with all kinds of other stuff, just lying around. It felt so wrong seeing her there. I needed to put her back where she belonged.'

I can't help myself. 'But it was dark – the grove is miles away.'

'It wasn't actually dark when I left. It was kind of dusk and I thought I could get there and back before it got properly dark, before you'd noticed I'd gone. It's not that far, really.'

'So you just set off into the woods by yourself?'

'I wanted to take Bluebell with me, but I thought you'd notice if she wasn't there.' The fact that Dolly thought I would notice a missing dog before a missing child is a pretty damning indictment of my parenting skills. 'Besides, I wasn't scared,' she says. I imagine her making her way past shadowy tree trunks and branches, hearing the rustle of animals and birds in the undergrowth. Seeing their eyes. It must have taken real guts; I'm not sure I could have done it. The belief that drove her to do it, that kept her going down that path, is no temporary whim or teenage fancy. In the heat of the August afternoon, I shiver.

'When you got there, what did you do?'

'I put her back.'

'That's it?'

'That's how it works. You have to make a figure to represent the person you want to come back,' she says doggedly. 'And lay it in the tunnel and say the spell. Then you wait.'

'And that's what you did last night?'

She nods.

'I had to say the spell again, in case you'd broken it when you moved her.'

'What did you do next?'

'I came back,' she says matter-of-factly. 'It was getting dark then so it took me longer.'

'Did you see anyone? When you got back to Fortune's Yard?'

'No.'

It's the speed with which the answer comes that makes me doubt.

'No one at all? Ralph must have been in the Fortune's Arms some time that evening.'

'I didn't see him, or Aunty Meg. Or anyone.'

'Meg?'

'She told me that sometimes she walks Drake in the evenings, but she must have done it earlier.'

'Were there lights on? In Ralph and Evelyn's cottage, or in the Fortune's Arms?'

'I don't remember.'

'You must have passed both buildings.'

'Do you still think I had something to do with what happened to Ralph?' Her voice is panicked.

'Of course not,' I say, but I do think there's something she's still not telling me. 'Dolly, you told me earlier today that Ralph was your enemy. What did you mean?'

'I just meant that he was horrible about Hannah and now he's dead.' I wait. 'When you saw him arguing with me it was because he'd found out Laura and I had been to Hannah's Grove. I told him about Hannah's spells and he said it was mumbo jumbo and against God, and he said I'd go to hell. But I don't care about Ralph,' she sounds tearful again, 'all I care about is my mum and the chance to see her.'

It makes my heart break that Dolly thinks a clay figure and a spell is going to bring her mum back.

'Dolly, you know your mum will always be with you?' She looks away, her eyes full of tears. 'You carry her inside you. You and your dad, and all the people who love her, will mean that she'll always be here.'

I keep my voice gentle. I want to put my arm around her again, but I'm still wary of whatever it is we're building up between us, and I don't want to ruin it. I slide my fingers over the table towards hers.

'What did you do to your hand?'

'Oh, it's nothing. I cut it on some glass earlier.'

'It looks nasty. You should be careful. It might get infected.'

272

'I washed it well.'

She sniffs, wipes away some of the tears. Her face looks less stricken. The return to the everyday has broken the sombre mood and, as if to acknowledge this, Dolly says simply, 'Can I go and watch *Friends*?'

Later, sitting at the kitchen table surrounded by the flapjacks I've just made, and that I managed not to incinerate, I sift through Dolly's story about what happened last night. I think I believe most of what she told me. It makes sense that Ralph would berate her about going to Hannah's Grove, and the story of taking the tiny clay figure back there is so odd that I feel like it can't have been made up. But as I get up to put the flapjacks away, a detail strikes me. The little coffin that I found – the one that Dolly says she returned to the woods last night – had a letter on it. The letter R. Not J for Juliet. And I know there's something about what's going on here, in this strangest of places, that I'm still missing.

On some level, though, Dolly really does believe Hannah can bring her mum back to her and, although my parenting skills are improving rapidly, I'm still not sure how to tackle this. For the first time, it occurs to me to wonder what Dolly might plan to do with me if she brought Juliet back. *It might get infected.* It's a disquieting echo of that moment in the car: *You might swerve going round that next corner and drive straight into a tree.*

Chapter Fifty

Beth

'How's your dad doing?'

'So much better.' I can hear the relief in Noah's voice. 'Almost like his old self again. He's going to be out of hospital tomorrow, so I'll just see him settled and then I'll be back with you on Friday. How's everything there?'

I swallow. I'm standing at the end of our garden, next to the creepy scarecrow family. It feels like months since I first saw them and thought they were real people, rather than five days. There's a fish pie cooking in the oven for dinner, and I've poured myself a glass of chilled white Rioja – in an attempt to keep a grip on normality. I have the glass in one hand and my phone in the other.

'A lot's been happening.'

I last spoke to Noah less than twelve hours ago but it feels like it was another lifetime, and hearing him now is like a forgotten link to an outside world. This place suffocates you without you even realising it. You forget that there are other lives and other people, and Laura, Noah, Meg and Stuart may all find that liberating, but I find it oppressive.

'How are you feeling?' he asks. 'I've been worried about you since this morning. It must have been a huge shock finding Ralph like that.'

It's a few moments before I can trust my voice. Noah's return on Friday seems an inordinately long time away. More than two whole days.

'I'm okay — well, not really. I mean I *am* okay.'

'Now I'm really worried,' he says lightly, but I can hear the anxiety underlying his tone.

'There's some stuff I should probably tell you about. To do with Dolly. She's fine,' I add quickly. 'She's up in her room at the moment. I thought I'd come out into the garden and give you a call.'

'What stuff Beth?'

I can tell he's trying to keep his voice calm.

'She's been quite shaken up by what happened to Ralph,' I start. While I was making dinner, I thought carefully about how best to tell him — even about whether I should tell him at all, or whether it would be better to wait until he's back, but I think it's important that he knows at least some of it. 'And she's kind of got it all mixed up in her head with the stories Laura's been telling her about the history of Fortune's Yard. You remember we talked the other evening about how interested she was in them?'

'The witchcraft stories, you mean?'

Noah's voice is wary.

'Yes. When you talk to me about them it's like they're some kind of nostalgic childhood ritual you all experienced when you were growing up and now it's Dolly's chance to enjoy them.'

'I told you the other night, I'm sorry. I didn't mean it to sound like that.'

'My point is that you didn't literally believe those stories, did you?'

275

'I don't know, we probably did for a while. Hannah Fortune and her magic powers.'

'What exactly did you think she had the power to do?'

'God knows. It was a very long time ago.'

'It's important, Noah.'

'Okay, then.' He sounds taken aback. 'I guess we thought she had power over life and death.'

'Specifically?'

'Beth, what is this? What's Dolly been saying?'

'I really need to know.'

'Specifically,' he says, 'we thought she had the power to bring the dead back to life.'

I feel a wave of relief. So, Dolly was telling me the truth about the figure in the coffin. It really was meant to be her mother, not Ralph. And the spell was to bring her back to life, not to end a life.

'Oh shit, Beth.' Noah has finally made the connection. 'Is this going where I think it is?'

'Yes, Dolly believes – and I mean truly believes – that Hannah Fortune can bring Juliet back. I'm sorry.'

There's silence. In the background I can hear Amy's kids shouting something to each other. Finally, Noah says, 'I'm such an idiot. When you told me before that she was getting too interested in Hannah's Grove, I should have thought about why.'

'You know that little figure I found in the coffin in the grove? Dolly made that.'

'*Dolly* made the figure you showed me?'

'Yes.'

'She told you that?'

'Yes.'

'I wouldn't have thought she was capable of it. It seems a weird thing to say, Beth, but it was so beautifully made. Dolly's never been any good at things like that.'

'She thinks it's her mum,' I say. It's a bit brutal but I need to break through his denial. 'She would have taken her time over it, she'd want it to be perfect.' I remember the second doll, far cruder in design, but maybe she hadn't finished it yet. And then I think about the other thing that's bothering me: the little R on the coffin and the feeling that I've missed something important. Something that will make everything fall into place. 'Noah, did Juliet have a nickname at all?'

'A nickname?'

'What did Dolly call her?'

'Mum. She called her "Mum". Why are you asking?'

'It doesn't matter. Just something that doesn't quite make sense.'

'Beth, I'm so sorry that you're having to deal with all of this. It's all my fault and I'm not even there.'

'There's no point in blaming yourself.'

The words come out automatically, but as I say them, I realise that a bit of me actually does blame Noah for this – not for exactly what's happened, I don't think anyone could have foreseen that – but for not realising, or not wanting to realise, just how damaged his daughter still is. 'But when you're back we need to talk about this properly, and decide what we're going to do. Dolly needs us right now,' I say, and for once the 'us' comes naturally.

'Of course. Maybe it would help if she started seeing a counsellor again. She saw one for the first couple of years after Juliet died.'

'Maybe.'

What I want to say is: *I think we need to get her out of here.* Back to Starbucks, drama club, trampolining and vaping on street corners. Back to normality, because whatever else this place is, it's very far from normal. But that's a conversation I need to have with Noah in person.

'It sounds like you've had a crash course in extreme parenting.'

'It's not all bad,' I say, wanting to share something positive with him. Not the false positive of perpetual optimism – I'm done with polite lies about Dolly – but something messy and real. At the same time, I'm slightly hesitant to talk about something that still seems so fragile. 'I think we're making progress, Dolly and me. I think from the start she's really resented me for trying to fill her mum's place – no don't say anything,' I add as he tries to interrupt me. 'I know that's not what I'm doing, but it's how Dolly sees it. It's how she's always seen it, ever since that first day you introduced us, and you pretending otherwise hasn't helped.'

There's silence thousands of miles away in San Francisco.

'It's my fault, too. I've been so hung up with all the stuff about my own parents, so unsure about the whole parenting thing, that I've let her get away with behaving the way she has. I should have challenged her long ago and I know I should have told you way back that we were having problems. The thing is, I'm telling you now because I don't feel like that any more. I'm not saying there will never be problems again, but I think the two of us have turned a corner.' He still hasn't said anything. I plough on, determined to make him understand. 'Things have got worse in a way – she's been so much more openly hostile since you went, but I'm starting to realise that might actually be a good thing. That it's better to have this stuff out in the open and to be able to talk about it. It's been really intense, and maybe it's always going to be difficult, but I'm realising that being a parent, or a step-parent, or whatever I am, isn't about always having a perfect relationship with your child. Sometimes it's chaotic and painful, but that's how the relationship builds, that's how you develop something meaningful. I don't want to run away this time, like I did with my mum and dad. I thought I did, but I don't. I want to stick it out. I want to find out how Dolly and I are going to end up.' I look back across the sun-dappled garden towards the Old Watermill. 'Noah? Are you still there?'

'I'm here.' There's another pause and finally he fills it: 'I should have said this before, but Dolly does find it quite difficult to form attachments to people. And when she does, they're sometimes a bit intense.'

I think of Dolly's puzzled voice saying *How can you be too friendly with someone?*

'Like with her friend Alice?'

'She told you about Alice?'

'A bit,' I say carefully. Noah must know that it was Alice's party that Juliet and Dolly were driving back from the day of the crash.

'Alice joined Dolly's class part of the way through primary school and it was like there was this instant bond between them. Dolly's always struggled to make proper friends. I mean, she's not unpopular, the other kids like her, but she tends not to have anyone she's close to, and then when she does find someone, it's like she goes a bit over the top. Dolly would have done anything for Alice. When her family moved to Spain it was really tough for her. It took her about a year to get over it, and she hasn't really had a friend like Alice since.'

I don't know if he's aware of the emphasis he places on the last word, but it makes me ask, 'What about before Alice?'

'She was just a young kid before that.'

'Noah, I know there's something you're not telling me. Dolly's my responsibility too. You said it yourself, if we're going to co-parent, we have to trust each other, and I have to understand Dolly's past.'

'You know all the big stuff.'

'Then tell me the little stuff. Tell me what's in your head right now.'

'Okay, there is one other thing, but this is going way back. She can't have been more than four. And it's not so much the thing itself. It's what she said afterwards. There was this one kid in her reception class – Jake – and Dolly adored him. She used to have these huge tantrums when it was the end of a playdate and Jake's dad came to pick him up. Once, Jake's dad was leading him out of the playground and she launched herself from the very top of the climbing frame and landed almost on top of him. He nearly fell over and of course she ended up on the tarmac and she was bleeding from this big gash on her leg, but she didn't react at all. She just went up and hugged Jake. When we were talking about it later, I said, "You could have hurt yourself really badly." And she said: "I could have killed myself."'

This time the silence is mine, as I try to absorb this, and try also to process the hesitation in his voice as he told me.

'What else?' I say finally.

'Isn't that enough?'

'I can tell from the way you said it that there's something more.'

'There really isn't, Beth.'

But, for the first time in our relationship, I think he's lying to me.

Chapter Fifty-One

The Grief Counsellor

In our last session you mentioned that there's one thing that does make a difference to how you're feeling, that helps you cope. Are you ready to tell me some more about it?

I'm not sure. I don't think it's a good idea.

You know you can tell me anything? These sessions are just between the two of us.

I know. But if I tell you, I'm worried you'll think I'm going mad.

I'm not here to judge you.

The thing is, it really does help. But I know it's wrong, and I know it has to stop. I just don't know how – I don't think I can face losing this too. Even I think I'm going mad sometimes. I know I need to tell somebody about it. I nearly did today actually. I think it's the only way I can make it stop. But then other times I don't think I can bear for it to stop. It's all I have now.

Who did you nearly tell?

A friend. She's not really a friend I suppose, not yet. But I think she might become one. She's going through a lot of her own stuff at the moment and she's been telling me about some of it, and there was a moment when I thought she might understand.

What made you change your mind?

It's just got too big. It's impossible to tell.

What is it? This thing that's impossible to tell. If you share it with me, it might stop being so frightening.

The funny thing is, I think I've done what you said I should do. I've found the thing you talked about – you said to find a lasting connection, do you remember? And in a way it *is* helping me to lead a new life, so maybe you were right all along.

It's good you've found that connection, but I'm not sure I understand. Can you tell me a bit more. What is it that you're doing?

I pretend. That's all. I just pretend. That's not so wrong, is it? Grieving is all about pretending.

Chapter Fifty-Two

Beth

It's pitch black when I hear her scream. I'd been deep asleep and it takes me a few moments to fumble for the light switch and sit up. There's another scream. I fling myself out of bed and onto the landing without even thinking. Downstairs, Bluebell has started to bark.

'Dolly, I'm coming. Don't worry!'

Barefoot I run down the landing and wrench open her door. The fairy lights are casting an eerie glow around the room. She's sitting bolt upright in her bed, white-gold hair fanning out around her shoulders, her cheeks wet with tears.

'What is it?' I can hear the fear sharp in my voice. 'What happened?'

No answer. She's staring straight in front of her. I take a deep breath and try to be rational about this. There's no need to panic.

'Did you have a bad dream?' I step further into the room and place my hand gently on her shoulder. She flinches and turns to look at me with unseeing eyes. All at once I feel frightened again. It's like she's in some faraway place where I can't reach her. I try to make myself sound matter-of-fact. 'Dolly, it's me Beth. You're okay now, lovely. You were just dreaming.'

I kneel down beside the bed. She's still staring at me uncomprehendingly. I stroke her hand; it's freezing. Slowly, she focuses on me.

'It was just a dream,' I repeat.

'It wasn't,' she says in a small voice.

'You're safe in bed. I promise.' Now that's she's spoken, the spell has been broken; she's back with me and I feel in control again. I pull some tissues out of the box beside her bed. 'Here, take these. Do you want to tell me what it was all about?' I remember the nightmares I used to have about falling from the top of a spiral staircase and how describing them to my dad always used to make me feel better – and a fraction of a second after I think this I realise how strange it is to have a purely ordinary thought about my dad, one that's not tinged with resentment or bitterness. I think it's the first time for nearly two decades that this has happened. I force my mind back to Dolly – I suspect her nightmares are less abstract than mine used to be. In fact, I think I know exactly what her nightmares are about.

'Was it about your mum?'

She shakes her head. I notice the Blu–Tack figure I found in the board game box is lying on her bedside table, and a trickle of ice creeps its way down my spine. She follows my gaze.

'Shall we get up and go and make some hot chocolate?' I say brightly. 'Bluebell's worried about you. Can you hear her barking? Let's go down and see her. Where are your slippers? Pop those on or you'll get cold feet.'

I pick her dressing gown up from the back of the chair and hold it out for her. She climbs slowly out of bed, like an old lady, and puts her arms in the dressing gown, almost like she's still dreaming. She lets me tie it round her.

'Now, I'll go get my slippers too and we'll head down-stairs for a midnight snack. We can give Bluebell one of those disgusting pig's ears she likes.' As I head back down the landing to my own room, I'm keeping up a constant stream of chatter in the hope that it will give her time to adjust to waking up. I search for my slippers under the bed, and as I do, I think again about the contrast between the crudely shaped figure beside Dolly's bed and the flawless miniature human in the tiny coffin I found in the grove. Are they really the work of the same person? Dolly has such faith in Hannah's powers – and she's learnt that faith from Laura. I think of the bond between Laura and Dolly. And I have the same dominoes-falling feeling that I had earlier. Dolly would do anything for the people she becomes attached to. Has Laura lost somebody? Could the first figure I found belong to her? And did Dolly take it back because Laura is so important to her?

I head back out onto the landing, but Dolly hasn't appeared from her room yet. My brain is still whirring. How was it Noah had described Laura? A classic high achiever. A perfect replica person made by a perfectionist. It would make sense. The first doll was made by Laura; the second by Dolly. I'm sure of it, and with that certainty, I feel like I'm about to make a breakthrough – that I'm finally going to understand everything.

'Dolly? Are you coming?'

When she appears on the landing, there's a different look on her face – less blank, more guarded. She's properly awake now. Meeting her deep blue eyes, I feel moment-arily uncertain, but I decide to ask the question. After all, only a few hours ago I was lecturing Noah about how important it is that we all talk to each other and don't keep things to ourselves.

'Dolly, there's something I've been wondering. Did the figure you took back to Hannah's Grove belong to Laura?'

'Stop interfering!'

She moves so quickly that I feel the shock of her hands against my stomach before I've had time to register the danger I'm in. I topple backwards and it's as though everything is happening in slow motion. With my left hand I reach out to break my fall, but it slips off the edge of the stair and I carry on tumbling. I'm falling head first down the stairs and if I don't stop myself somehow, I'm going to crash down onto the tiled floor of the hallway. I don't want to think about what's going to happen then. With my flailing arms, I make a grab at the banister and my fingers manage to get a hold on it. My shoulder screams in pain as my arm takes the weight of the rest of my body, but I've managed to stop myself falling.

'Beth?' comes a voice from the top of the stairs.

Panic coursing through me, I scrabble to my feet as fast as I can. I'm about halfway down the stairs, and I know I need to get to the bottom right now. Clutching hold of the banister that saved me for support, I race down the remaining stairs. One of my slippers has already made the journey ahead of me, the other is still on my foot. My instinct is to run out of the front door and keep running until I get to Meg and Stuart's. But in spite of my terror, something keeps me rooted to the spot – some kind of new loyalty to Dolly, despite everything.

'Beth?' This time she appears at the head of the staircase; a slight figure with a white face.

We stare at each other.

'I'm so sorry.' And she sounds it. Her voice is shaking. Her eyes have lost the suspicious look of earlier and are huge and frightened. 'Are you all right?'

'You pushed me,' I say idiotically, my voice coming out as little more than a whisper. Almost every interaction I have with Dolly is so fraught with her reinterpreting what's happened and what's been said that part of me must feel that it's important to get this on the record.

'I'm sorry,' she says again. 'I didn't mean it. I didn't want to talk about the figures again, but I only pushed you away. I didn't know you were going to slip on Bluebell's ball.'

I glance down. Bluebell's old tennis ball is on the floor at the bottom of the stairs, beside me. My eyes on Dolly again, I try to remember whether I did in fact step on it before I fell backwards.

'I didn't mean to hurt you.'

She takes a step down on to the staircase, and I auto-matically take a step backwards in the hallway below. The front door is just behind me. It's not too late to run. But I don't feel the same intense urge to do this that I did a few moments earlier. Some of the immediate fear has passed. After all, she's a thirteen-year-old child. Even if she did push me down the stairs deliberately, she's hardly going to follow up the attack now. All the same, I'd rather not be too near her right now.

'I'm going to check on poor Bluebell,' I say, moving slowly and deliberately towards the kitchen, although I don't stop to put my other slipper on. The hand that I reach out to open the kitchen door is shaking. I notice that the cut from earlier has opened up again, and my shoulder is shrieking in pain. Bluebell bounds out, tail wagging, jumping up at me. She's a blessed relief, and I want to bend down and hug her, but I don't quite trust myself to do it with Dolly approaching. She's now hovering in the hallway behind me. I reach for the light switch in the kitchen, and electric light floods the scene. Dolly follows me in. She looks wretchedly unhappy and seems oblivious to Bluebell, who sits her big white hairy form at Dolly's feet, as though sensing something is very wrong.

'I'm going to make us those hot chocolates,' I say.

'I can't go back to bed. I'll dream. Don't make me.'

'No, okay.' The most important thing right now must be to keep her calm. I go to reach for the jar of hot chocolate, but to do that I'd have to turn my back on her, and I'm still not entirely sure I want to do that. I'm suddenly conscious of the knife block on the worktop, and the fact that I'm even thinking like this makes me wonder if I should have run out of the front door while I had the chance.

'Why don't you go and watch some TV?'

She nods, miserably.

'Something fun. How far have you got with *Friends*?'

'Season six,' she mumbles. And, despite everything else, a part of my brain is still capable of marvelling at how quickly teens can make their way through a TV series.

'Well if you go and find the next episode, I'll make us a drink and bring it in to you.'

She hesitates. I keep the reassuring smile plastered on my face, but I'm not sure how much longer I can hold it together.

'I honestly didn't mean it,' she whispers.

'You could have really hurt me.'

Killed me.

'I know. I'm sorry.'

'I'm going to have some impressive bruises,' I manage. What I really need is time to process what's just happened and to decide what to do next. I need her to leave. 'Go and find *Friends*. I'll be right in.'

She nods and walks disconsolately out of the door. Bluebell trots loyally behind her. I edge sideways so that I can watch as the pair of them make their way down the hall and into the library. I need to be sure that she's gone – and that she's doing what I said she should do. I hear the TV spring to life and all at once I collapse onto one of the kitchen chairs like all the breath has been forced out of me. My whole body is shaking now and I choke back a giant sob, biting on my uninjured hand to stop the noise bursting out of me.

What the hell just happened? Did Dolly panic because she didn't want to talk to me, and forgetting her own strength, shove me so that I accidentally fell down the stairs? Or did my stepdaughter just make a deliberate attempt to kill me? I honestly can't decide. But even the former is pretty terrifying. And what exactly was she so upset about? She didn't answer my question about Laura, and I'm certainly not going to ask it again any time soon. I'll have to find out the answer another way.

I get to my feet and move automatically around the kitchen, which is already starting to feel more familiar, filling the kettle, and finding mugs and the hot chocolate jar. I even add little marshmallows, more to delay the moment when I have to go into the library and face Dolly again than because I think this is a normal thing to do for a person who moments earlier pushed you down a flight of stairs. But I can't delay for ever, and besides, I suddenly need to be sure that she's still there. I can hear the hum of the TV, but it's just occurred to me that the TV doesn't necessarily equal Dolly. What if I go in there and she's vanished again? What if she's gone outside into the night? Or, and somehow this is even worse, she's somewhere in the house, waiting for me?

Okay, I need to go and look. I pick up the hot chocolates, but then something else occurs to me: my phone. I retrieved it from the bedside table when I went back to get my slippers, and somehow it made it through the fall still in my pyjama pocket. In fact, I remember crashing down on it when I first fell – there's going to be a phone-shaped bruise on my thigh. I put the hot chocolates down on the worktop again and pull it out. There are two cracks running right across the screen that weren't there before, but otherwise it seems to have survived all right. My first thought is to message Noah, but of course I can't. What could I possibly say? *Think Dolly might have tried to kill me.* I feel a hysterical sob rising up inside me again. Sasha. I'll message her. She'll know what to do. I need to send this message quickly and go and check on Dolly, so I don't give myself time to think. I tap out:

> Just had a scare with Dolly. We were talking and she got upset and pushed me and I fell. I'm fine nothing broken but a bit shaken. Really need advice. Please message asap. Don't call, I might be with D

I hit send and then shove the phone back in my pocket, pick up the mugs and practically run down the hall, slopping hot chocolate as I go. My whole body, not just my shoulder, is starting to ache. I needn't have panicked. The scene that greets me from the library door is about as innocuous and homely as you can get. Outside, through the French doors, it's pitch black and the wind is picking up, but inside Dolly is curled up on the big sofa, the green-and-blue checked throw pulled up around her, her hair

291

hanging loose down her back. Next to her, also on the sofa despite the ban Noah and I have imposed, is Bluebell, joyfully and nosily chewing one of her feet. On the big TV screen, I'm briefly confused by the sight of Reese Witherspoon talking to Jennifer Aniston.

'Hey,' Dolly says, sounding much more normal again now. 'Did you know she played Rachel's sister? How weird is that?'

'Pretty weird,' I say handing her the mug of hot chocolate. I regard her warily. Because, after all, perhaps a return to normality is the strangest thing of all after what just happened to us both.

'Laura says the cameos are the best.'

The name jars but I think I manage to keep my voice level as I reply, 'I think there's one with Brad Pitt in later.'

I take the uncomfortable armchair, needing to keep some physical distance between us. I check my route to the door.

'Yeah?' Dolly says, less interested in Brad Pitt than I am. To her, he must seem ancient. This is so ordinary, so low-key, I'm already starting to question what just happened. Dolly has settled back on the sofa, her eyes fixed on the screen, her expression relaxed. Her hands, with their chipped yellow nail polish, are wrapped around the mug I've given her. Every now and then she leans forward to stroke Bluebell's head.

Over the next few hours, we listen to the wind whistle round the side of the house and watch episode after episode of *Friends*, and although it is surreal, it is also strangely soothing. I see Chandler admit he can't cry, Rachel and Phoebe moving out of their fire-damaged apartment, Joey audition for a series about a detective and his crime-fighting robot, and it all seems vaguely familiar and safe. Occasionally, Dolly will say something – usually a reference to something she's seen on TikTok or YouTube; she doesn't mention Laura again and neither do I – and I'll reply, but mostly we're silent. I watch the first few episodes in a daze, but after a while, my brain kicks back in and I realise that what I have now is exactly what I craved: precious time to think. Okay, I'm not by myself, which is what I really want, but I know where Dolly is and she's so absorbed that I can allow my mind to focus on something other than my immediate surroundings.

My eyes still on the screen, I try to formulate a plan. I need to do something and fast. Noah isn't back until Friday and I don't have that long. I need a plan now. Obviously there's something going on here that I still don't understand, and I think Laura might be the key to unlocking it. Dolly didn't answer when I asked if the figure from the grove belonged to Laura, but what happened next was surely an answer in itself. On screen, Phoebe is helping Chandler shop for a wedding ring. The carriage clock that belonged to Noah's parents and which they left on the mantelpiece tells me it's just gone six a.m. I make a decision. In a couple of hours, I'm going to take Dolly round to Meg and Stuart's. She seems happy enough in their company. Any other time I'd worry about imposing on their kindness, but I've got bigger things to worry about right now. My idea is to get Laura by herself, explain what's happened with Dolly and ask her if she can help. If I'm right and the first figure I found belongs to Laura, then Laura must be grieving for someone too. For the first time it occurs to me that the source of the bond between Laura and Dolly might be grief, and if Laura is grieving, maybe Dolly is just protecting her. After all, Laura and I have talked about some pretty personal things over the past few days, so I feel like I can ask her if she's lost someone. I need to know what's going on here before I can decide what to do next.

Having a plan, at least for the short term, brings me peace of mind of sorts and for the first time in hours I allow myself to relax just a little. I find myself actually watching what's happening on screen, and I feel a small spark of optimism that I can still get through this, and that when Noah is back we can sort this out together. As the credits roll for the umpteenth time, it occurs to me that Dolly has been very quiet for the past half hour. She's curled up on the sofa with the throw still pulled around her. I get gingerly to my feet, my bruised body protesting, and have a closer look. She's asleep. She looks so peaceful and so perfect, with her face relaxed and her hair fanned out around her. I suddenly worry that my whole plan is a bit overkill. Is running to the neighbours, who in reality I barely know, and telling them I'm worried my stepdaughter might attack me again really the right reaction to what just happened on the stairs? Isn't it a little bit, well, hysterical? I imagine Laura picking up baby Rosie and jiggling her up and down while she tries to hide the fact she thinks I'm a useless parent. I imagine her telling Meg about it later and Meg, mum to three teenagers in the past, rolling her eyes as she agrees that I overreacted.

In my pyjama pocket, my phone vibrates. I pull it out and see a message from Sasha:

> You don't sound safe. You need help. Call me as soon as you can.

294

Chapter Fifty-Three

Beth

'Good morning!' I say as breezily as I can manage.

Stuart blinks back at me. The wind has died down again and it's another beautiful August morning. My watch tells me it's 7:38 a.m. A little early for a neighbourly call. Plus this is the second time in two days that I've arrived before eight a.m. and last time I'd found a body. No wonder he's a bit wary of me.

'I made some breakfast muffins and it's far too many for just me and Dolly, so I thought I'd bring them round here while they're still warm.'

'That's very kind of you.' Stuart's social skills have kicked in. 'They smell delicious.'

He reaches his hands out to take the box I'm holding. This is the danger point, the point when he can just take delivery of the muffins and close the door. He meets my eye. I can see him clocking that there might be something else going on here. He steps back.

'Please. Come in.'

I don't think I've ever accepted an invitation so rapidly.

'Good morning, Dolly,' he says as she follows behind me. 'You're up early. Final few days of the school holidays, you should be taking advantage of that lie-in.'

'I couldn't sleep,' Dolly says simply. 'I had a nightmare.' She's wearing a purple hoodie that's a bit too big for her, so that just the tips of her fingers are hanging out the end, and her eyes are still puffy from the broken night and the crying. She'd looked briefly panicked at the thought of heading over to Meg and Stuart's, but when I told her about the muffins I'd baked while she was asleep on the sofa and asked her to go and find her shoes, she'd agreed docilely enough. We haven't talked again about what happened on the stairs, but it's there all the time casting its shadow over us.

'Ah,' Stuart says, shooting me another glance, like he might be starting to understand what's going on here, although I can't imagine for a moment that he is. 'I must find you a bottle of my anti-nightmare potion, then,' he says gravely. 'It goes well with muffins.'

Dolly smiles at Stuart – his flights of fancy somehow still appeal to her, even though I would have thought she'd be too old for them. He must have been a good teacher. I remember Noah saying how Stuart was the adult they wanted to hang out with when they were kids, the one who was always up for a game of make-believe.

'Coffee for you, Beth?'

I can hear the concern in his voice, and I feel a wave of relief. I've done the right thing.

'Yes please.'

'Take a pew. Meg's just tying up the tomato plants – we noticed some of them had flopped over in the wind last night – and I think Laura's still upstairs, but I'm sure she'll be down in a minute.'

'Ah great,' I say. I go over to stand next to him at the worktop. 'I was hoping to catch her for a chat. There's something I want to ask her.' Dolly darts a suspicious look at me. 'It's to do with a contract for my new baking business,' I improvise.

If Stuart is surprised that I've popped round to see his high-flying lawyer daughter at seven thirty in the morning about a baking contract, he manages not to show it.

'Right you are,' he says, as if this is the most normal thing in the world, and then starts to make the coffees. Dolly pulls out her phone and taps away. I sit beside her at the kitchen table. For a few minutes, I have the illusion that everything is fine. Meg and Stuart's slightly gloomy, old-fashioned kitchen is in what I now recognise as its perpetual state of chaos, but it's a homely sort of a mess and Stuart moves among it easily, finding mugs and a cafetière. The earthy smell of the coffee is comforting. By the time Stuart hands me a mug, I'm already feeling like the situation is more manageable.

'Can I get you a juice, Dolly?'

'No, thanks,' she says politely, putting her phone back in her hoodie. 'Can I look at the Fortune's Yard book again please?'

'It's back on the shelf in the other room,' Stuart says. 'Let me get it down for you.'

It's on the tip of my tongue to say I don't want her to look at the book ever again, but then I realise that right now I should welcome anything that gets her out of the way so that I can talk to Laura, and get to the bottom of what's going on here. Dolly gets up and heads for the hallway. Stuart follows her, holding his coffee, but when she's out of the door, he closes it softly behind her.

'Laura won't be long,' he says quietly. 'Stay here, and I'll tell her to come down as soon as she can.' And then, 'Are you okay?'

I nod.

'I'll explain later.'

He raises an eyebrow.

'Fair enough. Teenagers, eh? Never a dull moment.'

I attempt to smile back at him.

For a few minutes, I sit on my own in the kitchen, sipping the coffee Stuart has made me, but the urge to talk to Laura is now almost overwhelming, and I keep worrying that Dolly will come back. I can hear floorboards creaking overhead so I decide to go up and find Laura. She might be a bit surprised but I'm sure she won't mind when I explain about last night. As I pass the living room door, I can hear Stuart's voice, in the middle of another story. I only hope this one is not about magic and witches. Surely Fortune's Yard must have some boring, ordinary history to relate as well.

At the top of the stairs, I pause, trying to get my bearings. It's just as cluttered upstairs in the Old Farmhouse as it is downstairs. The landing is crammed with bookshelves, piles of towels and empty plant pots. I can hear a shower running somewhere. There's a row of open doors to my right. One of them must be Laura's room. Maybe I'll wait for her there.

The first room I come to contains a king size bed, an exercise bike, a vacuum cleaner and piles of books. If it wasn't so full of stuff, it would be huge and I think it must be the main bedroom. The next room must be Laura's; it's clearer and has a double bed and a cot in it. The bed's unmade and a beautiful bedspread with big multi-coloured flowers splashed across it has been discarded on the polished wood floor, near the door. The curtains are still drawn, but the sun is stealing in around the edges. There's a suitcase with a jumble of tops and leggings spilling out.

I stand in the doorway for a moment. Rosie is asleep in the cot, a mobile with dangling animals hanging over her head. There's a lion, an elephant, a giraffe and a cheetah – all made out of felt. Rosie is in a baby sleeping bag with rainbows on it, her head turned slightly to one side. From where I'm standing in the doorway, she looks so peaceful. Laura is lucky to have such a placid baby – I don't think I've ever heard her cry. I decide to creep in for a closer look. After all, I've been here five days and I haven't met Rosie properly yet. I'm not normally particularly interested in babies, but there's something soothing about the way she's lying there, without a care in the world. I'll be really quiet. Careful not to wake her, I steal into the room and over to the cot.

My world shifts on its axis.

Chapter Fifty-Four

Beth

For a few moments, my brain refuses to take in what it's seeing. Maybe I hit my head when I fell and my mind is playing tricks on me. Even once I get to grips with what is lying in the cot, I'm still reaching for some other explanation. The real baby must be here somewhere. I look round wildly, as though I might have missed her. This must be some kind of joke. Because this can't be what's really happening.

Laura's child, laid lovingly in the cot, is a doll.

A pretty convincing one, it has to be said. Her baby fists are balled, chubby arms bent slightly at the elbow, soft fair hair held back from her face with a pale green headband. Her mouth is slightly turned down, giving her a perpetually thoughtful expression. Plastic eyelids are shut over plastic eyes.

The floorboards creak behind me. I rip my gaze away and turn to see Laura, wearing a blue fleece dressing gown, hair in a towel, standing in the doorway to the room. If there was any doubt remaining that this is some kind of prank, it vanishes the moment our eyes meet. The expression on her face is a mixture of shame and terror. For a few seconds, we just stare at each other and in those seconds I have to decide which way to go – reality or illusion. I know instinctively that what I say next is more important than anything I've ever said before.

'I was saying hello.'

My voice comes out as a croak, because I'm frightened too. This is beyond my comprehension. Laura's eyes are huge, wary, but she follows my lead.

'She's sleeping.'

'I know, I'm sorry. I–I shouldn't have disturbed her.'

'She needs to sleep.'

'Of course.'

My one thought is to get out of there, but Laura's between me and the door.

'I'm going to take her out for a walk later.'

'Good idea.'

I'm backing away from the cot. Simultaneously, Laura starts to move towards it.

'Do you want to hold her?'

'Do I…'

'Do you want to hold my baby?'

'I…'

Her face twists.

'You think I'm mad don't you? I knew you would.'

'No, I don't,' I say quickly, relieved that, after all, we've had to revert to reality – relieved that Laura is capable of this. 'I don't know what to think. I'm sorry – it's a big shock.'

'I knew you'd find out. I wanted to tell you, but it's too big a thing and in the end I couldn't find the words. You were confiding in me and I thought I could confide in you, but I didn't know how to start.'

I search for the right thing to say, but I feel as though my brain has stuttered to a halt and all I can manage is: 'It's a lot to take in.'

I'm replaying every time I've seen Laura with her baby: waving at her by the millpond on our first morning, looking out of our bedroom window and seeing the buggy in the garden with Laura asleep on the grass, the buggy at the end of our drive when I was about to drive Noah to the station. I think about Noah saying that the last time he'd seen Laura, at Christmas, she'd been heavily pregnant. Was that a pretence too? I think about the baby photos on the table downstairs in the living room.

'I can explain,' she says in a small voice. 'Will you let me explain how this happened?'

'Beth.' Stuart's voice, from the doorway. We both whip round to face him. 'I asked you to stay in the kitchen.'

He speaks oh so softly, but with an undertone that makes the hairs on the back of my neck stand on end. He takes a few steps into the room and I can see Meg is there too, silhouetted behind him. For the long minutes since I glanced into the cot, I'd forgotten all about them, but now, for the first time, it occurs to me that this isn't Laura's secret. It's a family secret. And I wonder what kind of family could keep a secret like that. And what they might do to someone who found out about it.

Chapter Fifty-Five

Beth

'Dad?'

Laura sounds stricken.

'It's all right. It's all right, my darling. Why don't you take Rosie out for a stroll? Your mum and I will talk to Beth. We'll explain.'

Laura looks uncertain.

'I don't know...'

'I think she'd like a walk.'

'But I'm not dressed.'

'Take her into our room then.'

'Please don't go, Laura,' I say.

Because I very much don't want to be alone with Stuart and Meg. Laura is so much more damaged than I ever realised, but what about the two people who've been enabling her fantasy? But Laura scoops Rosie up as if she's in a trance and makes her way to the door. Meg reaches out a hand to touch her shoulder as she passes. In her other hand, as she turns, I catch a glimpse of something metallic.

'Don't worry, my love.' Meg's voice is tender. 'I'll be with you in a moment.' Then she steps into the room and shuts the door. I can see her face properly now and there is anger blazing in her eyes behind the big burgundy frames. 'Don't you dare judge her,' she says fiercely.

I hold up my hands as if that is somehow going to protect me from her fury.

'It really would have been better if you'd stayed down-stairs,' Stuart says, and although he's outwardly the calmer of the two, I don't think he's any less upset.

'I'm sorry. I had no idea...' I trail off. 'I just wanted to talk to Laura,' I manage. It seems very important to placate them – to get out of the house somehow – to get miles and miles away from this place. I knew from the start something in Fortune's Yard was very wrong.

'We need you to understand what's happening here,' Stuart says.

I can tell he's trying to sound reasonable and, after all, it's what I wanted: to understand what was going on. Only now I have the chance to find out, I want to run for my life.

'It's none of my business. Any of it.'

'Sit down,' Stuart says.

'I really should be making a move,' I say, ridiculously, as if taking refuge in platitudes is going to restore us to friendly neighbours, passing the time of day.

'Sit.'

I sit on the edge of Laura's unmade double bed. Meg goes over to the window so she's behind me and out of sight. I remember the glint of metal in her hand and wish I could keep both of them in view. Stuart is standing directly in front of me. He clearly has no intention of sitting himself.

'Do you know what it's like to lose a child?' he says.

I shake my head, although I've probably thought more about it than most people, although from a very different perspective. I've thought of my parents and the child they lost when she was seventeen because she wanted nothing more to do with them, and, however sure I am it was the right decision, I've sometimes wondered how they dealt with that.

'It's what happened to Laura, our poor Laura. She lost her baby. Her Rosie.' Stuart's voice chokes as he says her name. 'She was five months old. She was in the bath and Laura turned her back on her for a few seconds to go and get a towel from the cupboard on the landing. Just seconds – that was all – and in that time she lost everything. Can you imagine what it's like to live with grief like that?' He seems to be waiting for an answer, but all I can find to say again is how sorry I am. 'You have no idea. No idea what she went through.' Stuart shakes his head as if trying to rid himself of a troublesome image. 'She was consumed with grief. It was like it was literally eating her up – she got thinner and thinner, her hair started falling out, and the worst thing was how much she blamed herself. The guilt was even stronger than the grief.'

In that moment, in spite of everything, I understand properly for the first time what it was that drew Dolly and Laura together. There really is a special bond between them, even if Dolly doesn't know it, and it's not only grief – it's guilt. Dolly must have recognised an echo of her own agony in Laura. I wonder what Laura told her about the figure in the grove and what story she spun about why she was leaving it there.

'Do you understand what I'm saying?' Whatever I say seems to make Stuart more agitated, so I restrict myself to a nod. 'Laura blamed herself for Rosie's death, and no matter how many times Meg and I tried to tell her that it was an accident, that she wasn't responsible, it was like she couldn't hear us.' There's despair as well as anger now in his voice, and his own grief is there again when he says his granddaughter's name. 'Of course, that bastard she married made things even worse. Ewan. As if it wasn't bad enough Laura blaming herself, he blamed her too. He said he couldn't live with her any more – couldn't bear to be with her. Just like that. She's worth a hundred of him. When she most needed his support, he walked out on her. Can you believe it?'

He starts pacing restlessly up and down, but he's never far from the door, and although almost every instinct I have is telling me that I need to get out of this house, grab Dolly and drive as far away as we can get, something is keeping me in that room, other than just fear of what Meg and Stuart will do to me if I try to leave. My brain has started working again, and mingled with the shock, fear and compassion, I feel something else: curiosity. It's curiosity that drives me to say what I say next, even though another part of me knows that it's a really bad idea.

'But how was this ever going to help?'

He stops moving and turns to look at me, his expression briefly the old Stuart one of mild confusion, rather than the hostility of a few moments earlier.

'This?'

'How is…' I hesitate, searching for the right words to describe what this is. 'How is pretending helping Laura?'

'I'm trying to make you understand.' He sounds petulant rather than angry now. 'You have to let me finish. She's our little girl. They never stop being your children, no matter what. We'd have done anything for her, Meg and I, but we couldn't do the one thing she wanted. She came up to stay with us after Ewan left her, just for a few days she said. We thought being up here would help, but it didn't seem to make any difference. She was like a robot, going through the motions of living. I persuaded her to see a grief counsellor, but she said even that didn't help. Nothing helped. She just wanted Rosie back.'

He puts his hand to his mouth to suppress the sob that's trying to escape, and, without even thinking about what I'm doing, I get to my feet and reach out an arm to comfort him. He shakes me off impatiently. Meg comes over to stand beside him, and when she extends a hand, he seizes it tightly and briefly closes his eyes.

'Stuart started researching grief online,' Meg says briskly.

'I did so much reading. I was desperate, you understand?' I nod. I definitely understand the addictive torment of looking for answers online. 'I came across a piece that really struck a chord with me – it was about finding an ongoing link with the child you'd lost. It suggested that the bereaved parent should retain a memento, like a piece of bedding or clothing, as evidence of their child's presence.'

'It was your idea?' I say, comprehension dawning. 'You gave her the doll?'

'It really helped.' There's eagerness in his voice now. 'It was the first thing that made a difference. To start with, I suggested Rosie's old blanket, and Laura sat on the sofa stroking it for hours on end, and then I remembered the doll in the attic. I went up there and searched until I found it, and then I wrapped it in the blanket, and took it down to the living room, and I said, "You could take her for a walk, my darling," and she looked at me like I was crazy. But the next morning, when I asked Meg where Laura was, she said she'd gone for a walk, and I knew even from the way she said it that she'd taken the doll with her. When she came back, it was like a miracle, wasn't it Meg? It was like having the old Laura back – for a while at least. She was smiling. It was the first time I'd seen her smile in three weeks. She said it gave her peace. What parent wouldn't want to give their child peace after such trauma?'

'She knows it isn't real,' Meg says. 'We're all clear about that. It's a way of coping, nothing more.'

'The point is that for a while it enables her to *imagine*,' Stuart says. 'And that's enough. For a while, it was enough.'

'Until she started believing it,' I say, unable to help myself.

'No,' Meg says sharply. 'She still knows what's real and what isn't. I'm her mother. I'm sure of that.'

'She went back to work after her six months, like she was planning to, and of course it's all been very stressful and that makes having this release all the more critical,' Stuart says. 'We begged her to take longer, but she said she needed to go back, to be in a routine.'

'She told work,' Meg says. 'She told them she'd lost the baby. She's not living in some fantasy world.' Meg is studying me with the same intensity she inspected me with on the day I arrived. 'She only has the doll when she comes down here. At weekends. Even then it's just to take it for walks. Nothing more.'

'It helps her,' Stuart says. 'It's helping her to get through this time.'

'How could you possibly hope to keep this secret? You must have known it couldn't last.'

'It wasn't meant to last,' Meg snaps. 'It was meant to give her a chance to heal.'

'It's the perfect place to live a different version of your life,' Stuart says. 'It's always been a place of imagination, of freedom. Here she could be what she'd always wanted to be: a mother.'

'But even here people would find out eventually — just like I found out.'

Stuart's casting of Fortune's Yard as some kind of *Sliding Doors* parallel world is infuriating me. Can they not see the damage they've done?

'May I ask you to keep your voice down?' Meg says. 'Laura is in the next room and I don't want her to hear us arguing. Of course we would have told you. None of this fuss was necessary. As soon as we found out Noah was moving into his parents' house, we knew we'd have to explain. We were just waiting for the right moment.'

'The first time Laura took the baby out,' Stuart says, 'Noah's parents were already in the States. Ralph and Evelyn were staying with their son in Cambridge, so there was no one here at all.'

At the mention of Ralph's name, something twists in Meg's face. In that split second the suspicion of what really happened slams into me with nightmarish force.

Chapter Fifty-Six

Beth

'It's not the first time, is it?' I manage to say.

'What do you mean?' Stuart says.

'Ralph found out too, didn't he?'

As soon as the words leave my mouth, Stuart's expression goes blank, his watery brown eyes become hard and cold. A muscle in his neck is twitching.

'Ralph had no idea.'

I know I should just agree with him – that getting out of there might depend on agreeing with him – but I can't help myself. The words spill out before I can check them, because suddenly, I understand what Evelyn told me. Everything she told me.

'I think he did. I think he found out just before he died. Evelyn said he came back that day angry, and she even remembered what he was angry about: it was all about a doll, she said. But more than that, she actually told me: "Laura doesn't have a baby." I thought she was confused, but she was telling me the literal truth. Evelyn knows. Let's ask her. Let's call her son and ask her.'

The muscle spasms. He's blocking the route to the door, but I wonder if I can get past him. He must be nearly seventy, but he's wiry and fit.

'You're wrong,' he says.

'I even know *when* Ralph found out. He was alone in your house on Monday when I turned up just before lunch, looking for Dolly. He was searching for an earring Evelyn had lost. Meg, you left him to come and talk to me and when he came out to the kitchen he had this kind of weird triumphant look about him. I think he knew then. He was nosy, maybe he already suspected something wasn't quite right, and when you left him alone he couldn't resist going to have a look for himself. And I can't believe it's a coincidence that less than twenty-four hours after he found out, he was dead. I don't think the police will think it's a coincidence either.'

'This is nonsense,' Stuart says. 'You're basing all of this on the ramblings of a confused old lady.'

'What exactly are you accusing us of?' Meg has gone ghostly white, but her voice is still cool, logical. 'You think Ralph found out about what happened to Laura, and he confronted her and she, what, pushed him down the stairs? It's grotesque!'

'No,' I say, still working it out, 'I don't think he told Laura. I think he told you. He knew how much you love her and he liked having the power over you.'

'So you think one of us killed Ralph?'

'Meg,' Stuart says, warningly.

'I know Ralph found out that Laura was pretending her baby was still alive and that gives all three of you a motive to kill him. I think you'd both kill to protect your daughter. He was a threat to her and you had to remove that threat, because once he knew, he wasn't going to keep it to himself was he? He'd have told everyone eventually.'

'Most people already know,' Meg says tightly, her face set. 'I told you. Laura's work already knows.'

'They know her baby died. That's a tragedy – everyone will sympathise with that. But pretending your baby is still alive, taking a doll for walks? Well, they might still sympathise, but that's something else entirely. No law firm is going to employ a woman who can't tell truth from fantasy.'

'How dare you say that about my child!'

Meg advances towards me and finally I get a proper look at what she has in her hand: gardening scissors. My mouth goes dry. In that moment I know that she killed Ralph and now she's going to kill me. My heart pounding, I take a step backwards, stumble on the edge of the bedspread on the floor and grab hold of the bed to right myself, twisting out of her way. My breath is coming in ragged bursts. Meg takes a step onto the bedspread, coming closer to me, and at the same time, the bedroom door opens and Dolly stands on the threshold. If I wasn't so frightened, there would be something almost comical about the way her head jerks back and her mouth falls open.

'What's going on?'

'Go away, Dolly. It's not safe. Get help!'

'Dolly!' Meg says. She's still holding the scissors.

Dolly moves so quickly that I barely register what she's doing, but she must have reached down and yanked the edge of the bedspread that's nearest the door, because Meg goes tumbling backwards.

'What have you done?' Meg cries.

Stuart goes to help her up. Dolly looks from Meg to me.

'Beth, come with me!' she shouts. 'Run, now!'

I make a dash for the door. Stuart turns to look at us. I'm briefly aware of Laura standing, shocked, on the landing, but Dolly is already pelting down the stairs and I plunge after her. Meg is following us, shouting my name, telling me to wait. My mind is racing, the panic threatening to overwhelm me. Where are we running to? Who are we going to ask for help? Fortune's Yard has never seemed more cut off. We run down the hallway and into the big kitchen. Drake has appeared from somewhere and is jumping up and down around Meg, briefly delaying her. Dolly is by the front door, but I still don't have a plan.

Then, among all the detritus on the worktop, I see Meg's car keys.

Chapter Fifty-Seven

Beth

'She's right behind us,' Dolly says.

'Lock the doors,' I say. 'How do we lock the doors on this stupid car?'

'Shit. She's coming.'

I glance in the mirror and see Meg on the driveway. She still has the gardening scissors in her hand.

'It's okay, it's okay.'

I'm trying to work out how to start the engine on Meg's huge grey Range Rover. It's one of those weird keyless ignitions. Doesn't it work by proximity? I press a padlock button at the same time as Meg lunges towards the backdoor of the car and a fraction of a second later the engine miraculously springs to life. Thank God. I slam my foot down. There's a screech of wheels as they spin on the gravel – a noise I've only ever heard in movies before – and then we lurch forward and stop again. For a moment I think we've stalled, but the engine is still running. I just haven't got the hang of driving this thing yet.

'What are you doing?' Dolly shouts at me.

'Sorry. I'm sorry.'

'She's catching us up.'

I put my foot down again, more gently this time and the car moves off. I get to the junction and haul the wheel round to the left. We pitch sideways, and then we're pulling away, past our house and down the lane out of Fortune's Yard.

'It's all right,' Dolly says, turning back to face me. 'She can't follow us now.'

'Not unless she can run fucking fast,' I say. And something about the relief of it makes us both burst out laughing.

'I can't believe you said that,' Dolly gulps.

It's laughter verging on hysteria, but it feels good. There was a moment when I wasn't sure whether we were going to make it out of that house alive. I wonder if Dolly knew how much danger we were in. This can't have been good for her – trauma piled on more trauma. Right now, though, she seems okay, relieved, to be out of there. Her voice suddenly serious again she asks, 'What happened? Why was Meg attacking you?'

I know she needs to hear the truth, but I'm not sure I'm ready to explain yet.

'Can we wait until we've got a bit further away from here? I'll tell you in a minute.'

'She had scissors. It was pretty scary.'

'I know. You were great. Really quick thinking.' As Fortune's Yard recedes into the distance, I can feel a weight lifting off me. 'I don't think I ever want to go back there,' I say, without thinking.

'Maybe you won't have to.'

'I don't know where I'm driving to, by the way. I'm just getting us out of there. A police station I guess, or maybe we should stop and call them?'

'Not yet,' Dolly says, glancing over her shoulder. And I feel her superstitious dread of stopping, even though there's no way Meg or Stuart could be following us because we're driving their car. 'I know where we're going,' she says. 'Ipswich train station. Dad's there.'

'What?' I'm worried she's not as okay as I thought she was. 'He's not due back until Friday.'

'He flew back early to surprise us. That's what I came upstairs to tell you. He called me, but he said he'd been trying you as well. He wants us to come and pick him up.'

'Oh wow. Oh, thank God.' The relief of it floods through me. There is no one I want to see more right now than Noah.

'Please can we call from the station?' Dolly asks. 'Please can we not stop?' I don't want to stop either, but surely we've got far enough away now? And while there's no one else in Fortune's Yard for Meg to harm, I think the police need to get there sooner rather than later, although I have no idea what I'm going to tell them. *I think my neighbour pushed my other neighbour down the stairs.* I'll probably leave out the bit about the baby, and stick to Ralph. I suddenly remember Ralph's car, and the fact that Meg and Stuart have keys to Ralph and Evelyn's cottage.

'Okay, let's call from the station,' I say, putting my foot down on the accelerator again.

'Wait,' Dolly says.

'What?'

'What about Bluebell?'

My heart lurches, but it's okay.

'She's safe. We locked her in the house when we left, remember?'

'Do you think Meg would hurt her?'

'No, she's not going to touch Bluebell. I promise.'

Dolly nods, but her forehead is still creased in a frown line.

'We'll go back and get Bluebell. When the police are there and we've got your dad, we'll go straight back and get her.'

'I thought you weren't ever going back?' she says with that childlike simplicity that still sometimes surprises me.

'Well, I'm not sure I want to go back and live there,' I say, attempting a smile. I literally cannot imagine anywhere I'd less like to be. 'But I don't think avoiding it altogether is going to be possible.'

'Please will you tell me now why Meg wanted to hurt you?'

'I found out something she didn't want anyone else to know.'

'What?'

I suppose it's all got to come out eventually. Also, what Dolly needs is to talk. She's been keeping things to herself for years; we need to be a family who talk about things. The word family comes naturally into my head without me even thinking about it, and I realise that's what we are now. While Noah's been in the States, Dolly and I have been through a lot, but however difficult it's been, it's turned us into a proper family.

'It's going to be quite hard to explain.' I glance sideways at her.

'Okay,' she says levelly.

'Meg and Stuart care a lot for Laura, and a few months ago something very sad happened her, so they did something that they hoped would make her feel better and help her to cope with what she was going through. And for a while I think it did help.' I remember Stuart's face as he described Laura coming back from that first walk. 'But then it got out of hand. You see, it was only supposed to be for a short time and then she was supposed to feel better by herself, but that's not what happened. Instead, Laura became more and more dependent on—' I'm still hesitating about actually spelling it out to her. 'On what Meg and Stuart had done.'

'What happened to Laura?'

'Her baby very sadly died.'

'How?'

'It was an accident. She drowned in the bath.' Dolly's eyes have gone wide. 'It must have been an extremely difficult thing for her to deal with. She blamed herself and all she wanted was for her baby to come back.'

For Rosie to come back. I suddenly remember the R on the tiny coffin I found.

'Dolly? You know the figure you took back to the grove?'

'Yes.'

'It did belong to Laura, didn't it?'

'Yes.'

R for Rosie. I feel a ridiculous little surge of validation: I did work it out right in the end. The first figure was left in the grove by Laura to bring her baby back. The second figure, the much rougher Blu-Tack one, was made by Dolly to try and bring her mum back.

'So you knew Laura was grieving for someone?'

'I knew she was sad as soon as I saw her and she knew I was sad too.'

An image flashes into my head. I'm standing in the drive just before I took Noah to the station to catch his plane and I'm watching Dolly lean into the buggy and talk to the baby. And in that moment I realise that I don't have to explain anything to Dolly at all. Because she's known all along. She knows Laura's baby is a doll. She's not an audience for the fantasy. She's part of it.

Chapter Fifty-Eight

Beth

'You knew Laura's baby wasn't real, didn't you?'

'Is that what Meg was angry with you about?'

'Why didn't you tell me or your dad?'

'Laura asked me to keep it a secret.'

'Dolly, this was a really big secret.'

'They're the most important ones to keep.'

'Not always.'

She's frowning at me.

'I'm not blaming you, not at all. It's just that Laura needs help that's all.'

'Having the baby again is helping. She told me that. She knows it's only pretend and it's not for ever. It's just until the real Rosie comes back.'

The feeling of trepidation creeps down my spine again. I wish I could stop the car so we could have this conversation properly; so I could look her in the face, wrap her in my arms even. But now I've remembered Ralph's car, I can't stop. I'm approaching the junction to pull out onto the main road. We come to a temporary halt, and I glance sideways at her. Her brow is still furrowed, her eyes as they meet mine are defiant, but also pleading. I concentrate on the traffic, waiting for a gap in the stream of cars speeding past. The indicator clicks in the silence. I take my phone out of my pocket and risk a glance at it for the first time since we've left Meg and Stuart's. I'm expecting a missed call or message from Noah, but there's nothing. There's a message from Sasha though.

What's happening? You okay???

I still haven't called Sasha back and there's no time now. I type quickly.

I'm fine. Talk soon

'You shouldn't be using your phone.'

'Sorry, I know.'

'It's not safe.'

'I'm sorry. I'll put it away.'

I glance behind. Nothing in the rear-view mirror still. I pull out and we're moving away quickly, blending into all the other traffic. Less of a target. I'm getting used to Meg's car now. It's easy to drive: smooth, powerful and responsive when I put my foot on the accelerator. We're sitting high up on the road too. It makes you feel safe. I make up my mind. It's best to talk and I'm so much better at talking to her now.

'Dolly, those are just stories. About Hannah's powers. She can't really bring people back from the dead. No one can.'

'You don't know that.'

'I know you really, really want your mum to come back, and I'm so sorry about what happened, and what you've been through since and I promise we're going to work through this together as a family.'

'Laura says it can come true,' she says doggedly, 'and I believe Laura.'

'Laura is going through her own grief.' There's something else I can't stop myself asking her. 'Dolly, what would have happened to me? If you'd brought your mum back?'

She shrugs, playing with the elastic of the hairband around her wrist.

'I didn't really think about you.'

It's not exactly the most reassuring answer, but it's so much better than I'd imagined in my darkest moments. It sounds reassuringly teenager. For a while there is silence and then Dolly asks:

'Was Laura there when her baby died?'

'Yes.' And then conscious I'm treading on very difficult ground, I say, 'It's why she blames herself, I think. But it wasn't her fault, she didn't mean it to happen. It was an accident.'

'What are you going to do? Are you going to tell?'

'To tell?'

'About Laura. She doesn't want anyone to know.'

'I know, but sometimes it's important to tell, Dolly. Sometimes that's the way people get help.'

Dolly buries her head in her hands and her body is shaken by a huge sob.

'It really is going to be all right, I promise. I know how guilty you feel about your mum, but we'll help you, too. We'll go and pick your dad up, and we'll talk about what we're all going to do next, and we'll make it work. We'll be there for you.'

'Okay,' she whispers, taking her hands away from her face.

'I'm on your side, Dolly.'

I feel such elation. I've finally done this. I've finally broken through. We're close. She trusts me. I allow myself briefly to think about Noah, just pulling into the station. He must have been concerned about us both to come back early. I think about all he's going to have to deal with, but I'm not worried because I know he will understand when Dolly tells him why she blames herself for her mum's death, and I know he'll be relieved that she's finally felt able to share this secret that's been gnawing away at her for years. And I think he'll be proud of us, too. Proud of what we've dealt with and that we've come through it together. I think of Sasha again. *It's not going to happen by magic. You need something to bring you together.* Well, something has, and I think Noah is going to realise that as soon as he sees us.

I pull away from the lights and glance at Dolly. She's staring out of the window. Her face is ghost-pale, her mouth set, but her startling blue eyes are no longer tearful. They meet mine.

'I'm sorry,' she says.

'Oh Dolly, you've got nothing to apologise for.'

She gives me a half-smile. I return it with one full of reassurance.

It's also going to be important to get some help for Laura — help that isn't her parents. One of whom might well be arrested for murder. It's my word against Meg's, but maybe the police can find evidence that she was there. Even if they can't prove intent, manslaughter must be a possibility. My mind is running through the kind of things Meg might have left behind. Fibres from her clothing, hairs. Although would that be enough? Because of course she and Stuart go into the pub regularly. Maybe there are marks on Ralph's body that show he was pushed. There must be something, some physical evidence to prove what I know to be true: that when it came down to it, Meg couldn't take the risk of Laura being hurt any more. Perhaps it was premeditated and she arranged to meet Ralph in the Fortune's Arms with a view to killing him. She would have justified it to herself as protecting her child, and although I can't condone what she did, I can see why she would want to protect Laura.

I think of the shock on Laura's face as Dolly and I ran past her on the landing. I can't believe that she had any idea what really happened to Ralph, but maybe that's because I don't want to believe. I like Laura. Noah might have some ideas about how best to help her. Maybe she could go and stay with her sister – the one Amy's friends with, who also lives in the States. It would be a big change, but that could be what she needs. That and a really good counsellor. Which is exactly what Dolly needs, too. So much grief. So many lives destroyed.

We're nearing the outskirts of Ipswich and it hits me that in a few minutes I'm going to see Noah and, although it's been less than a week since I saw him last, so much has happened since that I feel like he won't recognise me as the same person. My stomach twists with anticipation. I'd wanted a new life and, strangely, at this moment I finally feel like I've got one: that I belong. I imagine the feel of Noah's lips on mine, strong and tender, and being held in his arms again. I picture the three of us climbing back in the car, and heading – where? The police station, I suppose. There's a lot still to resolve in this new life of mine, but I'm fully on board. I'm part of this. I put my foot on the accelerator.

'Almost there,' I say, turning to smile at her again.

'Almost,' she says.

My eyes back on the road, I don't see her first movement. I'm only aware of her hand, with its painted yellow nails, when it actually grips the steering wheel, and even then I'm so shocked that when the hand yanks downwards, my hands aren't ready to pull back. But in that split second my brain catches up. Dolly knew about the baby all along; Dolly would do anything to protect Laura. It's what Meg realised when Dolly opened the bedroom door. Meg wasn't chasing me because she was trying to harm me; she was chasing me because she knew I was in danger. She'd guessed what I've just realised for sure. My stepdaughter has killed once already.

The leather of the steering wheel slides through my light grip and the car responds at once, veering sideways across the inside lane of the dual carriageway. I try to pull back but it's too late. We're heading for the crash barrier and although we manage to swerve slightly as we approach it, I know we can't avoid it altogether. I slam my foot on the brakes. Dolly's hand yanks again and I try to fight her off. One hand around her thin wrist, the other on the steering wheel. Then there's a jolt as we make contact and we're through the barrier and in slow motion tumbling down the grassy slope, and I have time to think that my new life is over before it's even begun.

Chapter Fifty-Nine

School report for Dolly James
Lord Lane Primary School, Battersea
17 December 2014

Congratulations to Dolly for finishing her first term at Lord Lane Primary! Dolly understands the importance of persistence in achieving her aims, and her letters and sounds have come on in leaps and bounds over the past few months. She is also unusually adept for her age at watching and learning from other children, which should stand her in good stead as she progresses through school. Well done, Dolly!

On the social side, it's a big step up from Nursery and please don't worry because lots of children struggle to adjust to Reception. I know you were concerned in the early days that Dolly was quite isolated and didn't seem to be making friends, but it has been lovely to see Dolly become more confident as the term goes on, and in recent weeks she has made a very good friend in Jake and the pair of them appear inseparable.

Where we do still have some concerns is about Dolly's interest in the idea of dying. To an extent,

death is something that fascinates all young chil-
dren and is a key part of growing up. But as you
yourself mentioned at the start of the school year,
she does seem perhaps more than usually fixated on
it. For example, this morning there was a conversa-
tion that I would characterise as out of the ordinary
in my experience as a children's educator. During
break, Dolly was telling the other children not only
that they were all going to die, but describing very
specifically how they were going to die. Perhaps
this is something we could discuss further when
Dolly returns to school after Christmas? I don't
think there is cause for alarm at this point, but I do
think a joint approach on how best to handle these
situations would be helpful – I know you initially
suggested not reacting too much and giving it the
minimum of attention, saying that this tactic had
appeared to work in Nursery, but I wonder if the
time has come for a more direct approach. However,
I'm sure it is, as you say, something she will grow
out of with time.

Chapter Sixty

Meg

'I think I should say something.'

'It's better left alone,' Stuart says. 'Leave him to mourn, Meg.'

They both look over towards the church, where Noah is standing, tall and yet somehow shrunken, his long black coat wrapped around him. People are talking to him as they pass, but no one lingers; a few words and they're gone, as if his kind of cataclysmic bad luck might contaminate them. Or perhaps it's just that no one knows what to say. She shivers. It's an unseasonably cold September day and the wind is slicing through her thin blazer. Not for the first time, she feels a deep frustration with her husband.

'Wait for me in the car,' she says.

Stuart shrugs and turns away from her, heading along the path between the graves towards the gate that leads to the car park. She watches him go. There's no point in saying so now, but if she'd never listened to him in the first place, perhaps all this could have been avoided. She'd wanted to help as much as Stuart had – she was Laura's mother; she'd ached to ease her pain, for God's sake – but he'd been so certain it was a good idea, whereas she'd had her doubts from the start. And it had got out of hand so quickly. Even before Noah and Dolly – and friendly, lonely Beth – had arrived. It had already become an addiction. Laura came up to see them every weekend, and of course it was only natural that a bereaved daughter should want to spend time with her parents, but that wasn't why she came. The pretence had become a drug that she couldn't do without and the more she came to depend on it, the more important it became to protect her secret, but Beth had been right to say it couldn't stay a secret for ever, even in a tiny hamlet like Fortune's Yard.

She'd got careless that day Ralph was in the house searching for Evelyn's missing earring. More than that, she hadn't even thought when she left him alone to go and answer the doorbell that there was anything to take care about. She'd got almost used to the pretence herself. That was the thing about pretending: you become so accustomed to it that you forget the danger. But the danger's always there. Ralph must have gone upstairs straight away – maybe he already suspected something was wrong and the earring was just an excuse to snoop. She wouldn't have put it past him.

He hadn't confronted them then and there. He'd left; he couldn't get out of their house quickly enough, she seemed to remember. She knew from Beth that he'd gone home and told Evelyn what he'd discovered. *Laura doesn't have a baby.* It was strange to think of Evelyn stating it as a simple fact and Beth not realising the significance of what she'd said. Meg's not sure whether it's the biting wind, or the thought that Evelyn, now living somewhere in Cambridge, still knows, that makes her feel suddenly chilled to her core. But she continues to stand by herself in the graveyard, waiting for her chance to talk to Noah. The cold aside, she's not in any hurry. She has plenty to think about while she waits. She's deliberately stopped her mind going there over the past few weeks, but now it's almost a relief to run through it and try to make sense of it all.

Her next, and last, encounter with Ralph had come later that evening, when she'd been out walking Drake. He'd been lurking in the darkness, by the door to the Fortune's Arms. She'd called out a neighbourly good evening – they often crossed paths about this time of night, although usually at the gate to his cottage, where he would stand smoking those disgusting cigarettes. They rarely exchanged more than a few words. This time, though, he told her he'd seen a light upstairs in the pub and he'd got his keys and was going to have a look. *It will be someone up to no good.* The stupid thing was that her first thought at the time was that it might be Dolly. That first weekend when Dolly had come down with Noah and the removal company, she'd taken Dolly upstairs in the Fortune's Arms and shown her the scarecrows she was making as a surprise house-warming present. Dolly had helped her put the finishing touches to them, even finding her a silver scarf that she said belonged to Beth. Meg knew she shouldn't really use the pub as an extension of her home, but, at the end of the day, they had keys and the old farmhouse was such a mess that sometimes it was useful to store stuff in there. She'd even said to Dolly what a good hideout the pub would make. It was the kind of thing her children would have loved when they wanted to be by themselves.

She'd offered to go in with Ralph and have a look. He hadn't got a torch, so she'd given him hers, but mainly she'd gone with him because she thought that if it really was Dolly, she could protect her from the worst of his disapproval. But once they were inside, it was clear that the pub was empty. Or she thought it was. Afterwards, she'd assumed that he'd planned the whole thing: that he'd been waiting for her to take Drake on his walk and the story about the light had just been a ruse to get her inside the pub and make her feel trapped before he revealed what he knew. Because it hadn't taken him long to spill his venom. *There's all kinds of wickedness going on in this place. Did you think I wouldn't find out? Your daughter's not right in the head.* Her cheeks burn as she replays his words. *I'm going to write a letter to her employers first thing in the morning. No one will want to employ a looney lawyer who lies about having a baby.*

She'd fled home and told Stuart, and they'd stayed up all of that night trying to work out what to do. Even Stuart had eventually conceded that the best thing was to get in there first and explain to Laura that the pretence had to stop, and to help her contact her employer and explain what Ralph was going to tell them, so that at least they seized the initiative and could try to limit the fallout.

And then the glorious relief in the morning when they hadn't needed to. When Beth had burst in with the news about the body, she'd known at once that it was Ralph. If she blamed herself at all it was because she'd left him in the deserted pub without a torch and he'd clearly continued to explore and fallen. But maybe she should have asked more questions at the time, because, ultimately, when your luck seems too good to be true, it almost certainly isn't luck at all. It was Beth who had forced her to see that: Ralph discovered Laura's secret and less than twenty-four hours later he was dead. It could have been a coincidence, but Beth made her realise that, more likely, it was something much more sinister.

Meg knew she hadn't killed him – he'd been very much alive when she left and still hurling insults at her. Neither had Stuart. They'd sat in the kitchen together all that long night talking, and although it was just about conceivable that Laura had come downstairs in the night and overheard them, it was impossible to imagine her sneaking out and luring Ralph to his death. She knew her daughter. Laura was broken – she'd always been the most fragile of her three children, cursed with a brilliance that she quite often seemed to stretch to breaking point – but she wasn't capable of murder.

Beth had said no one else knew about the doll – Meg is determined not to refer to her as Rosie, it's important that she keeps a grip on reality – but that wasn't true. One other person knew. And here again, Meg had had her doubts from the start. It had been a bad idea to give Laura a doll to comfort her but it had been a disastrous idea to tell Dolly about it, but by the time she found out what Laura had done that first weekend when Dolly was down with Noah and the removal lorry, it was already too late.

It was only when Dolly burst into Laura's room as she and Stuart were trying to calm Beth down that Meg remembered her initial idea about Dolly being in the pub that evening, and it was at that precise moment that she began to think the unthinkable, especially when she remembered how protective Dolly was of Laura. It was sweet in a way, or it should have been sweet, but even at the time there had been something slightly unsettling about it. Something too intense.

Supposing Ralph really had seen a light on in the Fortune's Arms. If Dolly had been upstairs in the pub and had overheard the conversation between the two of them, she might have decided to take matters into her own hands. Not for the first time, Meg tried to picture what had happened after she left. Maybe Dolly had made some movement and Ralph had gone upstairs and found her. She might not even have realised what she was doing. She couldn't have meant to kill him. Probably, she just pushed him away and he fell and then, horrified by what she'd done, Dolly fled.

She'd tried to warn Beth, but the stupid woman had been terrified of her and gone running down the stairs and snatched up the car keys. She'd actually taken Meg's car and driven off in it. The police had wanted to know why and for a moment she couldn't think what to say. 'Her own car wouldn't start and she wanted to get to Ipswich.' It was the best she could come up with and the officer she'd spoken to had looked sceptical and said they couldn't find anything wrong with Beth's car, but for the police it was a minor puzzling detail in a much bigger tragedy, and, after all, her account was so much more likely than the truth. It even helped to explain what happened next, because Beth had been driving an unfamiliar car.

Meg both longs and fears to know what had happened in the car. The newspaper accounts didn't tell her much. The witnesses – and there had been several – said it swerved without warning through the crash barrier, down the slope and into the side of a warehouse. The driver and passenger were killed instantly and it was a miracle that there were no other fatalities. Meg knows, though, that Beth had been in the car with a deeply troubled child who had possibly already killed once. In her darkest moments, she wonders if Dolly had somehow caused the crash, and there had been a woman outside the church just now – Sasha, an old friend of Beth's – who'd been asking questions that had momentarily made Meg wonder whether she suspected something similar. But it must be Meg's own paranoia, because, after all, Sasha was nowhere near

Fortune's Yard at the time of the crash. What could she know? And maybe there was nothing to know anyway. Maybe it really was that Beth was unused to the car and, panicking at what she thought she'd uncovered, wasn't concentrating properly.

Either way, Meg finds it impossible not to blame herself. In colluding with Stuart to protect their daughter at all costs, she had not only caused more harm to the very person she was trying to protect, she had further damaged Noah's daughter and then set in motion a chain of events that had led him to lose Dolly entirely – and that had caused the deaths of Ralph and Beth as well.

It's not that she's planning to tell Noah any of this, but it's precisely because she has her own fears that she wonders if it might help him to have someone with whom he can share his. Because she's wondered a few times over the past, dark weeks. What does Noah think happened? How is he making sense of something so incomprehensible?

The stream of mourners has slowed to a trickle, and at last Noah is alone. As she watches, trying to think how to frame what it is she wants to ask him, he starts walking purposefully across the graveyard in the opposite direction to the car park. She follows but he's moving so fast that she has to jog to catch up with him, which is tricky in the low heels she's wearing and isn't used to.

'Noah!'

He doesn't break his stride. She calls again and then, when she's close enough, she reaches out and touches his shoulder. He spins round so fast that she almost cannons into him. He grabs her elbow and helps her stay upright and even once she's regained her balance they stand for a few moments clutching each other. It's as though they're in a bubble, just the two of them, outside time and space. She searches for a way into the conversation, knowing that the conventional expressions of condolence won't do, but he finds his words first.

'Beth's parents came. Did you see?'

She shakes her head, unsure why this would be remarkable.

'She's been estranged from them for years.'

'I didn't know.'

'No? Well she didn't talk about them much. She felt like they betrayed her. But they finally managed to track her down. I assumed they'd seen a photo of her in one of the papers and found out about her death that way, but the funny thing is that they got an anonymous email from someone who'd tracked them down online and wanted to put them back in touch with Beth. So if Beth hadn't died they'd have found her anyway. I actually quite liked them. Her dad was the only one who said what everyone else was thinking. *Two wives. Two car accidents. How could that happen?* Even the police didn't put it that baldly.'

They hold each other's gaze, feeling their way through this.

'Have they told you any more about what they think caused the crash?' she asks cautiously.

In spite of the thick wool coat he's holding around him, he looks freezing.

'We'll never know exactly what happened,' he says, and she gets the sense that, in a way, this uncertainty is what he wants. It's as though he's trying to reassure himself.

'I suppose not.' She can't just leave it there. 'It *is* a coincidence,' she hears herself say, the inadequate word hanging in the air between them. She watches as his expression hardens. She fears she's destroyed the bond that has enabled them to get this far.

'Sometimes lightning really does strike twice I suppose,' he says, his tone brittle. He half turns away from her so she can't see his face, but he doesn't walk off so maybe the connection is still there.

'Noah.' She keeps her voice very gentle. 'I've known you all my life. I was there in Fortune's Yard. I'm here if you ever want to talk. About anything.'

He doesn't reply straight away. In the distance, on the far side of the graveyard, visible and just about audible, a woman is berating her child of about four or five, in a bright red rain jacket, for some unknown misdemeanour. *You could have hurt yourself really badly!* The child starts sobbing, inconsolable. She wonders if Noah is watching them, too. She still can't see his face and she doesn't dare say anything more. He turns back towards her. There are tears streaming down his cheeks. She takes him in her arms and for a moment his body is rigid, but then he collapses into her, bending his head so that it's on her shoulder.

'Dolly's dead now,' he says, his voice muffled so that she has to strain to hear the words. 'It's all over.'

That's when she knows that he also thinks Dolly might be responsible – not for Ralph, he can't know about that. But for Beth. It's, strangely, a relief to realise that she's not alone, and she allows herself to acknowledge that this is what she wanted from the conversation all along. Eventually he pulls away from her. She reaches for something to comfort him.

'She's at peace.'

In the end, it's hard to avoid the established expressions.

'The things we do for our children,' he says, looking back towards where the woman was telling off the child, and wiping his eyes with his hands. 'The lies we tell ourselves.'

She finds a tissue in her bag and gives it to him.

'You could never have known.'

'That's one of the lies I tell myself.'

'Meaning?' she says, more sharply than she intended.

His face is haggard.

'You know Juliet was taken to hospital after the accident? Well, she regained consciousness. She talked to me, Meg.'

'I see,' she says, although she's still not sure she understands.

'She tried to tell me what happened. She told me that Dolly had taken the wheel. She made me promise to protect her, and I couldn't bring myself to take it in, so I pretended to myself that Juliet hadn't meant what she said, or had been mistaken, and I did such a good job of pretending, that over the years I almost convinced myself. Because I wanted to believe and that's such a powerful thing. It never occurred to me she'd do it again. So you see, I knew all along. I was just pretending, and hoping.'

His voice breaks. Appalled, she reaches out a hand to touch his arm, but this time she stops short of making contact. Somehow she finds the right words, though.

'That's what we're all doing. It's how we go on. Pretending and hoping.'

He gives a huge sigh, like all the air in his body is being expelled.

'Goodbye, Meg. Give my love to Stuart, won't you?'

She nods and turns away from him to walk back to the car, unable to bear any more. She stayed behind to talk to Noah because she was craving certainty, knowledge. And now she has far more knowledge than she wanted, and no one she can share it with. She owes Noah that much. She wonders if she will ever see him again. The Old Watermill is up for sale and maybe he will go and join his parents and sister in the States. She wouldn't blame him for wanting to get as far away from here as he can.

'Send my love to Laura too,' he calls after her. 'I know she's going to do great things one day. We all knew that, even as kids.'

She seizes on the thought of Laura to try and distract herself from what she's just learnt. At least, she thinks, wrapping her arms around herself to keep out the wind, Laura is doing better now. The one good thing to come out of this is that they've finally had a proper conversation with her and she's agreed that she needs to stop using the doll. She's even talked about it to her grief counsellor and he's supporting her. With time, she thinks, Laura will heal.

Epilogue

The looks the other parents give her as they pass, weary and conspiratorial. It's exhilarating. She's part of the gang again. A mother, just like them. It's the first time she's done this in London and she's chosen a walk along the Thames path, not far from where she lives. She imagines how the pair of them must look: the slender woman with the pale skin and fair hair, and the baby in the fleece romper suit. She's using the baby sling because the buggy is still down in Fortune's Yard.

As she walks, she feels a stab of guilt. She promised them all that she wouldn't do this again – her mum, her dad, her grief counsellor. But it's just this one last time and then she'll stop, just like they want her to. She needs this one final walk.

Some people don't seem to notice her at all – for them, parents are just not interesting – but this excites her, too. It's another sign that she belongs. She adjusts the strap on the sling, pulls the hood with the two furry bear ears on it further down over the tiny head, and the eyes of the group of young men she passes on the river path slide over her, as if she's become a non-person.

There's another category of walker too. Those who stop, despite the unseasonable cold, who want to talk. *How old? They're perfect when they're that age. Like dolls.* To these people, smiling, pulling up the slides of the sling: *I'm sorry.*

338

She's sleeping. She's not well today. One woman gets too close, reaching out arthritic fingers to touch a cheek, and she sees the confusion and then something else, something she thinks might be fear, on her face. It was the look Beth had too when she'd come into Laura's bedroom that day and finally seen for herself. That look isn't such a good look.

For a moment, the emptiness returns even more overwhelming than ever, but, it's okay, she can explain, just like she was going to explain to Beth if her parents had given her a chance. *You see, this is what was supposed to happen. What actually did happen for a few months. I really am a mother. I'm not mad.* But by the time she's found the words, the woman has gone.

When she gets home, she takes off the baby sling. Puts the doll down on the armchair in the spare room. Shuts the door. It's over: she's done with pretending. Just like they wanted.

Hours pass. She tries. She even sleeps for a while. When she wakes there's only one thing she wants to do. The door to the spare room creeks as she opens it.

And this time she no longer sees a doll; she sees a baby.

'I'm back,' she croons. 'I'm back my little one.'

She cradles her child in her arms, smooths her hair. Comforts her.

'Don't worry, I won't ever let you go, Rosie.'

A Letter from Joanna

Thank you for reading *She Wants You Gone*. It's exciting to be able to share the characters and world I've spent months creating and I love the idea of them coming to life in other people's heads, given how long they've been resident in mine!

She Wants You Gone is partly about families, and particularly about the relationship between parents and children – something that obsesses my main character, Beth. She's dealing with a difficult family history of her own, at the same time as she's starting a life with her new family. It's also about grief, of various kinds, and I've tried my best to tackle this painful subject sensitively.

The book arose out of two different but related ideas. A while ago, I read an anonymous column in a newspaper by a woman who was worried her teenage daughter hated her. The things she cited stuck in my head because they were small, but I could see how, cumulatively, they might be more disturbing than a big, dramatic fallout. It was hard to be sure from the column whether the woman was over-thinking what was normal adolescent stroppiness, or whether there really was something else going on. The behaviour she described was creepy and I made a mental note, thinking I might want to return to the subject one day. But it wasn't until I had another idea – one that I can't reveal here without a spoiler alert – that the daughter with the unsettling behaviour came back to me.

It was once I'd decided on the location, though, that both ideas really came alive. The book is set in a hamlet, with just three houses. I love visiting the countryside, but I'm very much a city person. In Arthur Conan Doyle's story *The Adventure of the Copper Beeches*, Sherlock Holmes and Dr Watson take a train to the Hampshire countryside and Watson tells Holmes that he can't imagine anything bad happening in such peaceful surroundings. Holmes replies: 'It is my belief, Watson, founded upon my experience, that the lowest and vilest alleys in London do not present a more dreadful record of sin than does the smiling and beautiful countryside.' Watson sees only beauty in the isolated houses, but Holmes sees the potential to commit crime with impunity. This is part of the fascination of a remote setting for me: the potential for keeping things hidden – not necessarily criminal acts but all kinds of things you don't want anyone else to find out. Even in the twenty-first century, might there be some secrets that it's easiest to hide in an isolated place?

I hope you enjoyed reading about Fortune's Yard, even if (like me) you're glad that you're not living there. If you've already read my previous psychological thriller *The Summer Dare*, thank you for coming back. If you haven't, please do look it up on Amazon, Waterstones or wherever you buy your books. If you'd like to follow me on social media the details are below, or you can visit my website to sign up to my mailing list.

Finally, if you did like the book, it would mean a lot if you told your friends, and left a review online or via social media. Word of mouth is so important – especially if, like me, you're a comparatively new writer. Thank you.

www.joannadodd.com
Twitter/X: @jkdwriter
Instagram: @jkd_writer

Acknowledgements

I need a thesaurus of positive words to do justice to everyone who's helped me with this book. First of all, thanks to the fantastic Lisa Moylett and Zoë Apostolides at my agent's, Coombs Moylett Maclean. Your feedback was invaluable and you have been so supportive throughout.

This is the second book I've been lucky enough to publish with Hera and both times it's been a great experience. Many thanks to the team there and in particular to my wonderful editor, Jennie Ayres. Jennie, we might not share the same view on the joys of living somewhere remote, but on everything else it feels like we're on the same page. Special thanks also to Kate Shepherd for her excellent work on the publicity side of things. The brilliant copy editor, Chere Tricot, saved me from several plotting oversights, and the proofreader, Vicki Vrint, spotted multiple errors I missed. Thanks to Lisa Brewster for creating such an eye-catching cover. I love it.

Other writers and book bloggers are such a friendly and inspiring bunch, so thank you to all the people I met at Harrogate Crime Writing Festival, the Crime Writers' Association and other book events, and to my fellow Hera and Canelo authors. Particular thanks to everyone who read review copies and provided quotes. It feels good to be building a community of writing friends.

Thank you, above all, to my family and friends, whose enthusiasm and encouragement mean a huge amount. David, thank you for loving the idea for this book from the start and for your feedback on the first draft. Thank you to Liz for listening to me ramble/talk through the plot one July day over dinner and helping me to sharpen it. Special thanks also to Maisie for talking to me about being a teenager, to Luanne for filling me in on school reports, to Claire for being one of my earliest readers, and to Fi for all her ingenious social media ideas. Thank you to all my friends for being so supportive. I realised I needed a dog in the book just before my brother and sister-in-law got Bluebell's real-life equivalent – I'm grateful to Texas for canine inspiration. This book is partly about parents. I'm very lucky to have lovely ones. Thank you to both of them for everything.